Model,
Incorporated

Also by Carol Alt

THIS YEAR'S MODEL

EATING IN THE RAW: A BEGINNER'S GUIDE TO GETTING
SLIMMER, FEELING HEALTHIER, AND LOOKING YOUNGER
THE RAW-FOOD WAY

THE RAW 50: 10 AMAZING BREAKFASTS, LUNCHES, DINNERS,
SNACKS, AND DRINKS FOR YOUR RAW FOOD LIFESTYLE

Model, Incorporated

CAROL ALT

AVON

An Imprint of HarperCollins*Publishers*

This novel is a work of fiction. Any references to real people, events, establishments, organizations, or locales are intended only to give the fiction a sense of reality and authenticity, and are used fictitiously. All other names, characters and places, and all dialogue and incidents portrayed in this book are the product of the author's imagination.

MODEL, INCORPORATED. Copyright © 2009 by Altron II, Inc. All rights reserved. Printed in the United States of America. No part of this book may be used or reproduced in any manner whatsoever without written permission except in the case of brief quotations embodied in critical articles and reviews. For information, address Harper-Collins Publishers, 10 East 53rd Street, New York, NY 10022.

HarperCollins books may be purchased for educational, business, or sales promotional use. For information, please write: Special Markets Department, HarperCollins Publishers, 10 East 53rd Street, New York, NY 10022.

On the cover: Dress—Cynthia Steffe at Lord & Taylor

FIRST AVON PAPERBACK EDITION PUBLISHED 2009.

Designed by Elizabeth M. Glover

Library of Congress Cataloging-in-Publication Data
Alt, Carol, 1960-
    Model, incorporated / Carol Alt. — 1st Avon ed.
        p. cm.
    ISBN 978-0-06-156597-7
1. Models (Persons)—Fiction. I. Title.
PS3601.L73M63   2009
813'.6—dc22

                                                                            2009012855

09 10 11 12 13   OV/RRD   10 9 8 7 6 5 4 3 2 1

Prologue

First class or coach, flying is hell when you've got a cold. It's barely 6 AM, my eyes are teary, my nose is as bright red as Rudolph's and the texture of sandpaper because I can't stop blowing it, and my voice is husky, at least two pitches below normal. In the state I'm in, I'm especially dreading getting on another plane, but even so, I hand my boarding pass to the uniformed gate attendant and try to manage a smile.

"Ms. Croft!" Despite the freezing cold, despite the ungodly hour, this girl is all smiles and small-town good manners. I wish I could borrow a bit of her sunny optimism to see me through this flight.

"Hi." I can't think of anything more charming to say, and in fact I'm so out of it I can't tell if she recognizes me or if she greets all of her passengers with the same enthusiasm. All I want to do right now is climb back into the warm, chauffeur-driven car that brought me here, drive back to the Four Seasons, collapse into the absurdly comfortable bed, bury my head under the down comforter and sleep for six weeks straight.

"Oh no! Pardon my saying so, but you sound terrible!" She

runs my boarding pass through the scanner's blinking red laser and hands it back to me, frowning with sincere concern.

"I know." I sip my piping-hot cup of green tea. I've spent the past three days straddling a horse, wearing only a bathing suit, my arms wrapped around Ivan Gladst's perfectly chiseled bare torso, in the middle of a barren field, in front of the dramatic backdrop of the Beartooth Mountains, in the midst of a full-on Montana winter. Between shots, the stylist's assistant thoughtfully wrapped me up in a thick cashmere throw, but still, my monster cold is hardly unexpected. Manhandling a half-naked super-model might sound like fun, but when you're at the mercy of a relentless perfectionist photographer like Steve Kline, trust me, it's anything but.

"You poor thing." She lowers her voice in a conspiratorial whisper. "I know something that might make you feel a little bit better."

"What's that?" I'm practically seeing spots. The only thing that could possibly make me feel better is some serious medical intervention.

"You're in 1-B today," she says, grinning, "and we have a very special passenger in 1-A." She pauses, then leans toward me across the counter. "Patrick Carroll!"

In my addled state it takes me a second to place the name . . . but only a second. I might be totally out of it, but Patrick Carroll is one of the most famous movie stars of all time. I'm sick, not brain dead.

"Great," I mutter. "Six hours on a plane next to a legendary heartthrob and I look and feel like death warmed over. Awesome." I'm not impressed by celebrities, but I am a red-blooded American girl. The thought of cozying up to Patrick Carroll is incredibly tempting, but why today, of all days, when I look and sound like a sickly, chain-smoking drag queen?

"Ms. Croft," the girl across the counter grins at me. "You might be sick, but I'd give my right arm to look the way you look right now. Welcome aboard."

"Allow me, please." Patrick Carroll hops out of his seat and takes the overstuffed Coach carry-on—a little something I scored on a catalog shoot this summer—from my hands. He deposits it neatly in the overhead bin, slamming the door shut, and steps aside so I can take my seat at the window.

"Thanks." I hope my fever disguises the fact that I'm blushing. He is, if possible, even better looking in person than on screen: tall, broad-shouldered, with a perfect chiseled chin and gleaming blue eyes. He's well into his forties, but looks every bit the heartthrob he was twenty years ago, when he burst onto the scene as the darling of independent '70s film, making low-budget dramas now widely considered cinematic classics. I can't tell if I'm lightheaded or actually swooning. I collapse into the wide leather seat and sip my tea, which tastes like nothing because I'm so congested.

"Patrick Carroll." As if I didn't already know that.

I shake his hand weakly, worrying a little about my clammy skin. "Of course," I say. "I know who you are."

"And I know who you are, Ms. Croft." His blue eyes sparkle, his smile folds into that famous dimple, and despite the touch of gray at his temples, he looks more like a randy teenager than a dignified Hollywood superstar.

I actually can't believe that this man, this legend, knows who I am. "You'll have to forgive me," I tell him. "I'm not feeling so great."

"I can hear it in your voice," he says. "But trust me, you look absolutely fantastic."

I laugh. The fever must be making me delirious.

"You're a lucky woman." Patrick gestures to the flight attendant. "I happen to know the world's most reliable cure for whatever ails you."

The smiling flight attendant leans over us. "Can I get you something, Mr. Carroll?"

"Yes ma'am," he says. "Some hot water please. And a lemon, and some honey, and two bottles of Dewar's."

"I'm not much of a drinker." The sun hasn't even come up yet and this guy wants a cocktail?

"Trust me," he says, though of course, Patrick Carroll, five times married and divorced, linked to every famous woman of stage, screen, and what have you, has such a notorious reputation, trusting him is the furthest thing from my mind.

One

When I first wake up, I think I'm dreaming—dreaming that I'm back home, in my old room, safe and cozy in my bed. I can almost hear Mom downstairs, fussing around in the kitchen, clanking pots and slamming cabinets. I can almost hear my brothers' voices arguing about the Jets or cars or whatever it is they find to fight about. I can almost hear my dad telling everyone to pipe down so he can hear the evening news. Then I realize I'm not dreaming, just delirious from having traveled thousands of miles with a cold on the verge of blossoming into full-on flu. I sit up. I *am* back home, in the same old bedroom, in the same old house, in small-town New Jersey. But I'm definitely not the same girl.

In the past few months I've gone from waitress (waiting on tables, waiting for my ex-boyfriend to come back from his first year at college, waiting for my own college career to begin) to model. I know a lot of girls would consider this a dream come true, but I never planned on being a model. I'm still not planning on it, necessarily; I want the same thing I've always wanted: college, a master's degree, a career as a nutritionist. But since I started modeling, that dream is closer than ever before; at this point, I could pay for medical school, if I wanted to. But even though it's closer to becoming a reality, now that I don't need to rely on scholarships and loans, school seems so distant. My whole life seems so distant; it's basically disappeared. Life now is waiting in the security line at the airport. Life is sitting in a chair on set, waiting for the photographer, sipping water through a straw so I don't screw up my lipstick, wondering what time zone I'm in while some stranger fusses over my hair. I do some quick mental math. I've been a model now for a full nine months. It seems an appropriate amount of time, because I've basically been reborn. Melody Ann—I don't even know who that is anymore. Mac? I'm still figuring out who she is, too.

Though I do know one thing about Mac: Apparently, she's the kind of woman who can charm one of the world's most famous men during a six-hour plane ride. Turns out Patrick Carroll wasn't lying; his cure-all magic elixir knocked me out before we even took off, and I woke up somewhere over the Great Lakes, my head on his shoulder. Lots of women drool over Patrick Carroll; I literally drooled *on* him, all over the poor guy's soft cable-knit sweater.

"Feeling better?" he'd asked me.

I'd admitted that I did. Patrick asked the flight attendant to bring us our meals (he'd skipped his while I slept—what a gentleman!) and over some not-too-terrible omelets and melon, we bonded. He'd asked me what I was doing in Montana—where it turns out he keeps a vacation house—and before we landed he asked where he could find me in New York. He insisted that I get better so that he could take me to dinner at Per Se, his favorite restaurant in the world.

I sit up and rub my eyes. The whole thing—from the first

go-sees and my first shoot with *Teen Vogue* to spotting my *Sports Illustrated* cover on the racks at JFK to chatting up Patrick Carroll while ensconced in my first-class seat—seems like a dream. But it all happened. It's only hours since I got off a plane, collapsed into a taxi, and somehow directed the driver to drive me back here, where my mom marched me upstairs and into bed. And that's where I find myself now. I yawn, stretch my hands above my head, and then, just out of curiosity, check my forehead, which feels cool to the touch. He cured me. Patrick Carroll cured me.

"Melody, my goodness, look at you!" Mom turns off the faucet and dashes toward me, like any good mother in emergency mode.

"I'm actually feeling a lot better." It doesn't matter: she's got one hand on my forehead, checking for a fever, and another hand gripping my forearm tight like she's afraid to let go.

"Well, your fever does feel like it's broken," she admits. "But your skin is so cold. And you look so thin! Wouldn't they let you eat in Montana? And were you shooting outside? I saw on CNN there was some kind of blizzard there?"

She's right; it snowed about nine inches on the second day of the shoot, but rather than cancel, artist that he is, Steve Kline had been overjoyed at the chance to get shots of Ivan and me with snowflakes melting on our bare skin. Besides, nine inches in Montana barely counts as flurries, though personally I'd like to take every man I've ever met there to show them exactly what nine inches looks like.

"Hardly a blizzard," I tell her. "And I do feel better." I am feeling more human, but I'm trying to convince myself that I've experienced a miracle cure: I need to feel better, because

I need to work. In some perverse way, being sick will probably help me on the go-sees I have scheduled for tomorrow—some bookers respond to the glassy-eyed, pale-skinned look. And what with all the jumping and shaking I've done for the past two days to keep warm, I've probably lost two pounds, and that certainly can't hurt. But work isn't my only motivation. Any minute now Patrick Carroll is going to call and ask me to dinner, and no runny nose is going to interfere with that.

"Look who's up!" Ted strolls into the kitchen, Ritchie following close behind him.

"Big bro!" I have to stand on my tiptoes to embrace Ted, my big brother in every sense of the word. We're all pretty close, Ted and Ritchie and I. Teddy's three years older, in his junior year at Rutgers. Ritchie is almost two years older, and closer to home, still living with Mom and Dad while he's at the community college part time. I think eventually he'll follow Dad's footsteps and train as a firefighter, but for now he's just kind of feeling things out. "What are you doing home anyway?"

"Just came down for the night," Teddy grins. "Mom told me you'd be passing through."

"Our sister, the jetsetter." Ritchie plops down at the table and grabs a clementine from the fruit bowl.

"Leave your sister alone, please." Mom sounds just like she did a decade ago, back when we really were kids who needed to be told to leave one another alone. She puts the kettle onto the stove. "I'm making you some tea," she says, "and then you're going to eat something young lady." She loves to throw in a *young lady* when she means business.

"*Melody! Oh my God!*"

I've never heard my dad cry out like that. For a horrible moment, I think there's something wrong—and I must not be the only one because all of us stop, and Teddy bolts out of the kitchen and into the family room to see what's the matter. I push past my big brother and into the room, where my father is frozen, half-standing up out of his chair, finger outstretched like he's seen a ghost, pointing at the television screen.

And there I am, on the television. It's one of those stupid Hollywood gossip shows that comes on after the news, and there's some weird voiceover talking about, well, me, and showing some behind the scenes footage from my *Sports Illustrated* cover shoot. I have no memory of anyone recording me while we shot, and I fleetingly wonder where this footage came from. But there I am, kneeling in the sand, hands behind my head, sweeping up my long, wet locks, smiling, then not smiling, and there's Cliff, circling me like a big game hunter, camera clicking rapidly as he lunges in and out on bended knee, changing angles and perspectives constantly, but silently, so all you hear is the camera, the surf, and of course, the inane patter of the *Entertainment Now* voiceover.

"There she is, the model everyone is talking about, the new *Sports Illustrated* cover girl, Mac Croft!"

Mom screams, an urgent, piercing scream—you'd think she saw a mouse dart across the room. Teddy and Ritchie just kind of stare at the screen and me, while Dad's still frozen, half-standing, half-sitting.

"I don't believe this," Dad mutters. "My little girl . . . on the TV news?"

"This isn't the news, Dad," I point out.

"My God, I can't believe this! Melody, honey, you're on the television."

I can't believe it myself.

"I didn't know many people read that magazine," Mom says.

"Yeah, thanks," mutters Ritchie. "I'll never be able to read it again."

"But everyone watches television!" Mom looks like she's going to burst with pride.

"Just think, right now, all up and down this street everyone is watching my little girl." Dad seems significantly more impressed with my being on television than on every newsstand in the country. "We have to go out and celebrate."

"Only if you're feeling well enough, Melody . . ." Mom looks worried again.

"I'll be fine," I tell her. "Let's go out and celebrate."

Life's a funny thing. If it hadn't been for a chance encounter with weirdo extraordinaire Jonathan Novak, the guy who technically "discovered" me, and first put me in touch with the good folks at Delicious Models, that could be me, unsteadily bearing a tray covered with little wooden bowls of house salads. But it's not me, it's some girl I've never met (her name tag says Karen). I'm the customer, the paying customer at that, too, since I made it clear before we left the house that dinner at the Porter House tonight is definitely my treat. As I scan the menu, I actually can't believe how cheap this food is; the Porter House is probably the nicest place in town, and has always been our special occasion restaurant of choice. But the most expensive entrée (the surf and turf: a charred hunk of meat surrounded by deep-fried shrimp and scallops) still costs less than the berries and yogurt I ordered from room service for breakfast two days ago in Montana. I try to imagine Patrick Carroll here, and the thought makes me grin. I can pick up the whole tab tonight for my family of five (though it's more like dinner for seven, considering how much my brothers eat) for less than you'd pay for dinner for one at Per Se.

Propped up in the middle of the table, displacing the standard-issue candleholder and salt and pepper shakers, is a copy of *Sports Illustrated*. Before we left the house, Mom mentioned to me that Dad's been carrying it everywhere with him, and sure enough, every time someone we know wanders past, which is about every ten minutes, my dad beckons to them, insists on showing it off.

"Hello there stranger," he calls, no matter who it is, standing and pulling his prey over to the table. "Have you seen my little girl . . ."

So far, my second-grade teacher, a lady who lives down the block, and the family of one of Ritchie's old girlfriends has wandered into the Porter House and been treated to a glimpse of little Melody Croft, all grown up and on the cover of a magazine. I'd tell my dad to stop, but I know there's no point; his pride totally outweighs my embarrassment, and anyway, I don't care. It makes me feel physically better to see Dad this happy. Since I've started this job, he's been only grudgingly supportive, but now he's positively glowing with pride. I've missed this, being together with the whole family. Sure, my brothers and my parents get on my nerves at times—that's just family life—but moments like this, graduations and birthdays, holidays and celebrations, we don't have them anymore. Or we do, but I'm away when they happen, on set or in yet another plane going to yet another location.

"So, supermodel sister." Ritchie unfolds a tiny foil-wrapped hunk of butter and spreads it on his roll. He pops the entire roll in his mouth and then leans across the table, extending his still-greasy butter knife in my direction like it's a microphone. "Tell our viewers at home what's next for Mac Croft? Paris? Milan? Movies? Hollywood? Inquiring minds want to know!"

"Cut it out." Teddy nudges his little brother in the ribs with his elbow. They're grown men, but whenever my brothers are together they can't seem to stop acting like teenagers.

"My little girl." Dad sips his beer and just kind of beams. "You idiots leave your sister alone. We're celebrating! This is her big night!"

"We are so proud, Melody," says Mom, spearing a mouthful of ranch-dressing–drenched lettuce.

I pick the croutons out of my undressed salad and take a big bite of nothing, chewing slowly, trying not to stare at the butter, or the bread, or Mom's salad dressing, or the huge platter of fried calamari our waitress just deposited in the center of the table. For a brief second, I think I'd trade it all, the cover and everything, for one deep-fried piece of squid, liberally dipped in marinara sauce. It's unlike me, because even before I started on this modeling track I'd have steered clear of anything crusty, gleaming with oil, and so obviously poisonous for the body. But today, somehow, it looks incredibly appealing.

"Thanks, Mom." I know she's happy, maybe not as happy as my dad is, but still happy that I'm making it. But she's worried. I know she'd be a lot happier to be here at the Porter House celebrating my midterms instead of my first *Sports Illustrated* cover. Suddenly, I want to cheer her up, and I can think of only one way. "Actually, Ritchie, I do have something big cooking."

"What's that?" Dad looks at me curiously.

"Cover of *Guns & Ammo*?" Ritchie picks up a huge piece of deep-fried tentacle.

"I met someone." I smile, remembering my three-hour conversation with Patrick. Three hours—that's basically a first date, right?

"Well, Melody." Mom looks pleased. She puts down her fork and smiles at me. "Tell me more. How did you meet him? Is it anyone we know?"

"Hmmm . . . Mom . . ." I chomp on a piece of carrot. Maybe this wasn't such a good idea after all. "He is someone you might know. His name is Patrick Carroll."

"Patrick?" Mom looks confused. "Was he in school with you? Wait, Ritchie, is he that boy from the baseball team?"

"No," I correct her. "Mom, he's not from the baseball team. He's not a *boy*, actually. Patrick Carroll. The actor?"

My dad starts chuckling. "Melody, come on now. Don't tease your mother."

"No, Dad, I'm serious. Patrick Carroll. I met him yesterday. I mean, this morning?" Suddenly, I can't remember what day it is. "Anyway, it turns out he has a house in Montana, and he was there for a couple of days and we sat next to each other on the plane and we got to talking and he's really great, and so nice, and so I think we're going to have dinner later this week. I mean, if we can. I hope. Anyway, that's kind of funny, right? Patrick Carroll? Me and Patrick Carroll?" I'm babbling but I can't help myself. I want to impress my parents, they don't care about Amy Astley sending me flowers, they don't care about Calvin Klein calling me beautiful. They don't know who those people are. But Patrick Carroll—everyone knows who he is.

"My ass, you and Patrick Carroll," my dad says. "Don't be ridiculous."

"What do you mean?" I can't help the little edge in my voice. I love my dad, but the more I work, the more I travel, the sillier it seems to try to live by his rules. He can hardly claim I'm still his little girl.

"What do you think I mean? Patrick Carroll is . . . he must be my age! And come on. How many times has this guy been married? You're on one cover of one magazine and suddenly you're a Hollywood player? Some kind of celebrity arm candy?"

"Dad! It's nothing like that. You don't know Patrick. Sure, he's been married before. Big deal. He's a nice guy. And we're just going to have dinner, not walk down the aisle." Suddenly it dawns on me that dinner at Per Se is wasted on me. What the hell am I going to eat? As it is, I can't imagine what I'm going to eat at the Porter House. I know the seared tuna I ordered is going to come slathered in a mayonnaise-based sauce, even though I explicitly asked our waitress to have the chef leave it off.

"Oh man, I can see it now: Melody Ann Croft Carroll. Mac-Ca-Ca. Wife number seven!" Ritchie laughs hysterically.

"Okay, darling daughter." Dad spreads his napkin on his lap. "I've got an idea. Why don't you invite your good friend Patrick Carroll to your family home? I think your mother and I would like to meet any man you're dating."

Dating might be an exaggeration, but never mind that: I have a problem. I almost choke on my dry lettuce as I try to imagine Patrick Carroll in my parents' living room. But I can tell by the look on Dad's face that he's not kidding, and a quick glance at Mom's face proves that she's with Dad on this one. There are no two ways about it; if I want the chance to not eat anything at the fanciest restaurant in New York City in the company of one of the world's most handsome men, well, first, I'm going to have to bring him home to meet my dad. Great.

Two

Maybe I'm spoiled or I've just forgotten—and that seems forgivable, since I've basically been around the world and back in the past eight weeks—but the trek from my parents' place to the Delicious offices takes forever. Seriously. It's a good thing I thought to bring along a couple weeks' worth of mail to occupy me on the PATH train. I find the whole day-to-day commute thing so boring. I hate sitting on planes too, but at least when you get off, you're far away. This just seems like torture; I don't know how my fellow commuters do this every day. To take my mind off things, I tear into my stack of envelopes. There's some junk mail, my cell phone bill, a card from my best friend Liza with some old pictures of us in high school that she says she came across while she was cleaning her room. We're deep under the Hudson when I tear into the thickest envelope of all, the one I've been purposely avoiding—the one from the University of Pennsylvania.

Deferring my admission last fall was one of the toughest decisions I've ever had to make, and I know exactly what this letter is going to be about, and frankly it's too soon for me to have to deal with this again. The school year doesn't start until September, but I know that this is the school wanting to know if in fact I'm enrolling next semester.

I pull the packet of papers out of the envelope, unfold them, and study the letter, tracing the embossed logo on the letter-head with my fingertip. I get as far as "Dear Melody" before I stop reading, fold the papers back up, and shove them hastily back into the envelope. There. Out of sight, out of mind. I turn and stare out the window at the dark, dank tunnel.

The train is moving along at a slow crawl, so by the time I emerge at Fourteenth Street I have no choice but to hail a cab—I'm scheduled to see someone at Origins for a new print campaign, the perfect commercial followup to my cover. There goes another fourteen of my hard-earned dollars. Or twelve, I guess, because traffic is so absurd I ditch the cab a couple of blocks early and decide to hoof it. I've learned a lot in a few short months on the job, and one of the best lessons I've learned is to stick to sneakers. My simple Converse All-Stars are easy on the back, and it's warm enough that I don't have to worry about lurking patches of ice. Or so I hope, as I dash down the sidewalk, weaving in and out of pedestrians. It's surprisingly warm for a winter day, the kind of day when you can kind of imagine that someday soon it will be spring again, with leaves on the trees, and little birds flitting around and singing, and people out in shirtsleeves and shorts instead of bundled into coats that look like sleeping bags. People are smiling as they linger on the sidewalks, not grimacing in the deathly cold gusts of wind that you only find in the concrete caverns of Manhattan. It might not be miserable, but it is February, so my sprint is kind of comforting, warming me up. Plus, when I make it to the appointment, my cheeks will be a nice healthy color.

When I push through the big revolving doors at 825 Broadway the security guy gives me one glance, then waves me right through. Well! The celebrity treatment. I shoot him my best million-dollar smile and rummage in my bag for the Post-it scrawled with the info about this appointment. What a relief—third floor. I take the steps (any chance to burn a couple of those troubling, possibly career-ruining calories) but when I burst out of the stairwell and onto the third floor, my panicked rush turns to shock. There must be two dozen of us, so many of us we're corralled in the hallway like . . . well, exactly like farm animals. I paid a cab for this?

"Hey." I spot a girl who looks kind of familiar, though in reality, we all look familiar: we're all wearing simple tees, jeans, and winter coats, hair pulled back to better show off our faces. I can't remember this girl's name, and can't think of where I might have possibly met her before. It could have been on set somewhere; it could have been in the office; it's possible we have the same agency—I have no idea.

"Origins, right?" She smiles, but her tone is cool and detached. I'm no friend; I'm the competition. "Check-in is up there. Then, get in line."

I try to smile back, but I don't mean it either. "Cool, thanks."

I head to the front of the line, past a wide range of types: a freckled redhead, a freshly scrubbed blonde girl next door, a black girl with wild, untamed hair, an almost albino with short cropped hair. The sad truth dawns on me: *Sports Illustrated* cover girl or no, I'm just another model, and we're a dime a dozen.

"Hey Mac!"

Sloane perks up the moment I step into the lobby of Delicious New York headquarters. At this point, she's got a

Wait, what? "Why was your sister on television?"

"Oh, you know, my sister's Susie Q. She used to be on TV all the time. But seriously, tell me all about Montana . . ."

"Susie Q?" I know that's someone, but I can't quite think straight—maybe it's the lingering aroma of peanut butter. "Wait, Susie Q . . ."

"Yeah, Susie Q, you knew that. Anyway. I need to know: Is Ivan that hot in real life? He can't be right? He must be gay . . ."

At last it dawns on me—a vision of a skinny girl with hair sprayed up as high as it can possibly go, and heavy blue eyeliner, in a slouchy sweater, possibly sequined, that slipped off her shoulders sexily. Susie Q.

"Wait—Susie Q? The singer?"

"The singer, yeah, you know, my sister. Let's talk about Ivan!"

"Wait a minute!" I can't believe what I'm hearing. I leap up from my seat and walk back to Sloane's desk, studying her face carefully. The first time I saw her, I thought Sloane was totally intimidating. But I think that has a lot to do with the minimal waiting room where she works, because though you might look at her perfect alabaster skin and sleek, almost white hair and think of some old-school screen siren, I know the truth: Sloane's a brassy and brash girl, with a throaty laugh, and a huge presence. She actually would have made a good screen siren—in silent films. She's so expressive that even watching her eat, I can almost taste what she's tasting. Almost. "Your sister is Susie Q, the singer."

"You knew that, right? Everyone knows that." Sloane gives a dismissive little wave.

I look at her more closely. Yes, her hair is pulled back, in an office-appropriate little bun, and yes, she's in a conservative little wool blazer, but there is a definite resemblance to Susie Q, the '90s pop siren with a fondness for fishnet gloves and leather jackets.

"I can't believe this! Your sister is Susie Q! I loved that song . . . Oh man, what was it called?" I try humming a few notes but can't quite get the tune that I distinctly remember dancing to at summer camp.

"'Show Me Your Love.'" Sloane sighs. "My God, I gave her such a hard time about that. Do you remember the video?"

I do, vaguely—Susie Q, writhing in a four-poster bed, purring and pouting. Hilarious. "I can't believe Susie Q is your sister! I never knew anyone related to anyone famous before." It's true. Sure, I just spent a few hours chatting up Patrick Carroll, but that was random coincidence—this is something totally different. I can't imagine what it's like to be related to an actual celebrity.

"Well, I'm not sure I'd call her famous, exactly." Sloane sighs. "She's thinking about doing this reality show. *One-Hit Wonders*? Anyway, she's my sister. I thought you knew. Sloane Quimby? Susan Quimby. Susie Q."

"Gosh. Wow. I'm so impressed." If my eleven-year-old self were here now, she'd really be freaking out.

"We need to get back to a more important topic. Ivan!" Sloane grins impishly. "Tell me he's gay. As a woman, I'm just not sure I can go on in a world where a man as hot as Ivan exists and yet is not sleeping with me . . ."

"Hate to break it to you, but he's straight as an arrow. I'm gonna go check in now. . . ." I make a quick detour to the communal kitchen, leaving a box of cookies on the counter, than continue down the hall toward Francesca's office. I hug the big box of cookies to my chest and give a tiny knock on Francesca's slightly open door.

"Come in, come in." Francesca waves at me through the frosted glass door.

I step inside. As usual, her sleek glass desk is submerged under an astonishing spill of magazines and tear sheets, and her modern office looks more like a messy teenager's room than anything. And behind the mess is Francesca, leaning back in her chair, phone cradled under her chin, nodding at something the voice on the other end of the phone is saying. *Sit, sit,* she mouths.

I drop my bag on the floor, place the box on the overcrowded desk, and sit, noticing, as I do, that a copy of my *Sports Illustrated* cover is teetering on the very top of the insane pile that is Francesca's desk. That must be a good sign, right?

"Yes, OK, fine," Francesca is saying. "But I think you might want to take a look at Mac. Hmmm. Yes, yes I know. No. No. Just trust me, OK? I'll send her over tomorrow! OK. OK. Listen, gotta run, but we'll talk tomorrow." She hangs up the phone. "Asshole," she mutters. "Jesus. Mac!"

"Me, Mac? You're sending me somewhere tomorrow?"

"You're the only Mac in the agency," Francesca says brusquely. "What's that?" She points at the box suspiciously.

"Just a little something." I smile.

"You're too sweet." Francesca snips open the twine and glances inside, inhaling the scent of the buttery baked goods. "Too sweet. Anyway, that was Karin Holder. At *Marie Claire.* I want them to think about you for the September cover. I know it's early, but it doesn't hurt. I heard they're planning something new for the fall. A redesign or something. Maybe they're going to finally ditch their fashion director. Anyway."

Francesca studies me. I swear she can tell someone's weight just by looking at them. "You're looking well," she says at last. "How was Montana?"

I guess by the way she says "well" that my post-Montana cold helped me shed a couple of ounces. "It was good. Freezing, but good."

"I have something very important to discuss with you. Hang on a second." Francesca rummages around in the mess on her desk. "I know it's here. Wait." At last she happens upon what she's looking for, giving it a good tug and sending a cascade of papers drifting to the floor. "Here it is. Damn. I need to clean up in here."

She thrusts a copy of the *Post* across the desk at me triumphantly. The paper's folded open to Page Six, and there's a shot of my cover alongside a tiny paragraph. I immediately pick out my name—my new name, that is—in bold type, alongside another, seriously boldface name: Patrick Carroll. It's a short item about the two of us hitting it off in the first-class cabin of an American Airlines flight to New York.

"Is it true? Tell me everything!" Francesca leans way back, kicking her feet up onto the desk.

"Not true at all," I tell her. I pause. "We flew Continental."

"Shut up!" Francesca laughs. "Patrick Carroll. Damn. You're something else, Mac Croft. Patrick Carroll. Damn, I am jealous. I've had a thing for him ever since *Commies*."

I shrug my shoulders. "All we did was talk. He's sweet. I hope we can see each other again, but I don't know. We'll have to see." I'm remembering my deal with Dad, and still none too pleased. Patrick Carroll and my father. Time to change the subject. "*Marie Claire*, huh?"

"*Marie Claire*. But wait, first tell me about the Origins. How'd it go? Was Stephanie there?" Francesca pulls her feet off the desk, sits up straight, and starts paging through her desk calendar.

"Yeah, well, I'm not sure I'm what they're looking for." Truth is they'd barely even glanced at me. Delicious had sent my portfolio down via messenger (convenient, except for the fact that I'm the one who has to pay for that little perk) and it was sitting on the table in front of a couple of people from the ad agency, lost in a pile of identical bound-leather portfolios. One of the suits behind the desk might have been named Stephanie; I wouldn't know. They hadn't said one word to me, just looked me up and down, smiled weakly, and said "Thanks." One of them didn't even bother getting off the phone the whole time I was in the room. That was it. Oh, and they handed me my book on my way out, so I could deliver it back. Charming. Of course, I've had go-sees like this, appointments where they don't even bother to take a Polaroid. But I thought those days were behind me. First *Sports Illustrated*, then Calvin Klein? I assumed I was finally moving up in the world.

"I almost forgot!" Francesca stands and reaches into the cabinet behind her desk. "I have a present for you!"

"A present? For me? Why?"

"Just for being you." Francesca hands me a dainty powder-blue paper bag. "I figured you deserved a little something. You've been having a spectacular couple of months."

"Speaking of which . . ."

"Business later, Mac. Open it, open it!" Francesca plops back down in her seat, clapping her hands like a little kid at Christmas.

I reach into the bag and pull out a heavy cardboard box that's the same powder blue shade as the bag. I untie the black ribbon, and lift off the top of the box, pulling back the tissue paper to reveal a beautiful navy blue pebbled leather wallet. "Francesca! This is beautiful."

"It's a travel wallet," she explains.

I lift it from its box and undo the clasp and sure enough it is, with deep slots for foreign currency and my passport and plane tickets.

"I thought it might come in handy for my favorite little frequent flier."

It does look pretty handy, with lots of space for the receipts and Post-its and business cards I constantly collect when I'm on the road. "Francesca, really, this is too sweet of you." I stand and lean across the desk, kissing her on the cheek. "I can't tell you how much I appreciate this."

"Anyway, hon, what were you saying? Origins? Tell me how it went."

"Uh, it didn't, Francesca. In and out. I wasn't even there for two minutes."

"Those bastards," Francesca mutters. "Screw them. I wanted something bigger for you anyway. That was some seasonal bullshit. I want something huge—TV spots, print ads. Hell, I want your face on the damn bottle."

Now this is good news. "I know, Francesca. I want the same thing. Which I kind of wanted to talk to you about. I mean, I'm glad we're on the same page. Because I'm starting to feel like these go-sees and all . . . they're starting to feel like kind of a joke." I gesture helplessly, feeling awkward all of a sudden. I can almost feel myself blushing from head to toe, kind of a welcome relief because ever since I got back from Montana I've had this weird, persistent chill.

"A joke?" Francesca gives me a funny look.

"I thought that maybe since we had a cover . . . and my portfolio. I'm paying to messenger my portfolio, and I have to go too? Can't I just send the book down? Is it really important for me to be out and about all the time like this?"

"Important?" Francesca leans back in her chair and looks up at the ceiling. "No, you're right. It's not important at all. Unless you want to keep working. If you're planning on retiring, then that's fine."

"I just thought . . ."

"Look, Mac, you did one cover. One cover. It's beautiful, it's major, don't get me wrong. We all couldn't be more proud. But it's *one cover*, Mac. It'll be off the newsstands in a matter of weeks. Then where are you going to be?"

"I didn't mean . . ." My cheeks are bright red and I feel hot and uncomfortable all of a sudden.

"And you realize, I'm sure, that you're still so early in your career. Why you're just a baby! We've got Maggie booking American *Vogue* covers and walking every show every season and doing that deal with that stupid shampoo, whatever it's called, the one in the green bottle that smells like vomit and pears. I'm afraid you've got plenty of go-sees in your future yet."

I wiggle around on my chair. "OK, I get it, Francesca, I do." I'm embarrassed. The truth is I still am a baby compared to some of the agency's biggest names. I feel stupid that I got ahead of myself. I know it's only been a few months, and I know the money's pretty good, but it is a lot of running around, and it is wearing me down, this model life. I want the same things Francesca wants: I want the ad campaign, I want the TV spots, I want my face on the shampoo bottle, because with that comes everything else—money, security, enough for the rest of my life.

"I hope you do, Mac, I hope you do. You're hard working, and you're talented as hell, but I'm going to need you to be patient too. *Sports Illustrated* is great, no question, but that's editorial, hon. You think Paul and Renee are going to let you climb up the ranks at Delicious before booking a serious ad client?"

Paul and Renee. Of course. It always comes back to them, doesn't it, the gods watching me from the top of Mount Delicious, watching my every move, waiting to see if I can do well before I am rewarded. "If a serious ad client is what it takes, then I want a serious ad client," I tell her.

"Hon, what exactly do you think Origins is?" Francesca frowns a little. I think she's starting to lose her patience.

"I know, I know." Gulp. I'm starting to get the feeling that today is definitely not my day.

"Well, fine, so, Origins, a no go." Francesca sounds suddenly so warm and maternal. "Whatever. Doesn't matter. You're better than them anyway."

Whew. What a relief—Francesca doesn't hate me.

"I am?"

"You are," Francesca nods. "Believe me. We all want the best for you, you know. Let's be honest—if you don't make money, I don't make money. And I'm not volunteering here, you know. We'll have you as the face of L'Oreal or Neutrogena or something before the year's out, this I promise you. But unless you're booked, you're going on appointments. Clients want to see girls who are in demand!"

"OK." I nod, feeling like a teenager in trouble at school.

"Look, I know the portfolio thing gets expensive." Francesca gives me a pitying look. "So, we can make a second book, one for you to carry around. If you're going in person, we won't messenger your portfolio down; you can just bring that one. Deal?"

I nod my head.

"Good. I'll have Oscar get to work on that." Francesca grabs a pen and digs through the mess on her desk until she unearths a piece of paper. She starts scribbling furiously, then hands it to me.

Tomorrow's appointments, it says. I glance at the page. "Three meetings," I say. "I can do this."

"Oh hon," Francesca grins. "That's just the morning. You can call in when you're done and I'll have Jude let you know where to go. We're going to get you out there and get you working."

"So I see." I nod. Guess I'll be wearing my comfortable shoes again tomorrow.

Three

I'll say this for Francesca: She's as good as her word. I've had an absolutely insane week, Montana well behind me, my cover shoot in Costa Rica receding into my memory to the point that the whole thing seems like a particularly vivid dream. If Dad didn't have *Sports Illustrated* displayed proudly on the mantel, I'd swear it had never actually happened. Not even one of the clients I've seen this week has acknowledged the fact that I'm splayed half-naked across every newsstand in the city. One snide woman did frown upon seeing me, saying only, "I thought she'd be prettier." I mean, imagine saying this right in front of someone? But other than that—nothing. And worse than that, no bookings, other than one stupid fashion editorial shoot for a yoga magazine: me and four other girls looking sweaty and flushed as we bent and thrust in fleece pants and tank tops. Boring—and not particularly well paying.

I'm trapped in a succession of seemingly endless, repetitive days that each feel like the last: Wake up with the rest of the workforce, drink some tea, catch the bus to the train station, take the train to the city, take the subway to the Delicious offices. If they gave frequent flier miles for mass transit, I'd be well on my way to a first-class upgrade. Unfortunately for me, all I have to show for it is $350 from my yoga shoot and some blisters on my heel, because it snowed two days ago and I'm tramping around in my heavy winter boots. The snow slows everything down, so I'm running behind schedule this morning, which is no big deal because I don't think my first go-see is until eleven. Still, I've made it my habit to camp out in the Delicious lobby. You never know when Paul or Renee is going to happen by, and I want them to see that I'm a team player, and that I'm dead serious about my work. Nothing on the books? No problem. I'm going to sit and wait, because for me, modeling is a career choice.

I push through the heavy glass door and into the almost stiflingly warm lobby. Sloane's behind her desk as usual, speedily and noisily tapping at her keyboard, and two other girls are lounging on the leather sofa, one whispering furiously into her cell phone, the other paging idly through one of the many coffee table books scattered around. I don't know them, but I give them both a quick smile out of model solidarity. The one on the phone ignores me completely, while the other—I can't tell if they're together or both just happen to be waiting to see their bookers—gives me a wry smile then goes back to her reading. Or page turning.

"Krispy Kreme," I announce. I open the box, turning my head slightly to avoid eye contact with the gooey treats. "Take one." The doughnuts were a last-minute pit stop—where else was I going to go when it's below zero outside?

Sloane looks up from what I assumed was work but is in fact the *USA Today* online crossword puzzle. "This is just what the doctor ordered."

I grin. I've probably spent the entire fee from my last shoot on treats for the agency. I guess it's worth it though; the other bookers know who I am, and Sloane and I are best pals now, so she gives me all the inside gossip on the other girls. "I live to serve," I say, as sunny as I can manage.

"You truly are my very favorite, Mac Croft!" Sloane claps her hands quickly, then pushes her chair back. From behind me, I can hear a little groan, and I turn in time to see the phone call model is chatting away quietly, but rolling her eyes. At me?

"Sloane, before you go, I was wondering if Francesca is free?" I've got no time for this inter-model bitchiness.

"I think she's with Sally." Sloane shakes her head. "Let me get her." She picks up the phone and jabs at the keypad. "Hi. Yes. I've got Mac out here." Sloane hands me the receiver. "There you go."

I smile my thanks. "Hi, Francesca. I was just stopping in . . . I brought doughnuts."

"Thanks, kid. I'll send Jude to grab me one." She pauses. "You've got *Glamour* at eleven, and then *Self* at eleven-thirty. And wait . . . I think you're down for Cover Girl? You are. Mitch and Helen, at Cover Girl, two o'clock, their offices. Get moving!"

"Cover Girl?" This is news to me. They do it all, and would be a huge get. I'm surprised that Francesca didn't mention this appointment before. Well, I guess it's not a booking, and she probably doesn't want to get my hopes up. Too late for that! I'm picturing myself splayed on billboards above Times Square and the Lincoln Tunnel, staring out from the back covers of all the magazines, starring in my own television commercials. Suddenly, the day is looking up. This is the kind of client I need, and I'm determined to land them.

ing through my hoodie. I haven't told my parents he's coming; Mom runs a pretty tight ship, but shouldn't I give them the heads-up so they can get the house to the point where it's ready to handle a movie star? You know, straighten the pillows, put out bowls of caviar and lots of extravagant cut flowers? I manage to place the call just before the train goes deep underground and I lose all cell reception.

Mom? Dad? It's me. We're having company tonight. Patrick is coming over. I'll see you soon is all I get out before the phone cuts off. When I hop off the bus and trudge through the snow, which is still coming down, but lighter now, it's clear that they've got the message. For starters, the place is lit up like it's Christmas—every light in the house is on, something my electric-bill–conscious parents normally won't stand for.

"Melody! Melody!" I turn to see who besides me is outside in this ridiculous end-of-days weather, and there's Mrs. McAuliffe, our neighbor across the way, who used to baby sit my brothers and me on those rare nights Mom and Dad wanted to get away to the movies or something.

"Mrs. McAuliffe?" I stop, then cross the street, tiptoeing cautiously through the slushy car tracks. "How are you? What are you doing outside in this weather?"

"Nothing, honey," she says, leaning on the mailbox, pulling her cardigan closed tight so casually, like it's not freezing and horrible out. "Just grabbing the mail!"

"Well, you better get inside before you catch a cold! I'll see you later!" As I turn to cross back to my place, I catch the eye of her son, Bud, a teenager now, leaning in the open doorway. He waves at me, smiling big. Weird.

Also weird: Not only is every light on, the driveway and front walk are totally clean and snow-free, even though it's still coming down. Even weirder: Teddy's car is parked in the driveway. What is he doing home in the middle of the week?

Slightly worried, I dash up the steps, ignoring the possibility of some ill-placed ice patches. The front door is open, which is even more alarming, and I yank open the storm door and step inside. "Mom? Dad?"

Teddy pokes his head around the corner. "Hey sis."

"Teddy?" I stamp the snow off my boots and look at my big brother. "What are you doing here? Don't you have class?"

"Well, thought I'd come by and see you!" My brother steps into the foyer and I realize he's wearing a tie. A tie! Something is definitely up.

"Why are you all dressed up?" I hang my coat in the closet and lean down to unlace my boots. "Are you sure everything is OK?" I study my brother's grinning face, and then step past him and into the living room, and suddenly I understand. There's my dad, freshly-shaven and grinning happily, and my mom, and Ritchie, wearing the sweater that I gave him for Christmas and sitting patiently on the sofa, legs crossed, sipping a soda. There's Uncle Kevin and Uncle Doug, who aren't blood relatives at all but guys from my dad's unit who we've known forever, and Mrs. Whittaker, our elderly next door neighbor who's kind of like a surrogate grandmother, and who my mom looks in on from time to time since her kids live out of state. Suddenly, I understand. Guess Mom and Dad did get my message after all.

Patrick pulls up about forty-five minutes later, but no one gets impatient in the least; they all just sit happily, beaming broadly, not even touching the bowls of almonds and the plate of broccoli and carrots Mom puts out, reaching some silent agreement that those are strictly for the guest of honor. It's a quiet night; the snow means most people are just staying in, but every time a car passes, Dad stands, walks to the front window, and frowns out into the night.

"You're sure you gave him good directions, Melody? Because you know it can be confusing when the exits split like that . . ."

"Dad, he's got a GPS. I gave him the address. He'll be here. Don't worry. He's not even due for another," I glance at my watch. "Well, OK, he's ten minutes late but it's snowing. Cut the guy some slack."

No sooner are these words out of my mouth, though, when we hear another car's wheels stirring up the snow outside. Dad peers out the window, then nods. "That's him."

I think Dad might be on the verge of running outside to embrace Patrick like some long-lost son, so I decide to head him off. "I'll go get him," I tell everyone. Back in the foyer, I pull on my boots quickly and dash out into the driveway just as Patrick is switching off the engine and emerging into the snowy New Jersey evening.

"You're a sight for sore eyes," Patrick says. "A little snow and the traffic slows to an absolute crawl." Patrick scoops me up in his arms and whirls me around like he's the quarterback and I'm the head cheerleader. "I'm so sorry I'm a little late."

"The snow is not going to be your only obstacle tonight," I tell him. He's wearing a thin khaki blazer over a thick ivory sweater, the kind with a collar and a big wooden button, and a bold blue button-down underneath that brings out his gorgeous eyes. His thick dark hair falls in perfect curly tangles over his forehead, and that distinctive voice sounds even sexier in person than it does over the phone. The last thing I feel like doing with Patrick Carroll is a meet and greet with everyone who ever knew me. Across the street, I spy Mrs. McAuliffe, casually checking her mailbox yet again, her son leaning in the doorway, trying surreptitiously to take our picture on his cell phone.

"Aren't you coming inside?" Dad's pushed the storm door open and is smiling like a madman.

"Brace yourself," I whisper, taking Patrick by the hand and leading him toward my dad.

"Mr. Croft? I'm Patrick." He offers my dad his hand, which Dad pumps enthusiastically. So embarrassing!

"Patrick, a pleasure. You didn't have any trouble finding our place, did you?"

"No, sir, none at all. Just a little slow going, what with this snow."

"Well, never mind that, now." Dad pulls Patrick in and away from me, putting his hand on the movie idol's shoulder. "Come in, come in. Everyone is dying to meet you. And you've got to see all our pictures of our little girl."

"Sounds great," Patrick says, sounding genuinely enthusiastic, which means he's an even better actor than I had suspected. Give this guy an Oscar, quick!

Four

"Come on, girl! Work it, work it, work it."

Work it? For a second, I can't disguise my disgust at the photographer, Ringo, and the stock phrases he insists on spouting as he dashes around the set, eyes shielded behind massive black wraparound sunglasses, ass crack clearly visible every time he drops to his knees, thanks to his skin-tight black jeans. I've worked with some characters in the past couple of months, but this guy is ridiculous.

"Mac, darling, frowning. That's a no-no. Look glamorous. Look regal! You're getting married!"

If I were getting married, I certainly wouldn't opt for the gown I have on: one hundred pounds of tiered tulle, speckled with glimmering glass beads. I look ridiculous—I feel like a figure skater in costume. But work is work, and the photographer is the boss. Or a collaborator, anyway. I smile, bashfully, happily, the way I imagine a bride might.

"Atta girl, Mac, atta girl!" Ringo cries, the relentless whirr of his digital camera echoing in the cavernous studio. "Kick off those shoes!"

I do as instructed, lifting the heavy beaded skirt with two

hands and kicking up my right foot, sending my silver Manolo sandal flying across the room, never mind that in the middle of the set is an artfully broken chandelier, spilling crystalline shards of glass all over the place and adding just the right touch to Ringo's vision of bridal meets punk. Or whatever. My flying shoe hits Ringo's assistant Karl square in the chest, but like any good photo assistant, he says nothing, simply following behind his boss, light meter and alternate lens in his hands. "Sorry!" I cry.

"No talking, models, no talking please. You're ruining my shot. Brides just are. Brides don't talk."

I turn and step, pivot and swivel, delicately, to avoid the glass. It's not without its risks, this business. Still, I'm a pro, and just tiptoe carefully. If I have to walk through broken glass, then I have to walk through broken glass. On a catalog job for Coach last summer I worked with this girl Maggie who refused—absolutely refused—to take off her shoes and tromp through the grass. And we were on a beautiful private estate in the Hamptons; no glass or dog doo in sight. If she were here now, I'm sure Maggie would do just what she did back then: storm off set, feet still very much inside her shoes, and sit backstage, arms crossed, pouting and texting her agent. Some girls.

"Now glow! Glow! New card!" Ringo stops, waving his free hand frantically over his head like a drowning man.

Karl scurries over, grabs the camera body from Ringo, and he changes the memory card. Ringo stalks over to study the images he's just shot at the computer bay, while the hair stylist Delphine swoops in to smooth out my hair. Her pinched, freckled face is inches from mine, like we're about to kiss, but she's not even looking at me. My hair is so teased out and full of product I can't even really feel her tugging and pulling at it.

"Theo! Zere is problem wiz ze hem!" Delphine steps back, nods, pleased with her handiwork, then frowns at my dress, but Theo, assistant to the stylist Zvi Zee, comes running, kicks his shoes off, and pads onto the seamless to inspect the part of the dress she's holding aloft.

"Where, where?" He's a little out of breath. In fact, everything about him is little. He's possibly the smallest and tidiest man I've ever seen, barely five foot seven, with immaculately parted thick brown hair, long eyelashes, a soft Southern accent, and quite possibly the world's cutest outfit: corduroy pants, perfectly-pressed blue gingham shirt, plaid bow tie, and cashmere sweater vest. "Oh, goodness, I see it."

From the horror and heartbreak in his voice, I'd swear he's actually on the verge of tears.

"Mac, would you mind terribly if I just pin you up here?" Theo smiles up at me imploringly. "I promise I'll be really quick."

This is quite possibly the first time any of the people I have ever worked with has asked me what I think, or for my permission before plucking at my eyelashes, or unclasping my bra, or jabbing a pencil into my eyelid. This is a pleasant change of pace—it's nice to be treated like an actual human being.

"No problem, Theo," I tell him. Ringo's still busy with the computer, scanning through the first couple of shots: me in a strapless dress with a ludicrously long train, gloves pushed up past my elbows, me standing perfectly straight in a slouchy bubble dress, heavy veil affixed to my head. Delphine is back in her little plastic chair on the periphery of the set, brush and spritz bottle clutched in her hands, ready for action. Annick, the other model on set, a Slovenian girl who doesn't seem to speak a word of English, is off somewhere being made up. This is the kind of rare downtime minute I've learned to savor when I'm on set.

I just kind of lose myself for a minute, standing and waiting. So much of this industry is standing or waiting; when the camera's clicking, I'm there, I'm present, I'm working. But when it's not, I've developed the ability to let my mind just shut off and wander where it wants. And I guess it's no surprise that it wanders to the subject of Patrick Carroll. I know he's got lots of awards and adoring fans. I know he's made some of the most celebrated movies in history. But that's not what's so cool about him, that's not what I like. What's great about him is that he's the nicest, most laid-back, down to earth guy I've met in a long, long time. In my opinion, modeling is just a job, and so, for that matter, is being a movie star; I don't care what you do, I care what you're like. But I must admit I didn't expect Patrick to be so normal. He drank beer with my dad and pored over the old family photographs, Dad pointing out every dorky snapshot of me from throughout the years. He posed for pictures with my mom, kissed Mrs. Whittaker on the cheek and nodded politely as she told him pointless stories about her two daughters, asked my brothers about college, talked to Kevin and Uncle Doug about his second wife's brother, who was also a firefighter. He was totally unfazed when the doorbell rang and some of the other neighbors dropped by, like it was any another night and they were just paying a social call, and shook hands and learned names and told stories and signed autographs like it was no big deal. And when Mom frowned because the snow was still falling, Patrick told her that instead of taking me into the city in the bad weather, he'd be much happier just having a simple dinner at home. *If you'll have me*, he said. If they'd have him? I could see my dad mentally planning our wedding already. I'm not sure how I feel about Patrick, whether we have a future, but I know this: Mom and Dad are in love with him.

So that's how it came to pass that my first real date with Patrick Carroll, matinee idol, legendary Hollywood romancer, was spent gathered around my family's formal dining table, eating pizza. Well, they ate pizza; I picked a couple of mushrooms off of one slice and ate those, plus a very hearty arugula salad and a nice glass of water infused with fresh lemon.

"It's a guy, right?" Theo's back, and carefully pinning up the hem of this ridiculous gown with safety pins.

"What's that?" I look down at him, feeling like Cinderella, talking to one of the little bluebirds that's dressing her up for the ball. Just then—whoosh. Lightheaded. Ugh. I blink my eyes, shake my arms a little to get the blood going. I can't help myself: I grab Theo's shoulder to steady my body, because for a horrible second it really seems like I might faint.

"You OK?" Theo looks up at me.

I nod, telling myself *I'm OK, I'm OK*, willing it to be true. I have work to do, after all.

"Forgive my saying so, but I'd know that look anywhere." Theo sticks an open safety pin into his mouth, then removes it and places it oh-so-delicately into the underside of the dress. "That look is pure reverie. And I'm guessing it's not the proximity to the creative genius of Mr. Ringo Tang that's got your eyes misting over like that."

"Those jeans are so tight I can see his creative genius from here," I say, snickering a little. The momentary spell has passed. I'm fine. Sure enough, Ringo is still preening and fretting in front of the computer, frowning over the morning's work.

"Oh my goodness, please don't make me laugh." Theo sounds a little panicked. "Once I start, I can't stop. And gosh, wouldn't you know I laugh like a horse in labor. Zvi can't stand it when I have a good time with the girls. Er, women. Sorry."

"Why don't you tell Zvi to lighten up?" I smile prettily down at Theo. Even if he weren't kneeling, I'd be smiling down at him. He'd have to stand on a stool just to button my trousers.

"From your lips to God's ears." Theo stands, brushes the nonexistent dirt from the knees of his trousers, and studies me critically. "Gorgeous. Just gorgeous. By the way," he adds in a dramatic stage whisper, "you are just the most beautiful woman I've ever seen."

This isn't the first time I've heard this line, but when it's spoken by a young man who clearly has no interest in getting me into bed—unless it's for room service and a midnight viewing of *Big Girls Don't Cry*—this compliment is strangely moving.

"Thanks, Theo." I wink, no easy feat considering I'm wearing both fake eyelashes and about three pounds of mascara. "I'll try not to ruin your handiwork."

"OK, girls." Ringo claps his hands authoritatively and storms back onto the set. "Back to work!"

Back to work. Work it girl. Make it work. Work, work, work.
Clearly, work is Ringo Tang's favorite four-letter word, and work we did. I've had long days before, but today was almost a record; a full ten hours after our call time of 8 AM, the crew finally wraps up. I'm trying to wriggle out of the gown that was

the day's final look, which is lighter at least, all shirred tulle, but is constricting and tight like some kind of bondage getup, and I'm caught, like I'm in a straitjacket.

"A damsel in distress," says Theo wryly, tiptoeing up behind me silently. He stands on a folding chair to release the hook-and-eye closure that's cinching the dress to my torso. The air comes flooding into my lungs, and I realize that this wedding dress makes me feel like I'm drowning. Is there a metaphor there?

"Oh thank God." I breathe in deeply, satisfied, wondering if this is how all the girls who smoke feel when they finally get out of wardrobe and get the chance to light up. "Thanks Theo." Then, realizing that I'm wearing only my La Perla thong, I cross my arms across my chest. "Uh, a robe?"

"A step ahead of you." Theo scurries over to the rack, grabs a terry robe, and then tosses it over my bare shoulders with a flourish. "There we go!"

"Theo! Did you call the messenger to pick up the Dior? Annabelle says she needs that dress on a plane to Paris *tonight*." Zvi Zee comes storming around the corner, dressed all in black, illuminated by the eerie green pulse of his ever-present, glowing Bluetooth headset. "Stop talking with the girls, and get those shoes packed up. It looks like Barney's on sale day in here."

Actually, the set's incredibly tidy, considering I've been in and out of seven bridal gowns, nine pairs of shoes, four pairs of stockings, one anklet, three diamond necklaces, one tiara, fourteen pairs of earrings, three veils, one pair of to-the-elbow gloves, two rings, and . . . I can't even remember the rest. Considering all the changes, and the two models, and the makeup and hair people, it's downright neat back here, and I know that's because of Theo, who is himself still neat and tidy, bow tie still perfectly done up.

"The messenger picked up three hours ago," Theo tells Zvi quietly. "And I was just helping Miss Croft . . ."

"Yes, yes, Croft, yes. Well, good job today, darling." Zvi Zee gives a weird bow and disappears.

I glance at Theo, who shrugs his shoulders and starts putting the jewelry into tiny plastic bags. I'm half tempted to help him, I feel so bad for the guy, but it's late, way late. I've got a couple of messages from Mom on my phone—I made the mistake of teaching her how to send text messages; she sends me one almost on the hour, no matter where I am—and I'm scared about writing her back and telling her that I'm just wrapping up now. Based on my past experiences with late-night train schedules, I've got a good ninety minutes yet before I can count on being home and in bed. Mom's going to be waiting for me, I just know it.

I smear some cold cream on my face, rubbing at the clownish makeup. "Theo—good luck! I'm taking off!" I dash toward the bathroom, playing beat the clock once again.

The way I'm yawning, you'd think I was coming from India, not Chelsea. My entire body feels like lead, and the only silver lining to the dark cloud that is late-night New Jersey transit is that I've got two seats all to myself, so I fold my body up, hogging the seat and not even caring about being polite, and try to rest. But even though I'm exhausted, I'm also too keyed up to just nap.

Being on set is a complicated thing; even though there are times it's as boring as watching paint dry, there's usually this energy, this electricity, and enough people running around, chattering, to make sure you stay awake and alert—or providing enough illicit supplies, if you're into that kind of thing, to make sure that you do. I'm not one for drugs, but I can't help get the natural high that comes from either working my hardest when I'm in front of the camera or being surrounded by a bunch of nervous, creative energy while I'm waiting to be in front of the camera. I think for a moment that I can't take much more of this, and then it dawns on me that I can't; but the thing I can't take any more of isn't modeling, it's commuting.

I've made some tentative stabs at moving out before—I holed up with Jade for a while, I spent one night at the Valencia, a fleabag hotel where Delicious deposits most of its out-of-town girls—but now it's time to really make a go of it. I've got to leave the nest.

I can just imagine the look on Dad's face. I mean, he almost had a heart attack over me staying with Jade, and her *mother* lived in the same apartment. I can just hear him now, his voice eerily present as if he were on the train right beside me: *No child of mine is going to go live in the city surrounded by drug addicts and prostitutes. Not a chance.*

In my head, I start arguing with Dad. I tell him about the money I've made, how it's all saved up, how I've been so responsible, and how it would be such a smart investment for me to move to the city. I tell him about the cab fares and bus tickets that are eating into my nest egg. I tell him about how factoring in a whole hour for my commute is adding an unnecessary burden to my already overstuffed days. I tell him I need a place to go between go-sees, which can sometimes be hours apart. I tell him that I need my sleep in order to be healthy, and I need my health in order to look good, and I need to look good in order to keep working. I tell him that lots of the girls in the agency live in the city. I tell him that lots of the girls get apartments together, pooling their resources to make it in this stupidly overpriced town. I tell him that it's perfectly safe—I tell him that it might even be safer for me to be surrounded by friends and not far from family in a city I know as opposed to all by my lonesome in some hotel in Montana or Montreal or Miami or Monterey.

It all sounds good to me, in my head, but I'm delirious from a long day, and can't be sure that my arguments really make any sense. And anyway, I'm not sure how interested Dad is going to be in logic. When it comes to his little girl and her safety, he can be pretty illogical.

Be that as it may, I know what I have to do. I have to just present my case, and be an adult about it. I'm a grown woman, and though I'd never say it out loud, we all know it's the case that I'm now making more money than my dad does. I still respect his opinion of course, but he's got to let me live my own life. For God's sake, I'm dating one of the world's most famous men. I think being allowed to move out of the bedroom I've spent my entire life in isn't much to ask. But I know my dad. And I know that the only way I'm going to get through to him is via my mother, and I know my mother, too, and I know that the only way I'm going to get through to her is with the facts.

First thing in the morning, I'm going to have to get out there and figure out where I can live and how much it's going to cost me. I'm going to have to figure out how much I can afford. Hell, I'm going to have to figure out exactly how much money I have. I think Francesca might have once mentioned something to me about an accountant, but honestly, I'm too tired to think about anything so serious. I dig around in my bag, looking for the tabloid magazine that I keep on hand for these moments when I need some mental junk food. Instead, I happen upon the envelope from Penn that I'd opened and then hastily restuffed only a couple of days before, even though that seems like years now. I definitely don't have the energy for this right now. I stuff it back into my bag, and turn to gaze out the window, but it's dark outside, so all I can see is my own reflection. For a scary moment, I don't recognize myself.

Five

Because I've lived with my mother my entire life, I'm not surprised in the least when I see, walking home from the bus stop on the corner, that the living room lights are still on. Friday night shifts at the Porter House ran just as late as it is now, and Mom never worried and waited up then, but things are different now, and I know she's inside, wrapped up in her warmest robe, probably drinking herbal tea and watching Letterman with the volume turned way down, so as not to disturb my dad, who's accustomed to popping out of bed at the slightest disturbance, which is just what happens to you after a lifetime of fighting late-night fires.

"Melody Ann." Mom's standing in the foyer when I push the door open, cradling a steaming cup of tea just like I knew she would be, softly shaking her head from side to side.

"Hi Mom." I plop down on the step into the foyer and tug off my boots. When I try to stand, my knees creak. I feel more like I've run a marathon than stood around on set all day—every muscle aches. But I've known this little secret for a while now: being a model is physically draining.

"*Hi Mom*? Melody Ann, I've been sitting here worried sick for the past hour."

"Didn't you get my text?" I hang up my coat and drape my arm around her shoulders, though her arms are still crossed in silent anger.

"I can't find any comfort in a ten-word message. I can only sleep once I know you're safe and sound."

"Maybe I'll have some tea, too," I tell her. She follows me into the kitchen. I'm freezing cold, and still have that same tired-but-wired feeling.

"I'll do it honey. You sit." Mom turns the knob on the stove, the click of the gas filling the quiet house. "You look beat."

"I am beat." I drop heavily into one of the wooden kitchen chairs. "Long day. Nutty day. You should have seen this one dress. I swear it weighed a hundred pounds."

"I'll never understand fashion." Mom reaches into a cabinet and pulls out one of those *World's Best Dad* mugs one of us must have given Dad for Father's Day or his birthday years ago. "And I can't see how it could take all day just to take some pictures."

"You don't know the half of it."

"I don't." Mom fills the mug. She places it on the table in front of me and sits. "I don't know the half of it, at all. Which is precisely what worries me."

"Don't worry, Mom." I blow on the hot tea. "There's nothing to worry about."

"That's just it, Melody." Mom sighs, long and serious. "I have so much to worry about. Instead of being off at college, my only daughter is jetting around the world, going on dates with men twice her age, spending all day doing God knows what with God knows who and coming home exhausted and emaciated. I don't know what to think."

"But I'm doing this for college . . ." I start to say—but then I remember that still-unread letter in my bag. I'm not sure that's true anymore.

"Melody, please. Let me talk. I might not know about fashion designers and runway shows and meeting movie stars. But there is a lot I do know." Mom looks out the window into the wintry suburban night. "I worry that I haven't taught you all the things you're really going to need to know."

"What do you mean? Mom, come on . . ."

"No, I mean it. You've always been grown up for your age; maybe because you have big brothers. If you were at Penn now I'd be worried, but I'd know I wouldn't have any real reason to be concerned. I know you're smart enough to be able to handle yourself at school. That's the world we raised you for, the one I prepared you for. But now, it's like you live in another world. You come in straight off a plane from somewhere, you're on television, you're going on dates with Patrick Carroll? I'm worried because I can't guide you though this. I can't be there for you in the same way."

"Mom!" I set down the steaming mug. "That's not true at all! This model thing, it's just a job. It doesn't change anything; just because I'm a model . . . I'm still the same person." I reach across the table to squeeze her hand. I've never seen her quite like this; it's not like I'm in trouble, exactly, not like when I was a kid. For maybe the first time in my entire life, I feel like an adult. And it's weirdly depressing. "Mom, modeling is just a job. Like being a fire-fighter is dad's job."

"That's the thing, Melody." Mom lets go of my hand. "Exactly. What your dad does is a huge part of his life. It's not all he is, but it's affected him, and us, and my life. It's a big deal."

I know I'm wrong, and I know Mom's right. This modeling thing is just a job, sure, but it's my job. It's who I am, or who I am becoming, and neither mom nor I ever planned on this happening. Suddenly I feel tired, and kind of sad. My accidental career choice, my way of making some quick cash for college, yes, being a model is those things, but it's also other things: it's who I am now, and it divides me from a lot of what I was before. I'm not Melody Croft, friend, daughter, college student, waitress. I'm Mac now.

"Promise me that you'll be careful, OK?" Mom asks.

I feel a twinge of guilt, thinking of the times I did have to be careful. I wish I could tell Mom about the tight spots I've had to talk my way out of. I wish I could tell her about my weekend in the Hamptons that turned into an accidental drug binge. I wish I could tell her about the number of times I've had to protect myself from some grabby slime ball. I want to tell her so she'll be proud, so she'll see she doesn't have to worry, but I know if I do, she'll just worry more. So I say nothing. "I promise, Mom. Please don't worry. You've taught me everything I need to know."

"Enough serious talk," Mom says. She stands and pours her tea out into the sink. "You know there's one thing I'm truly dying to know."

"Patrick?"

"Patrick!" Mom sits, a dreamy look on her face. All of a sudden, we're like the mothers and daughters you see on television shows—gabbing about boys over late-night tea at the kitchen table. "He's really something, isn't he?"

"He is something," I say, nodding. I drain the last of my tea, which has done exactly what I needed it to: calmed me down, warmed me up, and left me totally ready to collapse into bed.

"Your father's been planning your wedding all week . . ."

"It's a little soon to be thinking about me marrying anyone, don't you think?"

"Well, what do I know?" Mom stands, takes my empty mug and rinses it in the sink, her back to me. "Honestly, Melody, I'm beginning to think that nothing can surprise me anymore."

I can't help but laugh. "I spent the afternoon having two gay men put me into dresses that cost more than most cars, while I pranced around in my bare feet and tried not to step on the glass from a shattered chandelier. All while some weirdo in jeans so tight he's probably sterile took pictures of me."

"When you put it like that, Melody, it doesn't sound all that glamorous." Mom dries her hands on the kitchen towel and grins.

"It's just work. And it's exhausting. Which brings me to something we've got to discuss."

"You can quit anytime, honey." Mom looks serious. "That money might help, but it's only money. You have your whole life ahead of you. You have that scholarship!"

"Actually, Mom, that's not it. Look at you—waiting up. Look at me, rolling in late. I can't do it, Mom. I'm going to have to get a place in the city."

"I see." Mom folds the towel and places it on the counter. "You want to move into the city."

"We both know I'm going to need your help on this one." I stand and put my arm around her shoulders again. "I know it sounds crazy, but if I was in school right now, I'd be living on my own."

Mom sighs. "Leave it to me," she says simply.

"Are you serious?" I wasn't expecting her to be so easily persuaded.

"I'm not thrilled, but I understand. I'll talk to Dad. And by the way, Mac, it might not be the end of the world, but it is the end of an era." She pauses. "I'm going to bed. You should too." She drops a kiss on my cheek and shuffles out of the room.

I stand and stretch, yawning. Bed does sound good. I'm out of my mind with exhaustion, but I'm not so tired that I didn't notice that mom just called me Mac instead of Melody. All my life Mom's always been right about everything, which sometimes drove me crazy, and I know she's right about this, too; it's the end of an era.

Six

New York in the winter can be merciless, and its most persistently evil aspect by far is the wind, which races around corners, whistles through trees, and is right now slipping up both the front and back of my flimsy silk dress. I'm asking for it, being outside dressed only in this hot pink Zac Posen number while ice skating elegantly—or as elegantly as I can, considering I haven't done this in years—around Central Park's Wollman Rink. I'm overdressed for the occasion and underdressed for the weather, but we're not only selling dresses, we're selling a fantasy. Or so says Jen, the stylist and creative mastermind behind this gig. It's catalog, and the client is Lord & Taylor, and I've kind of been looking forward to this job since Francesca first texted me about it, because the client is prestigious and the photographer, once again, is Ringo Tang, who might be a weirdo, but is still one of the hottest fashion photographers out there.

"Mac, that's gorgeous," Ringo calls, his breath coming out in little clouds because it's just that cold.

I nod, not saying a word because he's still clicking away and I don't want to ruin the shot. The air's so cold against my skin it feels almost electric. In the fantasy we're selling, girls don't catch a chill, but in reality, where I live, being this exposed in near-zero weather is not good for you. Not that anyone on set cares about a little something like the model's health. Once, on set, a stylist rolled her eyes while she told me a story about another model stopping the shoot because she was just too cold—clearly, she was inferring that models are unreliable, sensitive creatures. I'm more empathetic though. If the stylist and photographer were working in sundresses, I bet they would be too.

"So nice, Mac, so nice." That's Jen, standing just behind Ringo in the middle of the totally deserted skating rink, wrapped up in a puffy coat and plaid scarf, sipping from a paper cup of steaming hot coffee. A hundred yards away, there's a crowd of tourists gathered, happily pointing and taking pictures of their own. It's got to the point that I barely even notice people gawking at me like an animal in the zoo. When I'm shooting, the world shrinks down to just me and the camera. Even the cold and the wind and the dull pain in my ankles that I'm pretty sure will turn into a full-on throb later today can't touch me. I'm just Mac, and I'm just doing my thing.

"You're such a pro, Mac," Ringo says appreciatively, swiveling his skinny hips and dropping down on one knee to shoot me from a whole new angle. "I love it."

And despite the cold, despite the pain, despite everything, I have to agree.

It's been, what, two years since I ran wind sprints? I'm suddenly grateful to Ms. McManus, our field hockey coach, for forcing me to run until my knees throbbed, my heart pounded in my ears, and my lungs felt like they were going to explode. She gave me a gift that's proving to be surprisingly useful—I can dash, I can run, I can sprint, and though I might break a sweat, I've got stamina, and damn I can move.

I'm proving that now, jogging down the clogged sidewalks of Fifth Avenue. I'm never late when I work, and I'm sure as hell not going to be late now, because I am on my way to see Patrick. It's rush hour, so I'm dodging shoppers, tourists, garbage, and the majority of the midtown Manhattan work-force. When I get caught in the crowd nervously waiting for the walk signal at Fifty-Seventh Street, I catch myself cursing them impatiently like any true New Yorker.

Now, naturally, my knees feel like they're on fire and my ankles feel like they might actually snap, but a date with Patrick is all the incentive I need to channel the high school athlete I once was. It's been more than a week since our first date, when Patrick managed to totally and thoroughly charm my parents—and me. All week, in fact, I've found myself literally dreaming about our second date, idle fanta-sies about walking the red carpet by his side at the Oscars, and one actual full-blown dream: it combined the plot of one of his most famous movies (Patrick as the seductive hairdresser with the heart of gold) with my life. Patrick was on set with me, working his strong hands into my thick hair. Sexy.

Of course, I'd prefer a romantic life that exists in reality and not in dreams, but it hasn't been possible until today. I was in Connecticut shooting a story for *Seventeen* for the two nights Patrick had free, and he had back-to-back dinners and meetings with producers and agents the nights I had free. But we talked and even exchanged text messages like a couple of teenagers—who would believe the actor acclaimed for his portrayal of the alcoholic screenwriter in *LA Deadline* is capable of sending text messages like *"cant wait 2c u. hot d8 wed?"*?

I squeeze between two Japanese girls dressed identically in long, flannel shirts and skinny, cropped jeans, clutching Abercrombie shopping bags and pink digital cameras. I think I might have just ruined their shot of the wintry New York cityscape, so I give them an apologetic wave as I sprint the rest of the way to the London, Patrick's hotel of choice when he's in New York, and our designated meeting place for the evening, ignoring the pains shooting up my shins. The first time we met, Patrick Carroll cured my cold. Maybe this time around he can soothe my aching body?

You need a special passkey to even press the button for the fifty-third floor, the London Suite, so the concierge used his to send me up. My stomach is reeling, and not just from the super fast elevator ride, when the doors whoosh open into the foyer.

"Mac Croft." Patrick's waiting for me, famous smile flashing.

"Patrick!" He looks terrific, but I'm momentarily distracted by the airy foyer and my first glimpse into the room beyond. I've slept in some pretty amazing places: the cottage on stilts in Costa Rica, with a trapdoor in the floor that led right to the ocean, the opulent Hotel Georges V in Paris, where my room came with its very own fireplace. They had nothing on this place, which feels more like a home than a hotel, and a damn nice one at that. So *this* is how the other half lives.

"Come in, come in."

Patrick kisses me on the lips, gently but firmly, and in the same slick movement helps me out of my coat.

"Thanks." The first thing I notice is that he smells terrific—clean, a mixture of soap and laundry detergent. "Nice place." This is the understatement of the year. I still can't believe it, even as I follow him up two steps and into the grand living room, which has a huge leather couch in the shape of a swirl right at its center, and a full wall of windows overlooking the park beyond. *Whoa.* Just when I thought I was over the fact that I'm kind of sort of dating a fabulously wealthy international superstar.

"I always stay here when I'm in town," Patrick says. "Can I get you a drink?"

"Just some water would be great." I'm sure the minibar is stocked with tons of exotic concoctions that I wish I could drink. I make my way to the windows and pull the curtains aside, gazing out into the rapidly darkening night. "You should open these drapes, Patrick! Look at this view!"

"Huh? View's great from here, trust me." He drops some ice into a tumbler and opens a bottle of sparkling water with a soft hiss.

Is he talking about me? I blush. "Do you mind if I sit?" First the skating, then the sprinting—my feet are killing me.

"Make yourself at home! Please. Mac. I've met your family. You don't need to stand on ceremony with me."

He's right. I've been looking forward to seeing him, day-dreaming about it even, but now that I'm here I feel shy or odd or something. "Sorry. You're right." I collapse onto the couch, which is even more comfortable than it looks.

Patrick sets my glass down on the marble-topped coffee table with a gentle clink. "Sparkling water for the lady. Is something wrong? You look a little . . . pained."

"It's my feet," I explain. "Long day. Ice skating."

"Say no more." Patrick settles in beside me on the couch. "It's a model's lot in life, right?"

"What would you know about that?" I teasingly nudge him with my elbow. "Do you know another model?"

"I might have met a few in my time," Patrick says. "But you're the tops, as far as I'm concerned."

That's quite a commitment, coming from someone who's probably bedded more models than are currently working with Delicious.

"Cheers, by the way." I knock my glass against his, which is full of dark red wine.

"Cheers to you," he replies. "I'm really glad we were finally able to get a couple of minutes together."

"I know. My schedule isn't all that easy on my social life."

"Never mind that now." Patrick reaches down and grips my calf firmly in his hand, pulling my foot onto his lap. "Let's get you out of those shoes."

"I don't want to mess up the couch," I start to protest, but he's already tugging at the suede lace that cinches the boot around my calf. Good thing I shaved my legs!

"Don't be silly," he says. "The amount I'm paying for this room they can replace the couch when I check out."

I relax into the sensation of Patrick's hands on my legs. I'm used to strangers undressing me—and the sensation as he tugs first one and then the other boot off is enough to make me swoon. Seconds later, he's caressing the bottoms of my feet with one hand and kneading the muscles in my calf with the other. "That feels so good," I tell him. "You better be careful or I'm never going to let you stop."

"Is that so?"

"That's so. I'll take you everywhere."

"I could get into that," he says. He leans over me, the pressure of his body causing the leather to squeak a little, and with his right hand reaches around the back of my neck, giving it a gentle squeeze. "I'm a pretty handy masseur."

"So I see," I tell him. "But if I were you, I'd quit while I was ahead."

"Why's that?"

"The whole reason you wanted me to come over was so we could try the incredibly fancy restaurant. And now we're never even going to make it downstairs."

"I've got an idea," Patrick says. "The penthouse comes with an in-room dinner, courtesy of the restaurant's sous chef. All I have to do is give him a call."

"You're kidding." He's still massaging my legs, and the sensation is pure bliss. "As long as you won't be too disappointed at staying in . . ."

"The dining room with a sick view of Central Park. And we'll have it all to ourselves. What do we need with a restaurant?" He smiles at me. "I can tell by the faraway look in your eye that dining in will suit you just fine. You sit and relax. I'll call them."

I pull my legs up to my chest so he can stand up off the couch, immediately missing the sensation of his hands on my body. I'd be lying if I said I wasn't curious to continue the massage, but I'm actually a little relieved for the chance to catch my breath. If I'm not careful, who knows what I'll end up doing. It's a good thing I'm drinking water.

I rest my chin on the back of the couch and take in the scene, which is exactly like something out of a movie. There's the handsome leading man, Patrick Carroll, grabbing the telephone and ordering up dinner. For some reason I notice he uses all five fingers on his right hand to dial—I've never seen anyone do that before. Patrick truly is different from anyone I've ever met, even when it comes to this simple thing. Behind him is the perfect hotel room, softly lit, and outside the many windows night is falling, while the love interest (that's me) sprawls on the couch. But this isn't a movie. This is my life. And I don't have a script to follow . . . what happens next is entirely up to me.

Patrick hangs up the phone.

"Done?" I ask.

"Done," he nods. "They'll be up shortly, and our first course will be on the table in forty-five minutes." He leans over the back of the couch, so close his eyelashes almost graze my face. "Now the only question is, what should we do for the next forty-five minutes?"

I was mildly impressed by taking the elevator up to the fifty-third floor. I thought the couch was pretty damn comfortable. The art collection on the living room walls surprised me, and I thought the heavy brass telescope on the downstairs terrace was a nice touch. But every last flourish and amenity pales in comparison to the master bathroom. For starters, it's about twice the size of my parents' bedroom, and there's a massive floor-to-ceiling window right in the middle of it, so when you step out of the shower you can just stand there, naked as the day you were born, and take in the glittering expanse of Upper Manhattan, which is precisely what I'm doing, thoroughly warmed by the powerful shower—and by the heated floor beneath my feet.

It's a cliché, but there's some truth in it: New York is a magical place. From above, the vast expanse of Central Park is dark, a massive void framed by brightly lit skyscrapers. The moonlight filters right into the window, right onto my body—it really is like my life has turned into a movie. Except for the fact that what should have been the climactic love scene, the handsome leading man tumbling into bed with the long-limbed, wide-eyed starlet, pushing aside the pillows and tearing off their clothes, never unfolded.

Forget sex appeal, Patrick oozes sexiness in everything he does, whether it's dialing the phone or just saying hello. No woman could possibly resist him. Maybe.

Patrick is pure gentleman, a pleasure to talk to, and just being near him makes me feel happy, almost giddy. We talked about everything—my work, his work, favorite places, trading funny stories about our friends, families, and life, and thirty minutes ticked by like seconds. In the movie of my life, every one of those seconds was building to one thing: the moment Patrick gripped my face in his hands, and pulled me closer to him, and kissed me, more deeply or meaningfully than any man has ever kissed me in my two decades on this planet. And that moment came and as I was sitting there on the world's most comfortable couch being kissed by the world's most eligible bachelor, the living room filling with the heavenly scent of one of the world's best chefs toiling away at our dinner I realized something: I just couldn't do it.

The shower was my idea. I tried to make the request to use his shower as un-sexy as possible, because I didn't want to give him any ideas, but Patrick took it all in stride, showing me up to the master suite, and firmly closing the door behind him, to give me my privacy. Which is just what I needed. I stood under the steady thrum of hot water for a good ten minutes, thinking through everything. I guess this is what people mean when they talk about taking stock of your life.

Standing here, naked, alone, I'm just myself again. I slip into the fluffy terry robe that's hanging on the back of the door and cinch it tight against myself. I walk back to the window and gaze into the night. An all too familiar feeling washes over me—hunger. I need to eat something, and then I need to get dressed and head home. As tempting as it might be to just give into the fantasy of a romance with Patrick Carroll, I'm trying to make a life for myself, a real life, not a fantasy one.

A soft knock at the door startles me back to reality.

"Mac? I don't mean to rush you, but the table is set and waiting for us."

I pull the door open, and Patrick steps through the escaping plume of steam and into the room. "Toasty. Feel better?"

Reflexively, I pull the robe closed a little tighter. "I do," I confess. "Much more human. Ice skating in a sundress. Can you imagine?" I turn away, examining my limp, damp hair in the fogged-over mirror.

"I don't want to." Patrick comes up close behind me, catching my eye in the reflection. "The things we do for a paycheck, right?"

"I can't complain too much." I grin.

Patrick leans even closer, kissing me gently on the neck. "Neither can I."

He's standing so close his words vibrate through my body like I'm the one who's talking. His stubble against my skin is making my knees feel all wobbly. "Don't," I mumble. "I'm all wet . . ."

Patrick chuckles. "I'm not going to make a joke," he says, kissing my neck again, and again, and again, then giving my earlobe a playful bite. "I'm a gentleman." He puts his hands firmly on my hips and twirls me around so we're face to face.

"That's a good thing," I whisper. "Here I am, all defenseless and naked . . . a lot of men might try to take advantage."

"Well, I'm not like a lot of men," Patrick says.

"No?" I look up at him, into those crystalline eyes, so close I can almost count every one of his eyelashes.

"Oh no." Patrick shakes his head, strokes my chin gently.

He pulls me closer to him, and I'm on my tiptoes, melting into him, kissing him hungrily, almost not noticing that my robe is slipping open. My heart is pounding so noisily Patrick must be able to hear it, and I suddenly feel out of breath, positively drained, like I need to lie down. But I can't do that; I don't quite trust myself to lie down anywhere near Patrick Carroll. Not yet, anyway. I pull my lips away from his and rest my head on his shoulder, breathe in his musky, outdoorsy smell.

"Don't fall asleep yet," Patrick says, his breath tickling the top of my head. "We haven't eaten dinner yet. You should see what they're doing down there in the kitchen."

Dinner sounds perfect—and I *should* go see what they're doing down there in the kitchen. Right now. I'm afraid if I stand here in Patrick's arms for one more second, I'll never let go.

Seven

"Passport?"

Yawning miserably, I hand my passport over the scratched plastic partition to the border patrol officer.

"Miss . . . Croft." She flips through the passport quickly, turns it on its side and studies my mug shot, glancing up at me to confirm that I am who I claim to be. I hate my passport picture. I heard once that Donatella Versace had Steven Meisel take her passport photo—maybe I should do the same thing. I wonder if Jason McDonald is available?

"Where are you in from?" She drums her fingers on her chipped Formica desk impatiently.

"Uh . . ." I falter. I desperately need to pee, my head is killing me, and I just got off what is I think my seventh plane in two weeks. Or eighth? For a horrible moment, I actually can't remember where I was yesterday.

She sits up a little straighter in her swivel chair and gives me a *gotcha* look. I can tell that she thinks I'm either some kind of terrorist or drug mule smuggling cocaine in my compact or, worse, some combination of the two. "Where are you coming from, miss?" she asks, a lot more seriously now.

"I'm sorry." I tell her. I check my coat pockets then dig into my tote bag. If I can just find my boarding pass, I'll be able to prove to this woman that everything is on the up and up.

"Miss?" she says icily. "I need to know what ports you visited while you were out of the country."

I shoot her my most dazzling million-dollar smile, pushing my hair out of my face. Can't she just look at my passport? I vaguely recall having it stamped at some point recently. "I am sorry. It's been a crazy week!"

"So, you, uh . . . don't know where you were?" She frowns at me.

"Lisbon!" I don't mean to shout, but the answer just pops into my head. The immigration line is getting longer, and I can feel the eyes of my fellow passport holders boring into my back, wondering what the hell the holdup is.

"I'm sorry. Lisbon." I breathe deeply, trying to sound less like a crystal meth-addled train wreck. "I was in Lisbon. In Portugal. I don't know how I forgot."

"Lisbon." She pauses, assessing me closely. She opens the passport again, starts studying it. "And the purpose of your trip was . . ."

"Work." I finish the sentence for her, feeling slightly more awake and human now that I've remembered who I am and where I'm coming from. I study her closely. She's got pointy features, with red hair and the classic redhead's complexion. Her thin lips tug downward in a natural frown, and though she's probably in her thirties she looks two decades older.

"And how long were you in Lisbon?" This lady is strictly by the book. I do feel for her—she's got a boring job, behind the same desk day in and out, asking the same stupid questions to every single American citizen who comes wandering through the international terminal.

"Uhh, one day?" I say it like a question because it doesn't seem like it could possibly be true. But it is: I flew out Tuesday evening, arrived Wednesday morning, shot all day, spent that night in some hotel and now here I am. It seems like a week has passed in the meantime.

She stops. "You were in Lisbon for one day?"

"That's right." I nod, trying to show her I'm an upstanding, hard-working professional.

"And New York is your final destination?"

"Yes, I live here." I give her my toughest *don't-mess-with-me-I'm-a-New-Yorker* look.

"All right then, what other countries did you visit on this trip?" She says it slowly, impatiently, like she's talking to a stupid child.

"Just Lisbon, um, just Portugal, just the one." I try not to fidget, but I'm truly scared that I'm going to pee in my pants. "Just the one," I repeat eyeing my passport. I wonder what would happen if I grabbed it and ran to the bathroom. Would she shoot me?

"Why were you in Lisbon for one day?" Her tone of voice makes it clear she thinks I was there building a bomb.

"For a . . ." I stop myself—the last word you want to use in an airport in this day and age is *shoot*. "For work," I tell her. "I was working."

"You were working, in Portugal, for one day?" She leans way back in her chair, arms folded across her chest, studying me seriously. I can tell she's decided I'm not a security threat, but I can also tell she wants to know what the hell kind of person flies across the Atlantic Ocean for thirty-six hours. I can't blame her; it's a damn good question.

"Actually, I'm a . . . I'm a model." I say it quickly, shrugging my shoulders a little like it's no big deal. I am a model, that's true, but saying as much, out loud. . . . Well, at best you sound frivolous and stupid and at worst you sound snotty and stuck-up. There are so many ways that one little sentence can go wrong.

"Is that right?" She studies me, head nodding slowly up and down as she takes it all in. "A model. Huh. You don't look much like a model to me."

Really nice. "Yeah, well, I am." I shrug my shoulders.

"Must be nice, the model life," she says. "Show up, stand around, look pretty. Get paid. I could get used to that."

"It's not so bad," I agree. I don't want to get into a whole big thing with a lady who carries a gun.

"Yeah, I could get into that." She's still holding my passport, and though she's smiling she's also somehow kind of scowling at me angrily. "Stand around all day, wear some fancy clothes."

I'm too tired for banter. I smile as nicely as I can, waiting patiently for her to relinquish my passport and let me go. All I want to do is stop at the bathroom, grab my bags, and get out of that airport, breathe in some fresh air, get into a taxi, and go home. "Careful what you wish for," I tell her.

"I don't know." She leans back in her little swivel chair, hands behind her head, grinning. "Flying around the world to stand around and have my picture taken. Sounds pretty sweet."

I've seen Sloane's sweet tooth in action before, but as always I'm shocked by how this prim and elegant girl chows down like a frat boy.

I can't stop myself from laughing. "Enjoy!"

"Francesca's waiting!" Sloane mumbles through a mouthful of chocolate.

I wave—not that Sloane is paying any attention—and hurry down the hall to Francesca's office. The door's standing open so I peek my head through. "Knock, knock," I say, jokingly.

"Mac, Mac, Mac is back." Francesca, seated as ever behind her fire hazard of a desk, waves me in impatiently. "How was Portugal? Sit, sit."

I do as told, dropping the candy onto her already over-crowded desk and sinking into the leather and steel chair across from her. "Got you a little something."

Francesca picks up the candy and grins at me happily. "You're too sweet. You're spoiling me! Anyway, tell me every-thing. You got back . . . yesterday?"

There's not much to tell, and what there is, I can barely remember. After a good night's sleep, my European sojourn feels like a dream, like a lifetime ago. "Yup. Back yesterday, slept and recovered, and now I'm back. Ready to get back to work."

"Glad to hear that." Francesca nods. "I think I can help you there . . ."

"Great!" I try my best to sound chipper and ready for the challenge, but even with a good night's sleep, I'm beat. Com-muting from Portugal is a lot more intense than commuting from Jersey.

"Great indeed." Francesca somehow unearths a pen from beneath the clutter and starts jotting on a piece of paper. "At one, you're going to *Town and Country*. You're going to see Angela. She's nice. And I've got you at *Allure* at three. And you're booked for three days . . . shoot, I can't remember when, but double check with Jude. It's *Modern Bride*. I know, I know, bridal is a drag, but money is money, right?"

"Bridal. No, love it." Of course, everyone knows bridal is a drag: massive, rhinestone dresses, ridiculous teased-out hair, crazy clownish makeup. But the memory of my last dressing-down from Francesca still stings; I'm definitely not going to complain.

"OK, Mac. I should go. I'm meeting Renee and Paul for lunch at Lever House." Francesca's all smiles, but it's clear our face-to-face is over.

"Great." I stand. "Enjoy the candy, have a good lunch . . . I'll let you know how it goes at *Town and Country*!"

I shuffle back toward the lobby, trying not to think about three days of bridal editorial, and trying to remember what it was someone—Sloane?—told me once: that all the important business at Delicious Models takes place over lunch at the Lever House. And that's where Francesca is dining. Francesca, my booker. I wonder if the important business on today's agenda has something to do with me?

In the lobby, I glance at the row of clocks above Sloane's desk, showing the time in Los Angeles, New York, London, Dubai, Tokyo, and Sydney. It's barely lunchtime; I've got hours to kill, and it's freezing outside. I might as well set up here for a while. Maybe later I'll drop in on Steve or Vicki, or see if Renee is around. It never hurts to make the rounds with agents. I drop my overflowing travel wallet onto the coffee table, shoving aside the stacks of magazines and books to clear a little space, and then sit on the floor, dumping out the wallet's contents: jangling coins, a thick wad of receipts, business cards, old boarding passes. I'll take advantage of this down-time to get my life in order.

I make a pile for receipts, smoothing the folds and creases out of the dozens of little paper slips, and divide them by date. I make another pile for business cards, which I collect every-where. It's a nice way to remember the endless parade of photo assistants, hair stylists, makeup artists, prop stylists, photogra-phers, creative directors, and other random characters I work with. It also comes in handy in other ways; last time I was in Miami, I grabbed a business card from the front desk on my way out of the hotel in the morning, which was smart because by the end of the day I had absolutely no idea what hotel I was staying in. People think models are dumb; really, they're just exhausted.

I've got a couple of Polaroids in there as well, though they're definitely an oddity because almost no photographers bother with anything as antiquated as film in this day and age. But I've worked with a couple of old-schoolers who refuse to make the switch to digital, which is cool with me; I like having these mementos. Usually, it's months before the pictures we shoot end up in print, and I've done plenty of jobs whose results I still have yet to see. This way it's like I have some proof, some tangible evidence that I really was in the Marais, wearing a Galliano pantsuit with my hair blown to ten times its normal volume in some formal garden whose name I've forgotten, or that I, in fact, did pose on the stage of some downtown jazz club dressed up like a tap dancer for a story about colored stockings.

"Wow. You've got a lot of stuff in there."

I'm so absorbed in sorting out my currency—I've got Euros,

Mexican pesos, and good old-fashioned American change all jumbled up in there—that I didn't even realize I'm no longer alone.

"Sorry." I scoop the pile of coins into my palm. "I should get this junk out of the way." I smile up at the girl who slumps in the seat opposite me, her long thick brown hair in glamorous disarray, her tiny face a little pinched, but not unpleasantly.

"Is no problem." She has an accent I can't quite place—Russian, Eastern European, definitely something. She smiles wearily, her teeth incredibly white behind lips slathered in purple gloss.

"I can't believe how much junk I have in here." I stuff the American change into my pocket. "I'm sorry."

"Is a bitch. Living out of a bag. Right?" She waves her hand in the air like she's trying to brush away a fly.

A fellow model. She understands. "It's getting to be kind of a drag." I nod.

"I don't even know where I am anymore." The girl exhales the words like the smoke from a cigarette. "One time I had to ask. I felt so stupid. But I asked anyway. I asked the photo assistant. I couldn't remember what city I was in. He laughed."

"I know how you feel." I do. I've been tempted to do the same thing dozens of times. "Sorry he laughed. It's actually not funny."

"No problem." She shrugged her shoulders. "I tell him I'm not going to fuck him now, because he laugh. That shut him up." She paused. "I'm Irin."

"Mac." I'm still plopped on the floor in what we used to call Indian style when I was a kid, but has probably since been rechristened for some yoga position. I reach up to shake her hand.

"Mac, Mac. This name is familiar. Oh, you're *Swimsuit Illustrated*?" She gives my hand a feeble squeeze. Her hand is, like mine, cold to the touch. All models seem to have cold hands. I think it's got something to do with your circulation.

"*Sports Illustrated*," I correct her.

"Cool." She pauses. "Mac, I ask favor? You from New York?" Her face is so open, so hopeful, she looks years younger than she probably is. In a plaid jumper, knee socks, and pigtails she could pass for thirteen, but I know she's not: Delicious requires the girls under seventeen to be under the constant supervision of an escort, usually a sad-looking mom living out her own glamour girl fantasies.

"I am." It's sort of true. I've spent so much time pounding the city pavement I feel like I qualify as a native. I think she's going to ask for directions, and I'm proud of my knowledge of the city's layout and the overly confusing subway system. "Do you need directions? You can get anywhere on the train. Don't waste your money on a cab." I wish someone had told me that nine months ago.

"No, is not train. I need apartment. I can't spend another night in this . . . Valencia Hotel." She shudders, visibly pained by the mere mention of the name.

I empathize. I had my own brush with that flea trap. If I try, I can almost conjure up the place's smell, a bouquet of mildew, hairspray, pot, and menthol cigarettes. But I'd prefer not to think about that depraved dormitory. "The Valencia, huh? I don't blame you. I crashed there once." Actually, I didn't even last the night through.

"So you know. You understand." Her eyes widen and she clutches at my wrist desperately like a prisoner in an old war movie. "I must cannot stay there one night more. But how to find apartment? I look on Internet but I no find anything."

Apartments. A hot topic I've been avoiding. Since Dad hasn't called me in screaming hysterics about how no daughter of his is going to pick up and move into the city, I'm guessing Mom hasn't brought it up yet.

"An apartment." Even the word seems dangerous to me.

"Yes, yes," Irin says, a little impatiently. "I cannot stand this living out of bag anymore. I need place like home. You understand? My family is far away. Is in Yaraslavl. I no go home, you know, unless I am in Milan or something and then I fly home for weekend. But that is so far away. Until then I need place."

"I know what you mean." I take a Euro coin out of the change pocket of my wallet and spin it like a little top on the glass table. "I've been running around like crazy lately. I'm still living at home, with my folks, in New Jersey."

Irin makes a funny face. "New Jersey? Is this far away? I should live there too?"

I stifle a laugh. I feel like I still fit in around Morristown—I can't imagine the looks this Russian glamazon would get if she showed up there. "No, you should really look in the city—or Brooklyn. I think that's the place to be these days." Or so the magazines say; I've never actually ventured across the river myself.

"You live at home. You don't like this? Maybe we should share place. I need, you need. Just room, closet, is all. I'm always away. You are, right?" Irin's smiling, excited.

I'm slightly less excited. I mean, I'm pretty desperate to get into a place of my own, but I've had some bad experiences with

other models, both boys and girls. I want home to be a re-
treat from the business, not a reminder of it. I don't want to
get caught up in the drama of competing for jobs or spending hours in the morning making sure I look better than my
roommate. Then, it might be nice to live with someone who
understands the life: the coming and going, the late nights and
early mornings. Plus, Irin seems normal.

"Roommates, huh?" I study her more closely, trying to size
her up.

"Just roommates," she nods. "I like clean. I like quiet.
When I work, I work. When I'm home, I sleep. Maybe watch
television. I love the cooking shows. We don't have these in
Russia."

Her message is pretty clear: just *roommates*, not *friends*.
That's fine by me. In fact, it might be better that way. She
needs a place, I need a place. And I'm going to need help with
the rent. I've got a big decision to make, and I do it, right now,
on the spot.

"Well, then. Roommates." I smile, trying to convince
myself that this is a great idea. "It's meant to be, I guess. The
only question now is how are we going to find an apartment?"
I look at Irin, who smiles back at me blankly. I wonder if she's
catching every word I'm saying or just generally piecing it
together.

"I don't know this how to find apartment," she says sadly.
"Maybe she'll know?" She points in Sloane's direction.

Sloane's busily chattering into her headset and simultane-
ously typing something urgently. I trust her with my schedule,
and I trust her with my secrets, but I'm not sure Sloane's the
woman I'd turn to for practical advice.

"I must know someone who can help." I start flipping

through the business cards, trying to match the names with my recollections of a parade of faces. Then it hits me: Frank Lindo. He's a high-powered suit-and-tie type who I first met months ago, just as I was getting my start. Francesca had sent me out to the Hamptons to do some test shots for my portfolio—which didn't even exist at the time—and the whole crew crashed at Frank's place. It ended up being a sketchy scene, with lots of bed hopping and drug bingeing, but Frank was a decent guy. I'm sure I've got his number somewhere, and I have a feeling he's the kind of person who can help me out. I just hope he's not going to expect anything in repayment.

"I think I have an idea," I tell Irin.

Eight

I'm stumbling out of the lobby at Four Times Square when my phone starts vibrating deep in the pocket of my shearling-lined coat, a little something I picked up for myself at Saks. If I'm going to hoof it all over New York City I need to stay warm, right?

I always keep my ringer off—it's bad form to be in the middle of a go-see and have your phone start ringing. I dodge a trio of tall, blond editors—everyone knows Conde Nast has the most beautiful staff in the business—heading inside, cheeks flushed, trailing cashmere scarves and that faint smell of cigarettes I've always found totally disgusting, and push my way through the revolving door, answering the phone as I go.

"Hello?" I don't recognize the number, but screening my calls is a luxury I simply can't afford. It could be some Delicious intern I've never met calling to tell me I'm supposed to be at Unilever in twenty minutes for the shampoo ad that is going to make my entire career.

"Mac Croft," says a gruff, vaguely familiar voice. "It's Frank Lindo, returning your call."

"Frank! Thanks for getting back to me." I pause outside, leaning against the building's granite façade with a pack of afternoon cigarette breakers, trying to ignore the noxious fumes. Secondhand smoke notwithstanding, it's nice to get some air; it's the first relatively mild day in weeks, and the weak winter sun feels refreshing, almost relaxing. It's that kind of mid-winter day that makes you dizzyingly optimistic, when you start spotting imaginary signs of spring, pretending the scraggly dead tree limbs are about to burst into bud. "How have you been?" I ask him.

"You know how it goes. Business this, business that. Just trying to leave some time for life's little pleasures, too, you know what I mean, Mac?" He pauses, and I can practically hear him smiling.

"I do, indeed." I catch myself—I'm flirting. There's something kind of charming about Frank, the gruff, seen-it-all business guy. He reminds me of Patrick in some ways: smooth talking, world-weary, and interested in only one thing. One thing I'm not all that interested in just giving up.

"You've been busy too. Spotted you on the newsstand the other day. Damnedest thing, too. The Hudson News, Grand Central. You know the one, under the staircase? Anyway, damned if they don't have about a hundred thousand copies of *Sports Illustrated*, all along the wall, in those little plastic display cases. Holy shit, I said to myself. Is that the same girl from last summer? Leaner, tougher, but still that same gorgeous face. Same girl!"

"Same girl." I repeat. Frank's a serial modelizer—once upon a time, he was even married to Caroline Gregory, the big '80s supermodel. So even though I know better than to fall for his sweet talk, Caroline's a legend. This guy knows what he's talking about. He might only be complimenting because he's after one particular thing, but right now I'll take whatever shots of reassurance I can get. I just left a semi-humiliating meeting: the bookings editor at *Allure* kept me waiting in the lobby—didn't even ask me into her office—for ages, shook my hand, looked at the first page of my book, then let me leave. Twenty-three minutes on the subway, eight minutes in the lobby; one minute of face time.

"But things have changed, clearly." Frank sounds proud, almost like he's responsible for my career success.

"It's been a whirlwind couple of months," I admit, trying to manage the delicate balance of my tiny phone and my heavy portfolio and my overstuffed shoulder bag. "And to think, you were there at the humble beginning!" I laugh, remembering that weekend. I was so green back then. That whole weekend-in-the-Hamptons arrangement was just an excuse to get a bunch of models into the beds of a bunch of rich dudes. It scandalized me at the time, but now it seems almost innocent.

"So tell me, Mac Croft. What is this all about—business, or pleasure? Please say pleasure. You're angling for an invite out to Long Island! I have been known to open the house in the winter, get the hot tub going, enjoy the silence of the off season . . ."

"Tempting, Frank. But I'm booked, well, constantly. I was actually calling to pick your brain." I steal a glance at my watch. I really am booked constantly, and should probably be on the train right now instead of standing around in Midtown.

"Can't blame a guy for trying." He sighs. I can hear all the ambient noise of a busy office—that electronic chirp of the telephone, the chime of an elevator, voices calling out to one another—in the background. It sounds hectic, but Frank

Lindo doesn't sound like he's bothered by it in the least; his voice has the laid-back lilt of the man in charge. "So, my brain. It's at your disposal. Pick."

"Let's say I'm a single girl moving to the big city." I dig into my bag and fish out my sunglasses. Some of the smokers gathered outside are looking at me, and it's making me feel paranoid. I can just imagine the post on Gawker tomorrow: *Midtown Model Sighting. . . .*

"Let's say you are."

"How does a girl like me go about getting an apartment? I mean, a nice apartment. I've got a girl I'm looking to room with, so two bedrooms. Some place clean and safe that will pass the inspection of an overprotective dad."

"Real estate, huh?" Frank gives a little whistle. "You tried the usual, the Internet, that whole thing?"

"Come on, Frank," I tell him. "You know this business. The last thing I can do is spend hours scouring the Internet for deals on some junky walk-up in some neighborhood you've never heard of in Brooklyn."

"I like the way you think, Mac Croft. You've got a problem, you want an expert. That's smart. That's the way it's done. Business school 101. I've got a name for you."

"I'm all ears!" I knew I was right to ask for help.

"Bullshit you are, Mac Croft. You're a sex kitten on long willowy legs. But that's another story. Call my friend Jim Segal. I'm going to have my assistant give you his number. He's in the real estate game, and if he can't help you, no one can."

"I owe you one, Frank," I tell him. Nothing has happened, but I feel so much better knowing the ball is rolling, good and proper.

"You certainly do," he says, the twinkle in his eye almost audible. "Now you be careful out there, or I might call in that favor someday."

"You've got to be my four o'clock."

I look up from the tiny, credit-card–sized map of Manhattan I keep in my travel wallet. Good thing I organized that mess. And so much for my bragging about knowing New York like the back of my hand. I managed to get totally turned around, forgetting where Park is in relation to Fifth, Madison, and Lexington Avenues. There's a construction site on the corner of Fiftieth and Madison, and both times I wandered past, clearly confused, a couple of guys loitering under the scaffolding tried to talk me up, offering directions to their place, but I just politely pointed out that I had a map and kept going. I've learned it's best to be polite but firm with guys on the street, who can be sometimes scarily persistent. I've had doormen, pedestrians, and even cops try to pick me up, just on the street, like I'm a hooker or something.

Those blocks across the city are long; my legs are sore from all the hoofing back and forth. But apparently I have managed to find 830 Park Avenue, and apparently the stranger who's loitering on the sidewalk is the man I'm looking for, Jim Segal.

"Mr. Segal?" I ask, because I'm actually not sure. He sounded nice enough when we talked earlier, but somehow I was expecting a recent MBA in a too-big suit, but the guy standing before me is older, and very distinguished: perfectly tanned, and wearing a crisp blazer and an ivory cashmere scarf around his throat. He looks like he just got off of a yacht. He's got flecks of silver in his close-cut brown hair, and beautiful, gleaming teeth, and perfectly round tortoiseshell glasses.

"Call me Jim. And you've got to be Mac Croft." He shakes my hand firmly. "Frank told me you were gorgeous, but man. This might be the first time in all the years I've known that bastard that he's not exaggerating." He leans in closer, still not releasing my hand from his death grip.

"So you talked to Frank, then!" I wriggle free of his grasp, eager to stay focused on business. It was a long trip to get here—a quick pop in back at the office, where there was still no sign of Francesca but there was the good news that I booked the *Allure* gig, then back on the subway uptown, followed by fifteen minutes of wandering around like a discombobulated midwestern tourist. But it was worth it: I'm here for a reason, and I'm finally going to get down to it and find myself a place to live. "I guess Frank probably told you what I'm looking for."

"If I knew what beautiful women were looking for," Jim says, "my entire life would be different. Why don't we walk and talk and you can fill me in for yourself? I could use a coffee."

I didn't trek up here for a coffee date, but this guy is my only lead on the real estate thing, so I figure I better play nicely. Besides, he's pretty cute—going along with his flirting won't exactly be the most painful thing I've ever done—so I nod and stroll along side him.

"So, did Frank give you any of the details?" I ask him.

"He said you were tall and gorgeous. But that was about as detailed as he got." Jim turns to me and grins. "Why don't you fill me in on the details yourself?"

I ignore his flirting. "Well, I'm in the market for a two bedroom. Something nice. Comfortable and clean, in a safe part of town. And I don't want to spend a fortune. Oh, and a doorman might be good." I figure the promise of a uniformed attendant always on duty will help put to rest Dad's fear that I'll be at risk of having my throat slit by some imaginary big city bad guy.

"A two bedroom, in a doorman building, in one of Manhattan's more charming districts. I don't imagine that will be a problem." We've reached the Starbucks on the corner, and he gallantly holds the door open for me.

We walk into the place, which is deserted. It's eerie how every Starbucks—even the ones in Mexico and Paris—is exactly the same.

"It's just that easy?" I ask.

"It's that easy," Jim agrees. "If you know what you're doing. The Manhattan real estate market can be tricky, but that's my area of expertise. And I'm happy to help you. I'm sure we'll find you something more than suitable."

What a relief—I can't wait to text Irin and let her know.

"What can I get you?" Jim asks.

"A small coffee, thanks." Lately I drink about ten cups of the stuff—most girls do—but I'm eyeing the glass case stuffed full of huge, elaborately iced sugar cookies in the shape of snowflakes, puffy doughnuts with cracked, sugary skins, and dense, rich brownies that look like they're made of mud. I feel a weird rush, and suddenly my head gets really heavy. *Whoa.* "You know, maybe I'll have some water, too."

"Whatever the lady wants," Jim says, paying for my bottled water and his medium coffee. He takes a big sip. "That's what I needed."

I gulp down half the bottle of water. My head stops spinning, and the cold liquid in my throat makes me feel awake, steady. "Me too, I guess."

We stroll back into the winter evening.

"So, where are you staying until you find a permanent place? Let me guess. The Mercer. You're the young, hip, type. Or no, the Waldorf? You're an uptown girl."

"A hotel?" I shake my head. The sun's going down, and it seems a little cooler out now. I dig into my bag for my scarf, wind it around my neck three times. "No. I'm staying with my folks. In Jersey."

"Your folks! No wonder you're ready to get a place of your own. Well, we'll see what we can do about that." His phone chirps loudly, and Jim reaches into his interior jacket pocket. He barely glances at the display, silencing it immediately. "Sorry about that," he says apologetically.

We're walking back in the direction we've just come, down Fiftieth Street and toward Park Avenue. The taxis and other traffic whizzing by kick up a breeze, and the sun dips behind the towering skyscrapers, so suddenly it feels much colder.

"You're shivering!" Jim sounds worried. "We need to get you inside, don't we?"

"I'm fine, I'm fine." I probably sound a little more impatient than I mean to—it's not that Jim's not a nice guy, it's just that I've got a goal here. "So, do you have some places to show me? Or do I need to do something else first? Is there a form to fill out?"

"A form? I don't understand." He drains his coffee cup and tosses it into one of those green mesh garbage cans that stand on all the city's corners.

I'm embarrassed all of a sudden. In a few short months, I've traveled the world, met a bunch of different kinds of people, and made more money than I expected to make in five years, but there's a lot I don't know about how to live like a grownup, starting with how to rent an apartment. "I'm sorry, Jim," I tell him, flustered. "You know, I've lived with my folks all my life, I never had to get a place of my own or anything. So I don't know much about how this whole thing works."

Jim grins. "This whole thing?"

He stops. We're back at the same patch of sidewalk where we first met.

"Right. This whole real estate agent thing." I study his face. Nothing. "Or is it broker? I'm sorry. I feel so stupid. But I'm not, and I'm serious about this, so if you can just walk me through what I need to do . . ." He's just looking at me, dumbfounded. I knew I was going to mix those two things up, and now I've offended the one person I know who might actually help me with this whole apartment thing. Great.

Jim starts laughing. "You think I'm a real estate broker, don't you, Mac Croft?" He stops, looks at me, then starts laughing again, a laugh that's the same distinguished, rich baritone as his speaking voice.

"I don't understand," I tell him. "I told Frank I needed a place, he said I ought to come see you. I just assumed . . ."

"You're lucky I don't have a fragile ego." Jim puts his hand on my elbow and gently turns me around so my back is to the street. With his other hand he gestures up at the massive skyscraper in front of us. "You see this building?"

"I see it," I tell him. "But I don't get it." I can feel my cheeks turning scarlet, and I'm at once cold and hot all over. Clearly I've made some kind of mistake.

"You tell me what that sign says, Mac Croft." He's pointing at an engraved gold plaque on the building's glass and marble façade. The one that says *The Segal Group*.

"So . . . you're not a real estate broker?" I try to smile but I want to hide under a rock.

"Close. I'm a real estate *developer*." He uses his hand to sweep up the entire height of the building. "This is mine. My flagship. My crown jewel. I build buildings."

"I'm so embarrassed." I feel all flustered and ridiculous. "Jim, er, Mr. Segal . . ." It feels wrong to call him Jim when his name is on the front of the damn building.

"I know how you can make it up to me," he says. "Let me buy you dinner."

I smile up at him. He's taller than me, and from here his square chin makes him look almost like he's carved out of stone. He smells delicious, in that way that some people just smell good; warm, spicy, but not overly cologne-d. Just right. I'm so used to fending off the advances of the men I encounter on a daily basis, I've forgotten that sometimes I *want* men to flirt with me. Handsome, interesting men. Men like Jim Segal.

I'm not sure what the right thing is to do. Patrick and I have been trying to schedule a third date, but he's back in LA for a couple of days, and I can't get away. Our schedules are incompatible, but that's not the only hurdle: I can't decide if I'm willing to try and build a real relationship with a man whose first and foremost commitment is to his own bachelorhood. Sure, we've been on a couple of dates, but I hardly think things are so serious that I can't see someone else for a friendly dinner. Right? Right.

"You've got a deal," I tell Jim. "I'm heading out of town, but maybe we should try and get together next week?"

"Wednesday," Jim says firmly.

"Uhhh." I wasn't expecting to make a concrete plan, but OK . . . "Wednesday. That should be fine." I double check my phone. "I'm back from California on Tuesday. So yes, Wednesday it is." I've got a shoot penciled in that day, but it's one day, in studio, in the city, for *Marie Claire*. No big deal.

"I already know where I'm going to take you," Jim says. "It'll be my little surprise."

"Cool." I nod, then I remind him that we've got serious business to discuss. "Maybe you'll have some apartment leads for me by then?"

Jim smiles, shaking his head. "Don't worry, Mac. I haven't forgotten. We're going to find you a great place to live."

At last. The ball is well and truly rolling.

Nine

The wind off the Pacific is icy and probing, whistling in my ears and whipping my hair back with a snap, but I don't mind. Sure, my slinky Luca Luca gown shows off plenty of skin, but I'm all wrapped up in an insanely long and luxurious Dennis Basso coat, and that wards off the chill. I turn slightly to the left, staring deep into Vera's eyes, because we've been instructed repeatedly (by Laurie the stylist, by Brian the hairstylist, by Fritz the makeup artist) not to smile.

"Don't make me laugh," Vera says, sternly, and even though her mouth is fixed in a straight line, I can see the laughter welling up in her inky black eyes.

"No laughing," Angelique chimes in. She's an absolutely stunning girl originally from the Ivory Coast. I've never worked with her before, but her reputation precedes her—mostly because the rumor has it she's dating a certain freckle-faced, much younger Hollywood starlet.

We've all been told to look fierce and serious, and we've also been told to interact—not to talk to each other, not to touch one another, but to engage. Those are the kinds of cryptic instructions a certain breed of stylist loves to give.

"I'm serious, Mac." Vera has the uncanny ability to speak without moving her lips. If her modeling career ever goes bust, she could get work as a ventriloquist. "Stop making those googly eyes at me."

"Girls! No talking, please!" shouts Laurie, a tiny wisp of a woman dressed all in black, hiding behind massive sunglasses and puffing on a cigarette. She sort of hops up and down to make her point a little more emphatically. Shelly Pine, the photographer who's technically in charge, says nothing. She's a legend, Shelly Pine—she's been taking fashion pictures for longer than any of the models on today's job have even been alive, most of them iconic shots from *Vogue* and *Harpers Bazaar*, of the sixties' most famous models sporting Vidal Sassoon bobs and flashy miniskirts. But like a lot of the so-called legendary photographers I've worked with, she seems disinterested, almost like she's on autopilot. Her three assistants do most of the work, setting up the cameras, tinkering with the lighting, keeping Shelly supplied with both film and Polaroid, since she's one of those old-schoolers who doesn't believe in digital cameras. Occasionally she'll whisper something to Laurie, and it's clear by her general air of boredom that she's happy to let the stylist run this shoot.

"This is serious, girls." Laurie sounds like a disappointed mom scolding a toddler. "The key here is sophistication. The attitude here is luxury. We need closed faces. Closed mouths. Closed faces. Closing time. Forbidden fruits."

I have no idea what she's blabbering on about, but I trust my instincts, so I just tune her out and fix my gaze on Vera again, not looking at her—looking through her. Even when I'm working with other models, I still have that same, intimate relationship with the camera. It's just the camera and I, everything else, even the other girls in the shot, fading. It all fades away now, even though there are so many distractions: the cold winter air, the stunning old mansion where we're shooting, posed on the oceanfront terrace, the other models, the crew, the sound of the surf crashing against the rocks.

I turn my head again, fixing the camera right in my gaze, staring it down like this is a life-or-death game of chicken. Moments like this, time stops, and there's only the feeling of the soft sable against my skin and the sound of the ocean hurling itself against the San Francisco coastline.

"Like Mac!" Laurie cries, tossing her cigarette to the ground and stubbing it out quickly. "Do it like Mac, girls. Do it like Mac."

I sort of register the compliment, but keep going, doing what I do.

The upside of shooting with a big name photographer like Shelly Pine is that there's no skimping on the budget. Even though we're in California shooting a cover try and fashion story for *W*, which is the bible of fashion magazines, and is known for being one of the more creative—but notoriously stingy—of the big American fashion magazines, we're not roughing it in the least. We're staying at the Ritz, and even though our call time was so early I was barely able to enjoy the many little luxuries of such a fancy hotel, I definitely appreciated the big, comfortable bed last night, since I've been working all week and was in pretty desperate need of a good, eight hours' rest. And now we're all of us—me, Vera and Angelique, plus Shelly, her three assistants, Laurie and her assistant Rebecca, the hairstylist Brian and makeup artist Fritz, the local producer Mark and his boyfriend James—causing a ruckus in what's supposed to be the city's most elegant and inventive restaurant, Quince.

I'm squeezed in between Vera and Rebecca, Laurie's bookish, kind of shy assistant. Rebecca's the girl who's responsible, on set, for keeping track of our shoes' mates, and making sure the diamond necklaces stay safely in their little tray, and that the dramatic silky gowns are utterly spotless, free of wrinkles, creases, or errant specks of dirt. I don't envy her.

Shelly has ordered the tasting menu for everyone at the table: fourteen courses, for thirteen people. The long table is littered with dishes, and every fifteen minutes or so four uniformed waiters and waitresses swoop in, their movements choreographed and perfectly in sync, to bring us even more food. The plates pile up, and never quite seem to disappear: a dollop of pate atop a buttery toast point surrounded by plump, almost dangerous-looking blackberries; one seared scallop with a candied Serrano chili balanced delicately on top; a lamb chop, pink and bloody at its very center, nestled in a tangle of frisée; a poached quail's egg, the yolk speckled with inky black caviar; three pillow-shaped ravioli stuffed with crispy pork cheeks and swimming in a broth of brown butter. I'm actually drowning in a sea of food I can't possibly eat. I use my fork to cut into each course, but so far I've only eaten the frisée, the blackberries, and one half of the ravioli—I just sort of shove the plates in Rebecca's direction. The table is so crowded, no one can keep track of their food anyway.

"Truth or dare, truth or dare," cackles Vera. She slurs the words, slightly, which is no surprise since she's downed two bottles of white wine by herself and we're not even halfway through dinner.

"What is this mean?" Angelique's accent is so glamorous, so dignified. She studies Vera from across the table.

"It's a game," Laurie explains. "You choose which you want to do—tell the truth, or do a dare."

"I don't know this game." Angelique picks her phone up off the crowded table and studies the display, distracted.

"You don't know the game, so you have to go first!" Vera's being way too loud for the fancy crowd at the restaurant, but she doesn't seem to notice. Besides, it's clear to everyone—well, maybe everyone but Angelique—exactly what she's up to. There's only one thing we've all been gossiping about all day. "So, choose truth!"

Angelique shrugs, and shovels the scallop, whole, into her mouth. I feel a twinge of jealousy. I reach across the table and pick the blackberries off of Fritz's plate and pop them into my mouth like they're pills.

"So!" Vera claps her hands delightedly. "True or false. You're dating Ali Saunders."

There are so many of us there have been about five different conversations going all night, but suddenly everyone gets very quiet, waiting to hear if the rumors of the May-December lesbian romance are true.

If her skin weren't the same impenetrably dark color of the blackberries, Angelique would probably be blushing. She clears her throat daintily and stares daggers at Vera. "I don't discuss these things," she says simply, shrugging.

"Can you pass the wine down here?" Mark asks, politely doing his part to change the subject.

"Come on!" Vera swirls her glass and downs the rest of her wine. "You're among friends."

"I wonder what the next course is," Rebecca says lamely.

"If you want to talk about Hollywood rumors," Angelique continues, "perhaps you ask Mac about this Patrick Carroll."

Twelve heads swivel in unison in my direction, and I can feel my cheeks turn scarlet. I guess she reads Page Six.

"Patrick Carroll?" For the first time all day, Shelly Pine herself seems interested.

"Oh. My. God." Vera's apparently pretty dramatic when she's been drinking. "Don't tell me you're both star fuckers! Get out of here." At this point, she's practically screaming, and everyone else in the restaurant is staring.

"I think maybe Vera's had enough." I pass the open bottle of wine away from us and down the table toward Mark and James.

"Don't play coy!" Vera laughs. "Someone please kiss and tell right now. It's a party!"

Angelique is completely ignoring all of the rest of us now, tapping her phone's keypad insistently, and everyone is still looking right at me.

"These berries are so good." I can't think of anything else to say. "If no one wants theirs, send them my way."

Laurie gamely offers me her plate, just as the servers sweep in once more, depositing tiny bowls on the table: lobster tails swimming in a buttery broth flecked with dill.

"You guys are no fun," Vera announces. She leans back into the velvet-covered banquette, digging into her clutch for a pack of Marlboros and some matches. She lights up, and there's an audible gasp across the room—you can't smoke indoors anywhere in California, and it's particularly bad form in hippie-dippie San Francisco.

"I don't think you can smoke in here," Fritz says politely.

Vera laughs, exhaling plumes of smoke from her nostrils. "Fuckers! Fascists. I should move to France, I swear to God."

The maitre d' rushes to our table. "Madame, I'm afraid you'll have to put that out immediately!" he hisses, politely but firmly.

Vera stares him down, takes another healthy puff on the cigarette, then stubs it out on top of her lobster, where it hisses and dies. "Happy?" she leans back into her seat, folding her arms across her chest like a sulking kid.

The maitre d' nods abruptly, whisking the lobster and ciga- rette butt off the table, and stalks away wordlessly.

"So," Laurie says, with forced cheer, trying once more to lighten the mood. "Bon appetit!"

The view is nice, and the shower is a little taste of heaven, but as far as I'm concerned it's the bed that makes this hotel worth every penny. Not that I'm paying. I'm sprawling right in the center of the bed, which is big enough that I can stretch out my arms and legs all the way and still stay warm and toasty underneath the covers. This is key because San Francisco is freezing. I somehow imagined that California would be a nice break from the winter weather back east, but I was sorely mistaken. Good thing we're shooting furs, and even better thing that I have the Ritz to come back to at the end of our long day.

Vera's drunken outburst put a damper on dinner. Every- one did their best to keep the conversation going—sticking to safer topics than Angelique's and my romantic lives—but when we piled back into our cars, I think everyone was pretty relieved. I'm just happy to be back in my room, safe from the gossiping crew and all those tempting dishes, and alone with my thoughts, which are right now about Patrick Carroll. And Jim Segal.

I haven't talked to Jim since we first met a few days ago. I've been on the road, and I don't want to bother him—I figure if he's got his name on a building, he's probably got more than enough to keep him busy. Besides, it seems somehow . . . wrong. Not that Patrick and I are all that serious. Much as I like him and enjoy spending time with him, I don't think Patrick Carroll is the kind of man you can get serious about. Or at least, he's not the man I'm going to get serious about. I like him, I do. I could love him, if I let myself, but I'm not convinced I could be enough for him.

Patrick is charming, kind, and fun, not to mention gorgeous, rich, and famous. You'd think any woman in the world would want him, but I don't. I can't. I've got to make the grown-up decision, and I know what's best for me is a guy I can rely on, a guy who can keep me grounded. Sure, my head starts to spin just remembering the scratch of Patrick's stubble on my neck. Yes, I loved the way he gripped my wrists firmly as we kissed, like he was afraid I was going to wriggle away and escape. But I'm not stupid. Patrick Carroll is not the kind of man you make a life with. I'm not looking to get married, but I'm not looking to get ditched, either. I don't want to read about our breakup in Page Six.

Our breakup. The word wakes me up like a double espresso. My heart is pounding, and though I can hear the wind whistling at the window, I'm sweating, anxious. I glance at the bedside alarm clock. It's eleven, and I really should get some rest, but until I deal with this, I'm not going to be able to sleep. At least Patrick's at his place in LA—that means that I won't be waking him up. Just breaking up. I dial the number, feeling suddenly very awake, and more than a little sad.

"Mac Croft." Patrick doesn't even bother with hellos.

"Hi Patrick." I lean back onto the bed, staring at the ceiling.

"To what do I owe this unexpected surprise? I've been hoping you'd call."

Wait, what am I doing? Why am I calling him? "I just . . . was thinking about you. Thinking about . . . us." I'm starting to panic—I can't quite catch my breath. It sounds like I'm making an obscene phone call.

"I like the way you think," Patrick tells me. "Where are you right now?"

"San Francisco." I look around the room. It's beautiful, luxurious, but totally anonymous. I could be anywhere in the world. I'm starting to realize that all hotel rooms are basically the same.

"You're in California?" Patrick sounds amused. "That's fantastic news. Seriously. You're coming to LA tomorrow, right?"

"Patrick." Now I've totally forgotten why I was calling. Why am I dead set on ending things with a man who can make me swoon from hundreds of miles away? "No, tomorrow I'm shooting . . ."

"Then the next day," Patrick says, like it's perfectly reasonable. "Terrific. You tell me what flight you're on, I'll send my driver."

"No, Patrick . . ." I'm about to tell him that I can't, that I couldn't possibly. But is that true? I'm shooting tomorrow, then it's Friday, and I'm going to be traveling most of the day anyway, and I don't have any appointments or anything to do in New York this weekend. All it's going to take is a quick phone call to Francesca to be sure, but I can probably get away to LA. Just for the weekend.

"You can't say no," Patrick says, warmly but firmly. "You're so close. Come on."

"Just this once," I tell him. He's right. I can't say no to him. Which is probably another reason I ought to break up with him. But if I am going to, I should at least do it in person, right? Or at least after one last weekend fling. . . .

Ten

Once again, I find myself on a plane, a familiar place, now, that's really no place at all. An airplane seat is nothing, just a gateway between places, in this case, between LA and Newark, but still, it's bringing back a flood of memories and sending my mind reeling. It's a good thing I have nothing more pressing to do than watch the in-flight movie. Would you believe it stars Patrick Carroll? The truth of my life is so much stranger than fiction.

That truth included a flurry of last-minute phone calls and scheduling adjustments. Then a quick flight to the warmer environs of LAX where, sure enough, Patrick Carroll had a driver waiting for me at baggage claim, holding a little cardboard sign with my name printed on it. Then I settled into the backseat of the maroon Bentley and was whisked away to Patrick's ridiculously beautiful Spanish-style villa. The whole scene was exactly like something out of one of Patrick's movies.

So I can be forgiven, right, for second guessing myself? It really was like a movie, and I was the leading lady who forgot her lines, lost her motivation. From the moment I saw Patrick standing in the door—those twinkling eyes, that tangle of hair above his forehead—I was right back to square one. I abandoned the script and just improvised.

Until that night. Dinner was amazing, and we lingered for hours after our plates had been cleared, saying hello to friends and the occasional fan (I've had people ask for autographs when I'm on location, but the attention I get is nothing compared to a regular night out for Patrick Carroll), and just talking. I lost myself in the moment, in the magic. But then, back home, sipping champagne and sitting out by the pool, I started to remember why I had gone there. I admit I was wondering what it would be like up in the bedroom, Patrick Carroll's bedroom, but my very first thought was *if those walls could talk.*

That was the wakeup call I needed, I guess. If I couldn't even sleep with Patrick, how could I possibly think we could make a life together?

"Patrick," I said, shakily. "I think we need to talk."

Then it all spilled out of me. It was like reading a script. When I got to the part about what I do, what I need, where life is taking me, Patrick interrupted, gently placed a finger on my lips, momentarily silencing me.

"I won't say I'm not disappointed," he said. "But you're a woman who knows what she wants. I respect that. I'm still glad you came to LA to see me."

And that was that. I never did get a look inside that famous bedroom of his.

I feel better now, lighter. Ours might not have been the most serious romance in the history of the world, but I'm glad we got one last hurrah. I'm glad I went to see him. I suspect I'll have more breakups in my future; I want to make sure

I've got good karma. And I think I handled this one well, but still I think the universe is screwing with me a little, because when the in-flight movie starts, and it's that gangster picture Patrick made last year, the one that got the rave reviews, the one he should have won all the big awards for (if he hadn't been inexplicably snubbed), the one that landed him on the covers of *GQ* and *Esquire* and *Men's Vogue* and *Vanity Fair*, my heart lurches and I feel like crying. It wouldn't be broken-hearted sobbing for how it all ended, it would just be me, crying a little over what might have been. But I fight back the tears and order a Dewar's. I never drink, but it seems only fitting, since I'm here on a plane, which is where I first met Patrick, after all.

"Everyone says this, Mac," he'd said to me. "But I really mean it. I want us to be friends—always."

"Yes, definitely," I told him.

"I mean it," he said. "It makes me very glad to know you're out there somewhere. The world is a more interesting place with you in it."

It wasn't meant to be, but even so, I raise my glass, to Patrick Carroll.

In the few days I've spent in California, something amazing and momentous has transpired, something I was truly beginning to think was never going to happen: Spring has arrived. It's not exactly time to break out the shorts, but there's no denying that we've turned some kind of corner—it's mild enough that the back of the cab actually feels a little stuffy, so I crack the back window and breathe in the fresh breeze happily.

"Where you coming in from?" The cab driver glances back at me over his shoulder, smiling broadly.

"California," I tell him, slipping on my sunglasses and studying the New Jersey sprawl. It's ugly, sure, but it's still good to be home.

"California," he repeats. "Sun and sand, huh?"

"Actually, it was freezing out in Northern California. But then I was in LA, which was pretty pleasant."

"I'm from India, you know." The driver shakes his head. "I'm not used to this cold."

"It seems kind of nice out today," I tell him.

"Yes, yes," the driver agrees. He mutters, leans on the horn, and curses the Hummer that's just cut us off. "Sorry. But yes, nice today. I've lived here a long time, though, and I'm still not used to these winters."

"I know what you mean." I don't actually mind the winter—I think the snow's kind of romantic, and can be beautiful—but I've had enough. A couple of days in warmer climates (Portugal, Mexico, Miami) has only whet my appetite for more.

"Spring is a good season," the driver continues, philosophically. "A time for new beginnings."

"That's true." He's right—the new season means I can make a new start. It's the end of one relationship, sure, but it could be the beginning of so much more: new clients, new gigs, new challenges. "You're quite the philosopher."

He shrugs. "I try."

I can't help but laugh. "You've got me thinking," I tell him. We ride on in silence, thoughts of what spring might hold occupying me.

* * *

Between the general sense of frenzy and madness on set (some shoots are like that, even when they're small and straightforward like today's job for *Marie Claire*), and the mind-boggling number of text messages and work phone calls (Cover Girl confirms our rescheduled meeting at last, then an hour later needs to postpone it, and meanwhile Francesca's got me going to Anchorage, Montauk, and possibly across the ocean to walk in London Fashion Week for Gareth Pugh and Vivienne Westwood), I forget I've got dinner plans tonight. The set is more chaotic than it should be, considering we're doing a pretty straightforward story, on new color combinations for summer dressing. Five shots, in and out. But the makeup artist is nervous and a little slow. She holds things up, and I'm distracted, worrying about whether Cover Girl is ever going to stop jerking me around. It's not until I break out my date book to double check my availability for this trip to Anchorage that I remember I'm supposed to see Jim for dinner tonight.

But now the day's wrapping up, and the photo assistants are packing the equipment, the stylist's assistant is packing the clothes, and I'm rushing to get back into my real life outfit (jeans, tee, and sweater), using cold cream to wipe the gunk from my face. But considering that it's almost the dinner hour, I decide to check in with Jim. I'm half-tempted to cancel—it's early enough that I could get back to Jersey for dinner with the folks, which would be nice, but I'm counting on Jim for apartment leads, and Irin's counting on me. I'm just not sure what we're going to talk about. The model and the millionaire? What do we have in common? I'm perched on the edge of a metal folding chair, lacing up my sneakers, when my phone rings. I glance at the display, and it's Jim, who has apparently not forgotten our date. Or maybe he's calling to cancel?

"Hi Jim!" I answer.

"Mac Croft," Jim says. "How are you, darling?"

"I'm doing OK." I stand and pull my black cotton sweater over my head. "How's life treating you?"

"Better now that I'm talking to you." I can practically hear Jim smiling through the phone. "You didn't forget we have dinner plans, I hope?"

"No, of course not!" I try to fluff my hair back into some semblance of shape, but all these back-to-back shoots have not been kind on my poor locks. I guess he's not going to cancel after all.

"We've got some business to discuss," Jim says cryptically. "But I hope from there the evening can segue into a pleasurable outing?"

"Business?"

"I'll tell you more over appetizers," Jim promises. "I'm in the car now. Where are you exactly?"

"I'm at Industria," I tell him. "It's a studio, in the West Village."

"Terrific. West Village. Text me the address? I'll pick you up outside in about fifteen minutes."

"Pick me up, huh? So old-fashioned."

"I know how to treat a lady," Jim tells me. "I'll see you soon."

I can barely sit still. My heart's . . . not racing, exactly, but fluttering, and so is my stomach, and for once it's not because I'm hungry, it's because I'm impatient. Jim's a man of his word, keeping his promise to pick me up precisely fifteen minutes after we talked, and keeping his promise not to talk business until we're seated, with appetizers and drinks on the table in front of us. That's why I'm fidgeting in my seat, flushed and anxious: because I'm waiting desperately for our waitress to show up with my beet salad and Jim's shrimp cocktail, because once she does, I'll be able to get Jim to fill me in on the great apartment search.

"You've never been here before?" Jim sounds like he can't quite believe it.

"It's true," I tell him. "I mostly end up walking around wherever I'm shooting, or near the Delicious offices. I haven't properly explored the West Village. I hope that will change if I find a place . . ."

"Uh-uh-uh!" Jim wags a scolding finger at me. "No shop talk until there's food on this table. That's the rule."

"Can't blame a girl for trying." I shrug, and finish my seltzer with cranberry juice.

"Blue Ribbon Bakery is one of my favorite places." Jim looks around the room appreciatively like we're in his house. "I come here, well, it's probably about once a week, but more if I can get away. Even though I live uptown I think of this as my little neighborhood place."

"Well, you must be a regular. You got the star treatment, and the best table in the house!" It's true: We're tucked into a corner table from which we have the perfect view of everyone in the restaurant and right out the huge plate-glass windows. The restaurant's right on the corner, so we get to watch the parade of pedestrians, one of my favorite things to do in any city.

"I've got news for you," Jim laughs. "They didn't give this

table to me. They gave it to you. It's good for business when there's a devastatingly beautiful woman seated right where everyone can see her. It's good business."

As he says this, the waitress descends with our appetizers. "Can I get you another?" she asks, taking my empty glass.

"I think another round?" Jim drains the last of his bourbon and hands her the glass. "Bon appetit!" He winks at me.

"Likewise." I take a bite of the salad—the beet is rich and sweet, and cooked to perfection.

"You're hungry!" Jim says it happily, like he thinks it's hilarious.

"I am," I admit. "My schedule, my diet. It takes a toll."

"I've got some news that might cheer you up." Jim dips a shrimp into the deep red cocktail sauce and pops it into his mouth. "You've got to try this, by the way. Amazing. Anyway."

I lean in closer across the tiny table.

"I've done some investigating, just as you asked."

"And?"

"And it turns out there's a space in one of my projects." Jim nods as the waitress returns with our drinks. He takes a tiny sip, sets his glass down and continues. "It's a beautiful condo building. Very modern, very chic. It's on Twenty-fourth Street, just across from London Terrace, right in Chelsea. Tons of galleries and restaurants—it's a very vibrant neighborhood. One of my favorites, that we're building in right now. I thought you might like to be somewhere kind of hip and young. Plus, you're right near the highway, so getting to and from the airports—all of them—is a snap."

"An apartment. You found me a place."

"I'm a man of action." Jim reaches across the table with

his fork and spears one of my beets. "I think you'll like it. I stopped by there the other day, and I'm pretty happy with it, if I do say so myself. You've got a view right down the High Line, you know, the old elevated train tracks that they're turning into a park? And you can peek right through the buildings across the way and see the Hudson."

"River views? Sounds incredible. But . . . you're sure it's in my price range?"

"Price range?" Jim looks at me like I'm crazy. "Don't worry about that."

"I have to worry about that!" I fork the last of my salad into my mouth and sigh contentedly. "I need to know what I'm getting into."

Jim waves dismissively. "We'll get you a good deal. Don't you worry."

"I don't know how to thank you." I lean back as the waitress clears our empty plates. "I appreciate this so much."

"Don't be silly! You came to me for help, you're the friend of a friend. I'm only doing what's right."

"Well, it is much appreciated. I don't know how I would have done this without some help."

"I have a feeling," he says, reaching across the table to place one hand one top of mine, "that you can do anything you set your mind to."

I laugh. But I don't pull my hand away. Somehow his hand on mine feels . . . right. Comfortable, and comforting. Reassuring. "Still, I needed some help, and you were there for me. That means a lot to me. I don't know how I can thank you . . ."

"I do." Jim looks at me, very serious. "You can get to know me. We're friends. You don't owe me anything. There's nothing I wouldn't do for the pleasure of your company. So what do you say we stop all this serious talk, and just find some pleasure? In one another's company?"

"That," I agree, "sounds great."

If I ever find myself on death row, I know what I'll order the night before they flip the switch: yellow snapper, whipped cauliflower mash, and haricots vert, right from the kitchen at Blue Ribbon Bakery. I can definitely see why this is Jim's favorite restaurant.

But between the heavy meal and the kind of work week I've had, I can't help but stifle a yawn or two, and Jim's too observant not to catch me in the act.

"I'm boring you." He shakes his head, like he's disappointed.

"I'm sorry . . . not bored. Just beat. I've had a crazy couple of weeks . . . I was just in Portugal and . . ."

"Well, you're here now. New York. The world's greatest city. With me. Forget Portugal." He pushes his empty plate away and leans back in his chair.

I *have* forgotten Portugal. I'm not even thinking where I have to be tomorrow, for what feels like the first time in months. "I know," I tell him. "I'm right here."

"And I, for one, couldn't be happier." Jim sets his drink down on the table, the ice clinking prettily. "Here's a question for you. Wake you up, get the old mind going. Tell me . . . tell me the most beautiful place you've ever been." He looks at me curiously, his icy blue eyes so penetrating and yet so warm.

"The most beautiful place I've ever been?" I rack my brain. Where have I been? "I think I have to say Alaska. Is that unexciting?"

"Plenty exciting. True, possibly. But there are so many kinds of beauty in this world, Mac. I agree. Nature can be breathtaking, really startling. But there's so much to see. The terracotta armies of Xi'an. The Taj Mahal at sunrise. Giza at sunset." He sounds truly moved, like he's there, mentally, far away from New York.

"That," I tell him, "sounds amazing." And it does. I want to get out there. I want to see the world.

"You know what, Mac Croft? I think I'd like to show you some of that. Pick a place. Let's go next week." He drains his drink—is he drunk?—and leans across the small table.

"Easy, tiger. Next week, I've got . . . *Allure*. Right. And something else. I can't remember what."

"I'm supposed to ring the opening bell at the stock exchange on Wednesday morning. Top that." He smiles. "I'd so much rather wake up in Biarritz with you, though."

"No question." The waitress comes to clear our dishes, and I pause until she's out of earshot. "I'd definitely rather be almost anywhere. But work is work. Besides, how else am I going to afford my rent?"

Jim waves his hand impatiently. "I thought we agreed. No work talk."

I glance at my watch. Shit. Somehow it got late. "Fine, fine. No talk about work."

The waitress reappears with our dessert menus, deftly clearing away the empty glasses and untouched breadbasket.

"I have to start thinking about getting home." I texted Mom right before we sat down, but she's probably starting to worry by now.

"Seems awfully soon to me," Jim says.

"Well, I've got to catch the train . . ."

"Don't be ridiculous." Jim signals to the waitress. "We are having dessert, and then I am escorting you home."

The Town Car—which has been waiting for us for the past two hours—glides silently through the West Village, starting and stopping, never picking up much speed because there's a stop sign at every intersection, but moving surely and stealthily west toward the highway. The deep thrum of the car's powerful engine, the comfortable leather seat, the heavy dinner, the intoxicatingly rich taste of raspberry sorbet afterward, not to mention my jet lag—they're all combining and conspiring to make me feel so sleepy I'm almost drugged.

Jim drapes his arm over my shoulder, protectively, and it's so cozy, so almost but not quite innocent, that I'm tempted to drift off into sleep. He smells warm and spicy, and has a hint of whiskey on his breath, which is more appealing than it sounds. The moon is steely and bright, even through the car's tinted windows, and it catches the silver on Jim's hair, though I can barely focus on that since my eyelids are growing heavier by the second. I shouldn't be getting quite so comfortable but I can't help myself.

"You don't have to drive me home." I'm mumbling, though, and clearly in no shape to navigate the dark streets toward the station, board the PATH train for Jersey, make a connection to the bus, and eventually find my way home.

"First off, I'm not driving. Anthony is." I can feel his warm breath on the top of my head as I slip closer to sleep. "Besides, what kind of a gentleman would I be if I didn't see you home?"

The car swings around a corner—I can't see because I'm slunk down far in my seat. Anyway, at night the streets all look the same, and even familiar ones seem alien from the inside of a car. But even though I can't see where we are, when the car stops I can tell we haven't driven far enough to be in Jersey.

"We're there already?" I wonder for a second if I actually fell asleep. I sit up.

The driver is out the door, and crossing in front of the car. Jim uses the opportunity to take my chin in his hand, pulling me toward his face for a quick kiss, before the driver pulls open the door, admitting a blast of cold night air.

"No, Anthony might be fast," Jim laughs, "but he's not that fast!"

"No ma'am," the driver says, smiling as he stands behind my open door.

I step out of the car, pulling my coat closed as I emerge into the night. It's brightly lit—there are fluorescent spotlights towering high above, as well as the headlights of the traffic speeding by, the traffic that seems to be behind us, somewhere else. Where are we? It looks like we're on the highway but actually we're next to it, between the road and the river, surrounded by a high, chain-link fence. And there, right in front of us, is a gleaming black helicopter, blades whirring slowly.

"You've got to be kidding me."

"I never kid," says Jim. He's carrying my bag in one hand, and places the other on the small of my back, guiding us toward the helicopter. One of the helipad attendants takes my other hand and I step inside, settling into the black leather seat. Jim pops in beside me, casually, as if he does this every day, and sits, taking my hand in his.

"This is too much." I feel wide-awake now, and giddy. I laugh out loud for no particular reason.

"Too much?" Jim asks. "That, Mac Croft, is precisely what you're worth."

My stomach lurches, but pleasantly, as we lift off into the night, the relentless whirr of the propeller just above our head kind of deafening, the seemingly endless twinkle of the city below us—does it go on forever?—illuminating the night like a magical carpet woven from stars.

Eleven

Days like today I love what I do. I'll gladly trade the nine to five grind for this. I'm *flying*. Technically, I'm strapped into an elaborate harness and hanging eight feet off the ground, gliding and leaping like an acrobat, my hair flying wildly, my legs kicked up dramatically, the better to show off my crocodile stilettos. After all, these shoes are the whole reason we're here. But as far as I'm concerned, I'm flying. And I love it.

"Gorgeous, gorgeous." I've known photographers who shout orders; I've known photographers who shoot in pin-drop silence, glowering at me from behind their big cameras. When he's shooting, Jason McDonald—yes, *that* Jason McDonald, he of the finely chiseled features, the perfectly placed dimples, the sandy brown hair and ridiculously long eyelashes—simply speaks, and politely too, using what my mom would have called, when we were kids, his indoor voice. "You're doing a beautiful job."

Floating through the air like this is intoxicating—though I worry it's because I can't get enough blood to my head.

"Shoes, Mac." Ringo Tang would have shrieked; Shelly

Pine would have glared, but Jason McDonald simply says it, calmly, and I bend my knee, and arch my foot so the shoe lifts up ever so slightly. Shoes are the whole point today. The creative director of *Allure* dreamed this shoot up, and entrusted it to Jason and the stylist Zvi Zee, and Zvi claims he wanted me from the get-go, though I have my doubts. He's nice enough, but he's hardly paying any attention to me—he seems to only have eyes for Jason's assistants, Matthias and Wes, who could be brothers and look like every other photo assistant in town: jeans, Converse sneakers, wrinkled Steven Alan button downs, a dusting of stubble, shaggy hair, skinny forearms, loads of tattoos.

"Gorgeous, gorgeous," Jason says again. It's his refrain. "Maybe we can try a smile now, Mac? A lovely, warm smile?"

I'm wearing a satin dress by some Italian designer I've never heard of whose name is full of silent *g*'s and lots of *c*'s, as well as a complicated but surprisingly comfortable harness and rope thing designed especially for this shoot by Jonesy, a big bearded bear of a guy, who told me before we started that I had nothing to worry about, because he's designed these things for Broadway shows and Vegas spectaculars. I wasn't sure at first, but now that I'm all rigged up I trust him completely—with my life, actually. Jonesy stands behind Jason watching me closely, which makes me feel even safer than the elasticized ropes that he promised me are strong enough to support the weight of someone four times my size.

The fan whips my hair out of my face, and my neck is starting to hurt, but still, I smile. I always do as told—at least, when I'm on set that is.

"Mac, baby," Jonesy calls, "push your arms out at your sides. Like you're on the swing set. That'll get you moving!"

"Thanks!" I'm barely able to get the words out because I'm in such a weird position. I don't know how Broadway stars sing when they're all strung up like this. I do as he says, pushing my arms out at my sides and sure enough, I pick up momentum, glide back and forth, the plain white backdrop behind me, nothing below me, the only sound the whirr of the fan, the frantic snap of Jason's shutter, and the electronic sneeze of the lights, which click on and off precisely every two seconds.

"I'm just losing the shoe a little bit," Jason says calmly.

I bend one leg at the knee, coyly, and kick the other out at full length, the better to show off my electric red crocodile Dior stilettos. The harness might pull a little, but still I'd rather float than stand in these suckers. They've got a thin heel made of gleaming stainless steel, about five inches of the stuff. Thanks but no thanks.

"I think we're good." Jason hands his camera over to Matthais. "Can we please get Miss Croft down? Gently, gently. Mac, that was great."

Wes and Jonesy scramble, kind of like firemen in a cartoon, hurrying over with a ladder. They set it up beneath me, and Jonesy scales it more nimbly than you'd think someone so big could.

"How are we doing then?" He places his big hand reassuringly on my shoulder.

"I'm fine," I tell him. "But I don't know if I'm going to be able to get down in these shoes, though." I can manage the catwalk, but a ladder and these heels—it's just not going to happen.

"Allow me, allow me!" Zvi's assistant Theo comes padding onto the set in his socks—Zvi has banned shoes for the day.

Ironic, since today is all about shoes. Theo is every bit as adorable as I remember, in his tidy button-down, grosgrain bow tie, and woolen vest. He perches on the ladder, not climbing all the way to the top, and delicately reaches up, slipping first one shoe and then the other off my feet.

"You're a gem," I tell him, as Jonesy unstraps me.

Theo cradles the stilettos in his arms like newborns.

"I try, I do." His Southern accent practically drips off every word.

Jonesy steps down off the ladder, guiding my feet toward it as he goes. "Easy does it there," he coos. "Easy."

I feel a little woozy, standing upright, the blood rushing back toward my legs. I climb down the ladder, my hand still in Jonesy's.

"And there we are," he says with a flourish as I step back onto the spotless floor.

"Amazing work, Mac." Jason shuffles over in his cute little argyle socks. His English accent is so distinguished, but his grin is pure schoolboy, and the overall effect is incredibly charming. "Do you think you're ready for another? Do you want to take a quick break?"

OK, I've never had anyone ask me *that* before. "No, I think I'm good to go." It's still early, but I'm starving. The sooner we get back to work, the closer we'll be to lunch.

"Terrific, then." He smiles. "Seriously, great work. Why don't you get some water, take your time. Then we'll do another shot and break for lunch?"

Lunch. The word makes me swoon. Or is it Jason who's having that effect? "That's great," I say. "Thanks, Jason."

Jason heads back to the computer to study the shots he's just taken. I head backstage, pushing past the rolling racks.

Theo's tidying up, even though it's already immaculate, and the makeup artist, a sweet, efficient girl named Natalie, and the hairstylist, a famous guy named Orbe, are waiting.

"And there she is!" Orbe claps his hands. "It's OK, it's going OK?"

"Going OK." I find the bottle of Poland Spring with my initials scrawled on the cap, unscrew it, and take a swig.

"More than OK!" Theo stands, pulling my hair back and out of the way as he unzips the back. "Mac's a real pro."

"You're such a charmer, Theo." Our eyes meet in the mirror's reflection.

"You're the only one susceptible to my charms." Theo sighs. His accent sounds almost like a put-on—his *my* comes out as *mah*—but it's pretty cute.

"Boy trouble?"

Theo tugs the zipper all the way down and it just slides right off me. I step out of the dress, which pools on the floor, and into my robe. "That could be the title of my biopic. *Boy Trouble*. Starring . . . who do you think could play me?"

"I don't think there's anyone in Hollywood cute enough." I wink at him and plop down into the makeup chair.

"You ready to go?" asks Orbe.

"Let's go!" I tell him.

And we go. For our second shot, I'm wearing a geometric printed Roberto Cavalli minidress (personally picked out just for me by Cristiano, their PR whiz) and little flats with long straps that wind up my leg, almost to my knee. My hair droops down in two long, calculatedly messy cheerleader pigtails, and once again I'm floating through the air like some kind of fashion superhero.

This time, the harness seems to creak more noisily.

"This thing is making quite a racket!" I call to Jonesy.

"Don't worry, doll. That thing could hold four of me. You're fine."

I don't find this all that reassuring, though I should. If it can hold Jonesy, I have nothing to worry about—I'm down to my lowest weight ever.

Jason doesn't say much, just huddles behind his big camera. Zvi perches on the edge of the set, sitting, arms folded, sometimes watching, sometimes blabbering into his Bluetooth headset, most often just checking out Wes and Matthias. Theo, on the other hand, watches my every movement, studying everything, though I know it's not me he's looking at—it's the clothes.

The sensation of the fan whipping my hair around makes me think of helicopters, and the magical end of my first date with Jim. It's ironic that what started as purely a business relationship seems to be on the verge of blossoming into something else. Or, I hope it is. I'm sure most women would think I'm insane to prefer the handsomely distinguished Jim Segal to the eerily gorgeous Patrick Carroll, but there was undeniably something between us the other night. Call it chemistry, I suppose. But there's something there, something I hope we get the chance to explore. So far, we haven't been able to make a concrete plan but I hope our schedules clear up soon.

"Mac, beautiful, just like before. Incredible." Jason sounds happy. He hands the camera off to Wes. "Another look, then lunch?" His blue eyes sparkle, and Jason's got an adorable dimple in his cheek. Normally, I'd be flirting shamelessly, but at the moment my mind is still on Jim.

We've breezed right through this shot, so it's still a bit early for lunch. I know Jason won't make me work if I don't want to, but I can't insist on eating at 11:30 without sounding like a stuck-up diva.

"Sure." I sound a little unsteadier than I want to as Jonesy helps me down from the harness. This time I'm wearing flats, so I can manage the ladder in the shoes. Or so I think. When I put my feet back onto solid ground I misstep, and weave like a boxer avoiding a punch.

Theo is at my side instantly.

"Gosh, are you OK?" He's got a firm grip on my elbow, and for a second he's all that's keeping me upright. Theo's small, but surprisingly strong. He looks me up at me worriedly.

"I'm fine, I'm fine," I assure him. And I am—immediately. I'm thirsty, maybe, but feeling fine. Steady. Solid as a rock, and ready for more. "We better get ready for the next shot."

"Don't be ridiculous," Theo whispers, quietly, into my ear.

Then, speaking in his normal tone of voice, he repeats what I've just said. "We better get ready for the next shot!" His keeps his palm firmly planted on the small of my back, helping me backstage, following me the way a nervous mom might follow a toddler.

Theo shoves the racks aside abruptly, ruffling and wrinkling the same silk dresses he's spent all morning steaming to perfection. The racks roll haphazardly in every direction, banging into one another, knocking over a pair of tall Hermes alligator boots. The clamor startles Orbe and Natalie, who leap out of their canvas folding chairs and look up at us like we're crazy.

"Ms. Croft needs a moment," Theo says in a tone of voice that leaves no room for argument.

"Everything is OK?" Orbe looks concerned.

"A moment!" Theo barks.

Orbe and Natalie dart away.

"Sit, sit." Theo guides me to the chair poor Orbe just vacated. He walks back to the racks, turning them on their casters so they once again form a protective wall of little silky dresses. As I sit, I realize I've totally ruined the pristine dress, wrinkling it all over. Good thing we're done with that last shot.

"I'm fine, Theo," I tell him. "You didn't need to make those guys leave."

Theo sighs and collapses into the seat beside me, studying my closely. "Please, Mac. Level with me. It's your friend Theo. Tell me the truth."

"Truth? Wait. You don't think I'm . . . on *drugs*?"

Theo laughs. "Drugs? Darling, girls on drugs do not have beautiful, clear eyes like yours. Come on. I'm no fool. I know you're not on drugs."

"I don't understand . . ."

"You're not on drugs, Mac Croft. You're starving."

What? I sit up straight, trying to look as tough as possible, but I'm shivering pathetically in this revealing dress and I can tell just by looking at him that Theo sees right through me. "I'm not *starving*," I protest. "I'm just . . ."

"You're just what, darlin'? Dieting? Come on."

"OK, maybe I got a little lightheaded for a second. But I'm fine. I just need some water."

"Mac, sweetie. Come on. Do you know how long I've been doing this? I've been assisting Zvi for five years now. You're going to have to get this under control. You faint on set, and your career is over. Jason's not going to stand for that, and the rumors are going to start, and before you know it you're shooting catalog in Iowa City with a bunch of locals." Theo crosses his arms and frowns at me sternly.

"Theo, you don't understand." I find my bottle again and drain it. The cold water helps me think a little more clearly. "I can't . . . if I gain even two pounds my career is over."

"Hush."

"I mean it. Basically, I can choose between eating, getting fat, and never working again, or not eating, staying skinny and . . . never working again. So what the fuck am I supposed to do? Of course I'm starving. I don't know any other way to keep thin." It feels good to get angry about this. Theo's right—if I faint, the rumors will swirl, and Francesca will be furious. The only way not to faint . . . is to eat.

"Darlin', I've worked with all the top girls. Natalie, Caroline, Adriana. You're not the only one in this particular predicament. But you've got to do something about it, Mac Croft. I don't want anything happening to you. Girl, you've got what it takes to be one of those top girls, I know you do. But only if you survive."

"Come on, Theo." I stand and pull the robe on over my dress. "You're overdramatizing."

"Am I?" Theo stares me down. "Let me guess. You're dizzy. Sometimes you're so hungry you feel like you're actually going crazy. You shake, even when it's not cold. You smell food everywhere you go, but instead of eating you drink water or coffee and pretend that nothing is wrong."

Everything Theo is saying is eerily familiar—it's like he knows what I haven't admitted to anyone, even myself.

"The girls talk, Mac." He stands and gets me an unopened

bottle of water from the makeup table. "And I listen. I've heard this all before." He starts to laugh.

"What's funny?"

"The thought of you on drugs," he tells me. "Gosh, this business can be so messed up, I swear. You think Zvi would notice if you were on drugs? He can from tell fifty feet away if your shoes are Alaïa or Balenciaga, but doesn't notice that you're starving. It's not funny. I shouldn't laugh."

I start laughing now, too, mostly because Theo's laugh is so warm and infectious. "I have a feeling Zvi would notice if Wes was on drugs."

"Please," Theo says, laughing so hard he's almost choking. "I'm sure he'd be thrilled. Drugs might make him easier to seduce."

"Seriously, though, Theo." I catch my breath. "I'm fucked, aren't I? I mean—even my skin has changed. It feels like plastic."

"Don't be ridiculous," Theo says. "You need to work, but you also need to eat. There's a way. Trust me. You need to see Dr. Gindi. All the girls see him."

"I don't want drugs! I was going to be a nutritionist. I can't pump myself full of chemicals," I protest. Filling your body with poison must be even worse than depriving it.

"Oh, sweetie, it's not drugs," he says. "Though to be honest, you're probably the only model in America who wants to just say no. Dr. Gindi is a nutritionist. An expert. From what I understand, too, he's a miracle worker. I don't know exactly how he does it, but it's got to do with supplements. Apparently the whole thing is like magic."

"I've tried everything else. I might as well try magic."

"I'll get you his number," Theo promises.

"You're the greatest. How can I possibly repay you?" I feel like hugging him, but I don't want to muss his perfectly tidy outfit.

"Number one, don't die," Theo says. "That's for starters. Number two? Let's have dinner. Saturday."

"Saturday. Dinner. I think I can do that." And I stand and do hug him, squeezing his compact little body close to mine.

"And promise me . . . at dinner? You'll eat something?"

I sigh. "It's not Saturday I'm worried about. We've still got three shots left!"

"Mmm. Good point, Mac Croft. Good point. We need to get some food in you, don't we? How about I just sneak out there and grab you a couple of bananas. While I'm gone, you slip into that Blumarine number. The leopard one."

I flip through the dresses, feeling better, but still kind of panicked. I hope no one else on set noticed my near meltdown. "You won't . . ."

Theo winks at me. "Our little secret," he says, then slips away, my knight in perfectly pressed khakis.

Twelve

Most days I earn my day rate. My workdays can start as early as seven with an early-morning go-see, then include a quick early morning job in studio, and wrap up on location way uptown, on a shoot that drags until midnight. And in between jobs, I'm not lunching at Le Cirque: I'm scrambling onto the subway and hoping I'm not going to be late. True, when we go long I'm technically entitled to overtime, but I never bother asking for that. The way I figure, I'd rather have a good working relationship with my clients than bicker over a few dollars. I believe in karma: I'm nice to everyone, because I want everyone to be nice back. And I do believe that eventually the universe does adjust itself, that everything falls into harmonious balance.

That's what I think today must be: the universe's way of atoning for all those fourteen-hour days. We start at nine and are done by one, even though it's a beauty shoot, and those are usually tricky, involving endless fiddling and readjusting of lights, constant touchups and blottings. But it's only one shot, my face in a tight close-up, illustrating the classic smoky eye and red lips. And the photographer and crew (whose names I jot down in my appointment book—I meet so many people these days I can't keep them all straight) are efficient and quick. Now it's only one o'clock and I'm strolling down Lafayette Street, a free woman.

I should get back on the subway and head uptown. I should drop in on Francesca, show her the Polaroids from San Francisco, and tell her how well today went. I should stop by and see Sloane, because I'm lugging around my portfolio and I'd love to drop it off. I should try for a chance encounter with Renee or Paul. But I'm not going to. I've got other business to take care of. I need a quiet place to sit, think, and cross some things off my to-do list. I remember some photo assistant I worked with—who knows when?—mentioning that he had some photographs hanging in a place called HousingWorks, a used bookstore and café in Soho that I think I'm near, but I'm not one hundred percent sure I know where it is.

I'm at the corner of Bond and Lafayette, and there doesn't seem to be much around here, but I know I'm walking downtown. I've got my map, though, so I dig into my bag and pull out my travel wallet.

"Damsel in distress! You lost, miss?"

The voice out of nowhere startles me, and I drop my wallet onto the pavement, spilling change everywhere.

"Oh, I scared you!"

I don't recognize him, but there's something in the way this guy is talking to me, so familiar, so intimate—I must know him from somewhere.

He drops to his knee, scooping up errant currency and handing it back. "I'm so sorry."

"No big deal." I take the change from him, toss it back into my bag.

He stands, handing me the wallet and a couple of old boarding passes. "Didn't mean to startle you." He's tall, so he smiles down at me, and I catch my reflection in his mirrored aviators.

"It's not a problem." I shove the boarding passes into the wallet, then drop it into my already overcrowded shoulder bag.

"Don't tell me." He pulls his sunglasses down his nose and studies me. "You're a model."

"I . . . yes, I am. How did you . . . oh, you saw my cover!"

"You kidding? I can tell just by looking at you. You've got it. It. No question."

"It? You think so?" I'm used to construction workers calling out marriage proposals as I walk by, but this guy seems relatively down to earth and sane. "Come on."

"Come on nothing. You don't think I can recognize 'it' when I see it?" He offers me his hand. "I'm Adam. Who are you with? Wait, don't tell me. Delicious?"

"Wow. Yeah . . . how did . . . ? I am. Hi Adam." I shake his hand quickly. I don't let the physical contact go on too long—but I'd be lying if I said I wasn't a little flattered. Sometimes I don't even recognize fellow models if they haven't been through hair and makeup, and this guy spotted me strolling down the street in jeans, sneakers, and my old volleyball sweatshirt—and he knows what agency I'm with. You've got to be an industry insider to be able to spot an agency's type.

"Listen, I don't normally do this kind of thing, but I'd love to talk to you. I'm actually working on a shoot back at my place. I do a lot of covers for Desire. You know, the romance novels? I shoot all of Barbara Dilling's covers. Have you done a book cover yet?" Adam tucks his hands into the pockets of his jeans. "It makes careers. And you're right here! We don't even need to go through the agency. It's a sign."

Now my mental warning bells go off. Francesca has made me swear up and down to never do any kind of business without consulting with her. "Sorry, Adam. My agent told me to refer all business to her. So I've got to consult with her . . ." I don't want to totally blow this guy off—what if he's some hotshot photographer I'm too dumb to recognize?

"I don't even know your name yet!"

"I'm Mac. And you're right. I'm with Delicious. But you understand—you're a photographer, you know I've got to check with my agent. Her name is Francesca. I'll tell her to expect your call?"

"Well . . ." Adam kicks the ground idly, disappointed. "I just wanted to help you out is all."

"That's so nice of you. But you know how it is. Don't want my agent to get mad. Anyway—maybe you can help me . . . do you happen to know where HousingWorks is?"

"I do." He gestures over his shoulder with his thumb. "You're almost there. Just cross Houston, turn right and walk over to Crosby. It's right there."

I knew I was heading in the right direction. "Thanks so much."

"I can escort you if you like. Maybe buy you a latte and we can talk shop? I also run this production company, you know, and I think we could talk about working together . . ."

"I can't do it now. Running late. Sorry! But definitely call Francesca. She'll hook us up, and we can get to work together soon." My back aches, so I pull my heavy shoulder bag around to my front and hug it close to my chest. "I've got a lot to take care of today. Maybe you can just give me your card . . ."

"Listen, by tomorrow I could have found some other girl to make famous."

This guy is starting to creep me out. He's getting a little pushy.

"I'd really love to talk to you about some projects I'm working on," he continues.

"Well . . ." I think I can guess exactly what kind of project he has in mind for me. "I have to take a rain check. I can't be late. It's so unprofessional! But I'll see you soon."

"Beautiful lady, listen. I know the business. And now I just want to know you . . ."

"Give Francesca a call!" I shoot him my biggest, warmest smile and quickly step into the street. "Thanks for the directions!" I hurry across Bond Street, praying he's not going to follow. I don't want to have to resort to kneeing this jerk in the balls. It's not until I get to the corner of Houston that I realize. I'm such an idiot. I know he was hitting on me, but I was flattered that a total stranger could see me looking my worst and still find something magical in me, still sense that I'm a model. But of course it wasn't magic: my huge portfolio is sticking right out of my bag, the Delicious Models logo right there for all the world to see. Now I know why Francesca insists I send potential business her way—she might have just saved my life.

I settle into a creaky wooden chair in the one little sliver of sunlight that's managed to work its way into the Housing-Works bookstore. The place smells wonderful, a mix of old books and coffee. Though there are some pretty tempting treats on offer at the counter and I'm so hungry I'm shaking, I settle for a cup of raspberry tea, which has a sweet aroma that makes it almost feel like I'm eating dessert. Almost.

Before I can get to work, I need to set up my workstation. I arrange my travel wallet, my cell phone, the letter from Penn, a tiny notebook, and a pencil on the table in front of me. Now it's time to make a list.

> *Text Irin—see apartment on Saturday?*
> *Talk to Mom & Dad re: apartment*
> *Call Penn*
> *Francesca—reschedule Cover Girl mtg?*
> *Dr. Gindi—make appt.*

It's not a ton of stuff, but it's funny how even a short list can be so daunting. I decide to start with the easy stuff. I grab the phone and tap out a message to Irin: *Found an apt. Chelsea. 24th Street. Want to see it Sat?*

OK. That's done. I cross that off the list and feel strangely satisfied. But this is no time to pat myself on the back. I scroll through my messages until I find the one Theo sent me yesterday with Dr. Gindi's telephone number, and I dial without giving it another thought.

"Hi, I'd like to make an appointment with Dr. Gindi."

My tea has gone cold, the warm patch of sun is long gone, but I've crossed off everything on my list.

Even though I'll probably see her later tonight, I called Mom and told her we're seeing the apartment on Saturday. I called Francesca to plead to reschedule my already twice-postponed meeting with the execs at Cover Girl. I hate to do it but I don't have much choice—this is an emergency after all. My appointment with Dr. Gindi is a matter of life and death. I've got plans for Irin and me to meet Mom and Dad and then go see the apartment together on Saturday, and then to meet up with Theo for dinner afterwards. Maybe at dinner I'll give Mom and Dad the biggest news so far: I called U Penn.

It was easier than I thought it would be. I guess I'd built it up in my mind to the point that it was an impossible decision, a major turning point. And I expected to feel a lot of regret, a twinge of sadness about the road not taken. But I don't. I simply called the admissions office and told them, essentially, thanks but no thanks. I never expected to be on the particular path I'm on, but now here I am, and there's no going back. Instead of juggling classes, I'm trying to stay on top of my bookings. Instead of laying the foundation for a career, I'm actually building that career. Every job takes me closer to success, closer to Mac and further from Melody. I thought that once I made that call I'd feel different, but instead I feel relieved. It was almost anti-climactic, and now things are falling into place.

My phone starts vibrating, clattering against the wooden tabletop noisily.

It's Jim. "Aren't you supposed to be signing big business deals and opening the stock exchange and things like that?"

"I am," Jim says seriously. "But I know how to prioritize. And as far as I'm concerned, the board can wait, the contracts can get signed tomorrow, my lawyer can leave me a voicemail."

"That's funny." I finish the last dregs of my tea, which is cold now. "I just so happen to have the afternoon free."

"No kidding?"

"Seriously. I'm just sitting here at a café in Soho, getting things done." As I say this, I use my pencil to cross off the rest of the items on my to do list, and feel a strange inner peace.

"I can get away if you can," Jim says.

"I think I can manage that," I tell him.

"Let's hole up at the best table in Pastis, then. What do you say?"

I glance at my watch. It's still early yet. "I say I'll be there in fifteen."

Inside the restaurant I do something I haven't done in a long time: I turn off my phone. Unless I'm airborne, my phone is my constant companion. I trust the alarm more than the wake-up service at even the finest hotels, and just because I'm sleeping somewhere in the world doesn't mean that Francesca's not trying to get me on the line, so I leave it on, all night. But now, something comes over me. I don't know if it's the freedom of being out in the middle of a workday, I don't know if it's the comfort of being in New York, a place that feels more like home every day, or if I just want to concentrate on being with Jim. But this afternoon belongs to me. What's the worst that can happen if I'm unavailable for a couple of hours?

The restaurant is almost completely empty—it's hours until dinner, a little late for a weekday lunch, and too early for happy hour unless you have a real problem—so the hostess lets us seat ourselves, and we pick a table by the window that's the perfect vantage for people-watching. I zone out, my mind straying to the scene outside, the random parade of perfectly put-together women carrying shopping bags, business-suited men barking into tiny telephones, nannies pushing strollers, dog walkers doing their thing.

"Mac? Mac?"

Oops. Must have zoned a little too far out. "Sorry."

"No need to apologize." Jim swirls the ice in his glass and drains it. My sparkling water is still here, barely touched. "But a penny for your thoughts, as they say."

"A penny?" I shake my head. "They're not even worth that much. Just zoning out."

"I hope I'm not boring you . . ."

"No, it's not that." I feel like I can be honest with Jim, like no matter what I say, he'll truly listen. I meet so many new people every day, but it's rare for the conversation to rise above *Where are you from/Where do you live/Who do you know* pitter-patter. Jim seems to care what I think.

"I see something on your face. Something. Tell me about it. Maybe I can help."

He says this so seriously, so unassumingly, I just . . . open up. "You know what it is? I'm always going. It's always work. And there's downtime, sure, waiting for the photographer, waiting for the light, waiting at the airport, waiting in traffic. But even when I'm waiting, I'm still working. It's that pace, that hurry up and wait pace that takes its toll. It's just so nice to sit here and not think about anything, not worry about where I have to be next, or who I'm working with, or what the weather will be like, or how late we'll go, or how I'm going to get home, or whatever. I needed this break."

Jim whistles. "Tell me how you really feel."

"I'm sorry." I feel my cheeks reddening. "I don't mean to complain. I've had a weird day."

"Weird? Interesting choice of words." Jim smiles. "Not bad. Not good. *Weird*."

"It's a long story . . ."

"You're like me," Jim continues. "Married to your work. I respect that. What the hell is the point of doing something, anything, for a living if you're not going to *do* it well? It's the same if you're an auto mechanic or a preschool teacher or a senator or a real estate developer or a model: whatever you do, do it to the utmost of your abilities. That, I respect. Any less and I'm not really interested."

"I feel like I'm constantly trying to get people to take what I do for a living seriously, to take me seriously." I can't help but remember that bitch at the immigration counter—was that this week? Last week? Who knows anymore?

"The key, Mac, is to take yourself seriously." Jim signals to the waitress for a refill. "Until you do that, until you commit yourself to being Mac Croft, model, you can't blame anyone else for not taking you seriously."

"But I am committed, Jim . . ." I start to say, but he holds up a hand, stopping me mid-sentence.

"I've been in business . . . well, a long time. You know what I would tell you if you worked for me?" The waitress deposits another tumbler onto the table, and Jim nods his thanks, then leans across the table toward me. "I would tell you I want to see more."

"More?" I don't have more to give, I want to say. I want to remind him about the crazy hours, the insane demands, the fact that I'm starving myself to do this, and I do everything I'm asked, and I do it all with a smile on my face. I can't possibly do more. But I don't say any of that. This is one of the richest men in New York City (I know—I Googled him) and one of the country's most successful private real estate developers. And he's sitting here, giving me free career advice. Any halfway intelligent person would kill for this chance. I swallow my pride. "How do you mean, more?" I ask him.

Jim claps his hands together, and the sound echoes through the empty restaurant. "That's it!" he cries. "There. That's it. I just told you, to your face, that you're not working hard enough, when I know damn well you work yourself like a farm animal. And you thought about it, smiled, and asked me what else you can do. That's it. That's how I know you've got more to give. Because you're willing to. You're willing to try." He takes a sip of his drink. "If you worked for me, I'd promote you right now. In fact, if this modeling thing doesn't work out, you should come join the Segal Group."

"So, your expert advice is for me to do more," I tell him. "But what does that mean? I mean, more what? What should I do, specifically? I'm trying as hard as I can."

"Bullshit." Jim jabs a finger at me, almost angrily. "You're holding back and you know it. Something is holding you back. What is it?"

I let my gaze drift back out the window. It's getting dark again—it's early but it is still winter—and a girl in a fur coat shuffles past, trailing a tiny Boston terrier. I don't want to have this conversation anymore. I've taken a lot of big steps today: talking to my parents, saying no to college, reminding Francesca that I'm out here waiting for my next big break. I'm not afraid of hard work, and I even agree with Jim that I could probably be even craftier than I've been so far. But I want to start tomorrow.

"I'm picking on you." Jim sounds apologetic.

"I've just had a momentous day, in some ways." I pop a piece of ice in my mouth and chomp down on it. "I turned down my scholarship to Penn. I've been putting off dealing with that. And I told my Mom about the apartment."

"How did that go over?"

"Not like the lead balloon I was expecting," I tell him. It's true. Mom was weirdly calm about the whole thing. Of course, I'd already prepared her. "She wasn't thrilled, I don't think, but in the interest of making this quick and painless, she agreed to get Dad on board and come out and see the place with me on Saturday."

"That's terrific." Jim smiles. "I look forward to meeting them. Saturday, you say?"

Meeting the parents? That's something I didn't prep Mom for, but I guess it's going to happen in a couple of days. I'll cross that bridge when I get to it. "Saturday."

"You have had a big day." Jim finishes his second drink. "What do you say we go out and celebrate?"

"I could eat," I admit, which is the understatement of the century. It's a good thing I made that appointment with Dr. Gindi. Here's hoping he'll be all Theo says he is.

"Let's go to dinner." Jim signals for the check. "How about the Odeon? Unless of course you want to go somewhere in the neighborhood . . ."

"Jim? Are you kidding me?" I grab his wrist gently. "Look at me! I'm not dressed for a fancy restaurant." Maybe McDonald's. Maybe.

"You look incredible to me. Besides, you're a model. Models can dress how they like, and go anywhere they want!" Jim hands his credit card to the waitress without even inspecting the tab.

"That shows how much you know about women!" I laugh. "Model or not, no woman wants to go to dinner dressed like she's been cleaning out the attic all day."

"I think you're crazy to worry," Jim says. "With eyes like yours, hell, you could wear that to a state dinner at the White House. But, have it your way."

The waitress returns, receipt tucked into a little leather book.

"Let me ask you," Jim says to her, signing the receipt and slipping his credit card back into his wallet. "Where can my friend here go in the neighborhood to pick up something suitable for dinner?"

The waitress is gorgeous—she might be a model too: tall, with skin so dark it's actually truly black, and dazzling white teeth and huge, brown eyes. "Hmmm," she says thoughtfully. "There's great shopping around here! There's Catherine Malandrino, just across the street. And Theory. Also, there's Stella McCartney, of course. And Alexander McQueen . . ."

"You see?" Jim says, looking pleased with himself. "Thanks dear," he adds to the waitress, who flashes another incredible smile and vanishes with what I bet is a hefty tip. "If you're feeling under dressed, we can remedy that so easily."

"I think you'll agree that it would be a bad business decision for me to spend my entire day rate on a dress at Alexander McQueen."

"Don't be ridiculous." Jim stands and slips on his soft cashmere blazer. "This is on me. We're talking shop, aren't we? So it's a business expense."

I pull my coat on and follow Jim out of the restaurant, feeling a little like Cinderella, prepping for her makeover before the big ball. He's right: I've had a momentous day, and now I'm ready to relax. I don't even bother to check my phone. I know it's risky, but tonight, I just don't care.

Thirteen

"Is it Melody, then? Or is it Mac? Which do you prefer?" Dr. Gindi smiles at me, his eyes twinkling behind his big glasses.

"Mac is fine," I tell him. It's true: more and more, I'm getting used to going by Mac.

"And how are you feeling now, Mac?" Dr. Gindi settles onto a little stool on wheels and makes some notes on my chart.

How am I feeling? When I got back from Puerto Rico on Tuesday, the doctor's office called to inform me that in preparation for this appointment I would have to go on a twelve-hour fast. Ironic, considering the whole reason I made this appointment is so I can eat. When I showed up this morning, the nurse informed me that she was going to take my blood. Fine. Except she wanted to take my blood . . . every fifteen minutes. So in the past two hours not only have I been pricked eight times, I've lost what feels like a gallon of blood, which would make anyone lightheaded, especially if you haven't eaten. By the third go, I couldn't keep it together, and broke down in tears as the nurse wound the little rubber hose around my upper arm yet again. It was like something out of a nightmare.

"I'm feeling a little lightheaded, to tell you the truth." That's an understatement.

"I'm not surprised." He closes my chart. "What we're seeing here is quite common. But also quite serious."

"Am I sick?" I wasn't planning on being diagnosed with anything—I just thought he'd give me some magic pills and send me on my way.

"You're not sick, dear. You're starving."

"I'm . . ."

"You're starving. Your body is very confused. It's so under-nourished that what's happening is the body is shutting down."

"I don't understand . . ."

"So you see, what's happening is when you do finally eat something, your body is storing it. It's saving it up, because your body isn't sure when it's going to get some more food. This is why you're having a problem balancing your nutritional intake with your weight gain. The whole system is out of whack."

This does sound eerily familiar. I grip the edge of the rubber padded bed, the tissue paper crinkling underneath me. "Isn't there something I can do?"

"You can eat!" He laughs.

"You don't understand." I feel faint. "I'm a model. I've got to . . ."

"I do understand," he interrupts. "Listen. You're a model. But you only get one body in this life. You've got to treat it well. If you don't start now . . ." He consults my chart again. "You're only twenty years old, dear. I don't see you making it to twenty-five unless you drastically change the way you're living your life."

"I was under the impression that you might be able to help me." I'm shaking. "I need to know . . ."

"You need to know *how* to eat," he says gently. "Believe me, it is possible to eat a healthy diet and still maintain your ideal weight. You simply need to think more carefully, and make the right decisions."

I'm in danger of breaking down again. My heart is pounding in my ears, I'm freezing cold, I'm shaking. My nose is running, the tears are welling up in my eyes, and I'm just so goddamned hungry.

"You don't need to look so panicked, my dear." Dr. Gindi places a reassuring hand on my knee and gives it a squeeze. "I'm here to help you."

I'm still a little lightheaded, even though I did devour a banana, a yogurt, and a bottle of juice, which nudged my blood sugar back up into normal human territory. I do feel much better, but I'm scared of fainting, and the visions of myself swooning and falling onto the tracks in front of an oncoming train were just too scary. That's why I'm stepping out of a taxi, like some *I-don't-get-out-of-bed-for-less-than-whatever* supermodel with money to burn when I run into Renee, strolling out of the Delicious building following closely behind Paul Anders, who ambles coolly out the door like he owns the place which, of course, he does.

"Mac!" Paul spots me from across the sidewalk, and I'm embarrassed to be seen getting out of a taxi. For some reason, it matters to me that both Paul, who owns the agency, and Renee, who oversees the ultralucrative commercial division, know that I'm the kind of hard-working girl who respects the profession enough to take mass transit. Until, that is, I prove myself. But first things first.

"Paul! Renee!" I slam the taxi door behind me, and step cautiously onto the sidewalk, meeting them halfway. Paul is his usual self: perfectly tanned, even in winter, hair neatly trimmed and flecked so artfully with silver that you'd almost think it's fake. His pinstripe suit fits his tall, muscular frame so precisely it's got to be custom made. Renee is wearing some kind of kooky avant-garde coat with a stand collar that rises halfway up her head, so she looks kind of like a painting of a medieval queen.

"Moch, darling," Renee coos, trilling her R for some reason. I swear every time I see her she's working harder to affect a French accent. It's such a put-on.

"Hi Renee! How are you? Long time no see!" We exchange cheek kisses, one on each, the international modeling-world greeting.

"Mac Croft." His voice is so smooth, so sexy that Paul manages to make the simple act of saying my name seem downright seductive. He bends down and deposits a kiss on each one of my cheeks. He's intoxicating—his reputation as a legendary ladies' man is well deserved. "The name on everyone's lips."

"What do you mean?"

"I've just been hearing things," Paul says, maddeningly mysterious. "Good things, don't worry."

Of course, you only ever tell people not to worry when they should be very worried. Great. Is my neck on the chopping block?

"Well, I worry," I tell him. "It's my job, right?"

"No, dear." Paul grips my arm reassuringly. "Your job is to make magic. It's my job to worry. My job, and Renee's, and Francesca's. And we're doing a damn good job of it, too."

"You are, you are!" I agree quickly. I don't want him to think I'm unhappy at the agency.

"Moch, dear," Renee interrupts. "We are late. You must excuse us?"

"Of course!" I back away, sort of half-bowing like you would if you were leaving the presence of royalty. "I didn't mean to hold you up . . ."

"Fuck them," Paul says. "They can wait." This makes Renee's eyes fly wide open in panic. She digs out her Blackberry and starts typing furiously. "You've been good, Mac? Interesting jobs?"

"Definitely. I'm just back from Puerto Rico. It was great." In truth nothing could be less interesting than the last couple of gigs I've had, but the last thing I'm going to do when I've got Paul Anders' attention is complain. "I've been having a great run. I'm so happy. I hope you guys are, too, of course."

"That explains that gorgeous tan of yours," Paul says. "I only hear good things, you know. I think I heard something about Cover Girl, was it? That's a big fish."

Cover Girl—a big fish indeed, and one I've been trying not to think too much about. I was supposed to see them weeks ago. They called to reschedule, then called to postpone. Then it was my turn to back out so I could see the doctor. Then when they finally called to say they were ready to see me immediately . . . I was on a date with Jim Segal. The one day I turn my phone off and I miss the most important call of my career so far. I smile to cover up my wince. "Cover Girl would be great." I nod happily.

"We'll just have to see what happens, eh?" Paul winks. I'm hoping he knows something I don't. Actually, I can probably bet on the fact that he does.

Renee creeps up behind and taps Paul gently on the shoulder. "Paul, we must . . ."

"I shouldn't keep you." I can tell she's desperate, so I give Renee an out. She shoots me a grateful look.

"I suppose we should get going," Paul agrees. "Mac? Stop by and see me sometime, OK?"

"OK, love you darling!" Renee calls out, basically shoving Paul toward the curb, where their Town Car is waiting. I wave goodbye and head into the warm embrace of the building lobby, which is a welcome relief from the grim early evening chill.

In the elevator I start processing what's just happened. Only the top girls get to hear directly from Paul Anders, and even though he hasn't given me any news, I'm relieved that he still knows who I am. Either he's telling the truth and my name is making the rounds or he thinks highly enough of me to lie about that fact. It's kind of a win-win situation.

These are the thoughts I'm torturing over when the doors whoosh open and I stroll into the lobby. *Shit.* As soon as I see Sloane, I realize I'm empty-handed.

"Mac!" Sloane rips off her headset and drops it on her desk. "How's my favorite girl? Did you love Puerto Rico?"

"I did," I tell her. "I can't even tell you. It was so nice to be out in the sun."

"Right?" Sloane rolls her eyes dramatically. "I'm glad spring is here and all but I am ready for shorts weather, big time." She releases me from her embrace, and hurries back to her desk, where the telephone is chirping insistently. She jabs a button and the ringing stops. "Nothing important." She giggles and sits. "My little trick. Screening calls."

"Our little secret," I agree.

"You look a little worn out, Mac." Sloane sounds concerned.

"I've just . . ." I'm still feeling a little woozy from losing all that blood. "It's nothing." I drum my fingers on the counter-top. "Say, Sloane, I just ran into Paul and Renee outside . . ."

"Those two." She clucks her tongue. "They're up to something."

"What do you mean?"

Sloane glances around but we're alone. "You didn't hear it here . . ."

I lean in closer. "Didn't hear what?"

"No, that's all I know, Mac. They're up to something. I don't know what it is." She shrugs. "Wait, did you talk to Francesca? She was pretty pissed the other day."

Indeed she was. Francesca left me three messages, and Sloane left me one, but by the time I turned my phone back on the day was over and it was too late for me to get up to the Cover Girl offices as requested. I've apologized several times, via telephone, via text message, but I still don't think Francesca's over it. I guess the story hasn't gotten around though, since Paul and Renee acted like nothing was wrong.

"I know." I frown. "I tried. I fucked up, I guess. I'm never turning my phone off again."

"Famous last words." Sloane giggles, then lowers her voice. "Don't worry about it. Those assholes at Cover Girl will get over it. You'll be the new Cover Girl before the year's out, I'm sure of it."

"I wish I had your confidence! Anyway, I'm just back from the doctor's . . ."

"Everything's OK, right?" Sloane looks worried.

"Fine, fine. But you know, if there's nothing pressing, I think I might take the rest of the day . . ."

"Rest of the day?" Sloane swivels around to consult the row of clocks on the wall. "It's almost happy hour, Mac. Go. But leave your phone *on*. Francesca or Jude will call if anything comes up."

I salute, like a good soldier. "Aye aye, captain." I pause. "Sloane, you truly are the best."

"I know it." She slips her headset back on. "Go say your hellos to Francesca, then get out of here. Go enjoy what's left of the day."

"You would not believe my day." Theo deposits our drinks on the table and hops up onto the tall stool. "I know you've had a tough one too. So, cheers to us." He very carefully picks up his martini glass and salutes me.

"Right back at you." I take a sip of my seltzer and cranberry. "This is a cute place! You were right." It's a narrow, whitewashed room, not much more than a bar on one side and some tables pushed up against the wall opposite, but it's bathed in sunlight from the back garden, and bustling with the noise of happy-hour drinkers and the Stones on the stereo system.

"I love this place," Theo says. "Abbot's. I come here all the time. When you move into the neighborhood you will too! It'll be our regular spot. We'll have a regular table, and they'll always seat us without making us wait. It'll be so fun!"

"If I move into the neighborhood," I correct him. "I still haven't seen this place."

"Whatever." Theo rolls his eyes. "I know that building. It's basically across the street from me. Fancy! You're going to love it."

I am excited at the prospect of already having a friend in the neighborhood. It's almost as much of a selling point as the views Jim talked about. "It's not me I'm worried about. It's all about getting Mom and Dad's approval."

"They'll love it too. I'm sure of it." Theo reaches across the table and takes my hand in his. "I'm glad we're doing this! It's so fun to hang out away from the set!"

I nod. "This is just what I needed. I'm glad you called." It's true. I was walking back to the train station when Theo's call came through, and I'm so much happier to be here, in this unassuming little neighborhood restaurant in Chelsea, than on the PATH train, dealing with yet another commute.

"I had to make sure you made it to Dr. Gindi. I might seem nice, but I can play bad cop, too, you know. So you better stay in line." He wags his finger at me comically.

"Yes sir."

"Anyway, tell me everything. Was it OK? Did the doctor help you?" Theo swirls the martini ever so slightly, and studies me eagerly.

"Did he help me? That remains to be seen, I guess. He was nice," I tell him. "But man, they did a number on me. Have you ever been tested for hypoglycemia?"

Theo shakes his head.

"Don't ever do it. It's probably the closest I've come to torture." My poor veins throb at the mere memory of this morning.

"That bad, huh? I'm so sorry. He is supposed to be the best though." He glances around to make sure no one's listening. "I hear *Caroline Gregory* sees him."

"You should see what he gave me. Enzymes. Pills. Hundreds of them." I reach behind me to the tote bag slung on the back of my chair. I give it a shake, and the clatter of the pills rattling around in their plastic bottles is startling. "Supplements. The doc swears they're going to help regulate my metabolism."

"Magic pills, huh? Do you think they'll work?"

"I hope so," I say. "I don't want to ever feel like I'm going to faint on set again. And he told me to eat! I'll be the only model in the world who actually eats. The foods on the list are all raw and unprepared, so I can eat all I want. Seriously, it sounds too good to be true."

"For real?" Theo drains his drink with relish. "Ooh, that's gonna go straight to my head. Anyway, yes, I don't want to hear about you fainting on set. Come to think of it, you're one of the only girls I never hear any gossip about. Seems like everyone else is always misbehaving."

I laugh. "Maybe I should misbehave. That'll get people talking—and word of mouth is the best PR."

"Speaking of word of mouth . . ." Theo grins naughtily. "Let me tell you about my day on set! I was working with Tom Adler . . ."

"Tom Adler . . ." The name sounds familiar. "Who is he again?"

Theo gasps in mock horror. "Mac, he's simply the most divine gentleman I've ever seen. I mean . . ." He whistles. "It's unreal. Bruce Weber discovered him, *of course*. He's from Montauk. A fisherman. Can you believe it? He's like a Greek god."

"Maybe I should ask Francesca to try to get me booked with him!"

"Mmmmm." Theo shakes his head emphatically. "Don't bother, Mac. The man only has eyes for himself. I swear, I've never seen a model spend more time gazing in the mirror. It was hilarious!" Theo claps his hands, and is laughing so hard he's shaking.

I remember some of the male models I've worked with in the past—it's so true. They don't spend as long in makeup and hair as the girls do, but they manage to spend so much time gazing at themselves in the mirror. I once caught one going through my makeup, powder in hand. Not all of them, though. There was, of course, Duncan, the male model I almost, kind of sort of fell for. . . .

I start to laugh too. It's not really funny, but his laugh is infectious. And even more, I need a good laugh. I need to forget about the doctor, and my accidental meet and greet with Paul and Renee, missing the call from Cover Girl, and the apartment and well, just about everything.

Theo stops laughing, and looks at me very seriously. "What do you say we get a table and order ourselves some dinner?"

I smile. "I say yes. I'm starving. Literally!"

Fourteen

"It's just up here on the left!" I point excitedly, rushing along the sidewalk at my usual clip—I must be used to city life, because I move a lot faster than Mom and Dad. "Come on, come on," I call back to them, feeling suddenly like an eager kid on Christmas morning.

"You're sure the car is OK back there?" Dad looks worried as he hurries up to the corner of Twenty-fourth Street, where I'm waiting.

"Dad, this neighborhood is full of millionaires and art galleries. I don't think anyone is going to break into the truck." I give his shoulder a reassuring squeeze.

"It's so noisy!" Mom says. "With all this traffic I don't see how you could get any sleep around here."

She's not wrong—the racket of buses, trucks, and cabs roaring up Tenth Avenue is deafening. But Jim said the apartment had a river view, so I'm assuming it's not right on the avenue. I hope. "I'm sure it's fine, Mom," I tell her. The signal changes and as we cross I spot the tiny figure of Irin in the distance, waving hello.

"That's my roommate, guys!" I wave back. I wonder how

this is going to go. Irin's a lot more . . . exotic than the friends I normally introduce Mom and Dad to. "You're going to love her." If I think it, maybe it'll come true?

"Mac!" Irin drops her cigarette on the ground and stubs it out delicately with her stiletto-clad toe. She's wearing a vintage-looking fur coat, the kind of thing you'd see on the evil female lead on a nighttime soap from the '80s, and her scraggly hair is tucked under a huge knit cap. She hurries to me and kisses me on both of my cheeks. "I so excited to see apartment. Is good to see you!"

"Hey, Irin." She's kookier than I remember. But there's no going back now! "These are my folks. Mom, Dad, this is Irin." As I turn back to the folks, I realize that Dad's disappeared.

"I'll be damned!" Dad's wandered off down the block to the apartment building's neighbor: a firehouse. This must be a good omen. "Look at that. Engine 341—right next door."

"Sam!" Mom sounds exasperated, like she's scolding one of the kids. "We can stop in and say our hellos later. Hi Irin," she says, hugging her as if she were one of her own. "It's so nice to meet you."

"I hope you're not planning on smoking in the apartment. Your health is your business, but did you know that cigarettes are the number one cause of death by fire? My dad's a firefighter," I explain. "Sorry."

Irin doesn't seem like she understands what's happening anyway.

"Right, right." Dad rejoins us, offers Irin his hand, and she shakes it limply. "What do you say, ladies? Should we get this over with?"

"Dad!" I complain. "You said you were going to keep an open mind."

"Look. No one ever said Sam Croft was anything less than open-minded."

"All right then." I pull my phone out of my pocket and text Jim: *We're here.* "Let's go inside, shall we?"

"Here we are. 9F." As the doorman promised, the apartment is unlocked, so I push the door open and step inside. "It's gorgeous!" Of course, I haven't even seen it yet, but I'm pulling out all the stops for Mom and Dad's benefit. If only the Cover Girl execs could see me now: I definitely know how to sell. I switch on the hallway light and lead everyone inside.

Then I get inside and realize it's true—it *is* gorgeous. There's a tiny foyer, not much to speak of, but when you round the corner the apartment simply opens up. It's a big room, flooded with light, because two of the walls are almost entirely windows, framing a view down Tenth Avenue to the south and to the Hudson to the west. From above, the taxis speeding up the avenue seem like toys, and the river in the distance, visible in the sliver between two towering buildings the next avenue over, glimmers beautifully. The wood floors are stained dark, almost black, which makes the white walls and sunlight seem all the brighter. A huge marble island separates the galley kitchen from the living room, and at the far end of the living room the wall of windows becomes a glass door, which leads onto a tiny terrace.

"This is amazing!" I can't believe it. I check my phone again—a message from Jim: *There in five mins.*

"Mac, is good place!" Irin rushes down the hall, her heels clattering on the floor. "You come see bedroom!"

"Melody, this is gorgeous!" Mom hurries into the kitchen. "Gosh, from here you can see right into New Jersey!"

my way. I look around at the room, and though it's empty, it already feels a little like home.

Feeling emboldened, I announce to everyone: "So what do you say we sign this lease then?"

"The papers are at the front desk, waiting for you," Jim says.

This should be a big day, a momentous day. This should be my first night in my new apartment, but it isn't: after we move my boxes in, I'm going to take the suitcase I've already packed with all the essentials and head out to Kennedy, because I've got to be in London tomorrow. I've got a bunch of shows lined up: Gareth Pugh, Vivienne Westwood, Eley Kishimoto, House of Holland, and Nicole Farhi, plus appointments in between at Saatchi, British *Vogue*, and British *Harpers Bazaar*. I won't get to sleep in my own first apartment for another six nights.

Since I'm traveling today, I'll earn some money—a lot of clients will pay a fraction of your regular rate, in this case I'm making fifty percent, for days you're stuck on a plane. That's why I've chosen this as my moving day; this way I won't lose any money while I'm dealing with my personal life. When I mentioned that to Jim, he was thrilled. He says I'm thinking like a CEO already.

Jim offered to help me with the move, but I couldn't take him up on it. He's already been so helpful, finding the apartment, getting Irin and me an insider's deal on the rent, and I really think Dad wanted to help me, even though all day he's been pretending to be totally put out by the whole thing. All morning he pestered me with those parental questions that there's no answer to: *You're really taking all these boxes? Are you sure you want to pack that ratty old sweater? What time is your flight again?*

Dad stops the car and opens the window, handing a tattered bill to the toll collector.

"Thanks!" he says cheerily, and she wordlessly hands him his change. "Off to the big city, I guess." He merges into the late Sunday afternoon traffic, the Holland Tunnel and the city beyond looming just ahead. "It's not too late to change your mind, you know."

The radio signal starts to break up, so I turn the volume down low. "What do you mean, change my mind?" I glance behind me, at the backseat loaded with cardboard boxes and luggage.

"I'm just saying," Dad says, drumming a little solo on the leather padding of the steering wheel with his fingertips.

"Saying what, dad?"

"I'm just saying." He pauses. "I'm just saying, you know, you can still call Penn and tell them you changed your mind. You don't even need their scholarship money anymore. And you've got the grades. You could apply to NYU, and still model on weekends or locally or something."

"Well . . ."

"Or forget modeling. You could put that money into an IRA, sit on it for thirty years, and you'll be set. Or don't. Buy a car. Buy an apartment. Blow it all."

"Blow it all?" I reach over and feel his forehead. "Dad, are you feeling OK?"

"I'm not saying you *should* do that," he corrects me. "I'm saying you could do that."

"I don't understand." Traffic slows to a crawl. The yellow

lights inside the tunnel are casting a sickly glow on my skin. "What exactly are you trying to tell me, Dad?"

"Sometimes you sound like you're stuck, Melody. Like you're a hostage, or you just have to do whatever it is that Francesca decides you should do. But I hope you do know that's not true. You really could be doing anything at all you want. Anything." He sighs. "I've always believed in you."

I know he doesn't have the easiest way with words, necessarily. Most of the time, growing up, the most we'd get was a stern *I'm disappointed in you* or the occasional *Job well done*, and that was usually only around report card time. I know he's always been proud of us though, me, and Teddy, and Ritchie. We've all ended up on such different roads, but I know Dad's genuinely happy with how all three of us turned out. It's just not his style to say so. "That's nice of you to say, Dad. I appreciate it."

"What I'm trying to tell you," Dad says after a minute, "is that *if you* want to stop, you stop. You want to come home, you come home. I don't care what apartment your stuff is in. Morristown will always be your home. You know what I'm saying, don't you?"

"I do." I turn to my right and look out the window. At last we're pulling out of the tunnel, into the gray early evening. It's like the sun set and all but disappeared in the few minutes we were under the Hudson River. The landscape is so different, immediately: luxury apartment buildings and huge warehouses line the street, tourists carrying shopping bags stroll the sidewalk, bundled up against the early spring chill. Then it dawns on me: this is home. "But I think I'm going to give this a try."

Dad starts to laugh. "I knew you were going to say that. You're just like me, you know that? Stubborn as hell."

I can't help laugh myself. "Maybe I am," I admit, "but that's what's going to get me through, at the end of the day. Because I am going to make it."

Dad turns to me, taking his eyes off the road momentarily, and locking with mine. Despite what he's saying, despite the fact that he wants me at home, safe and sound, I can see in his eyes he knows that's not going to happen. I know what he can see, when he looks in my eyes: the future.

"I'm going to make it," I say again.

Dad laughs. "I don't doubt that for one second," he says, as he slows the truck in front of the apartment building—my apartment building. "I don't doubt that at all."

Fifteen

Some days pass like years. Sometimes, sitting there in the chair while some stranger dusts powder or bronzer across my cheeks, teases out every one of my lashes with some gunky mascara wand, smears creamy lipstick across my mouth, every minute is an hour, and my mind wanders—thinking about to-morrow, thinking about the past, thinking about nothing at all. Other times the days, even weeks, slip by like minutes. I'll find myself on the plane, midair, mid-flight, reflecting on the fact that I'm leaving—Mexico City, Marrakech, Montreal, wherever—and heading back home, marveling at how the day or days or week or even weeks somewhere else slipped by, the entire time in another city, another state, another country a memory, like a vivid dream. That's what the past few weeks are: a dream, gone now, and I'm here, in a noisy downtown restaurant, back in New York, surrounded by my friends, back in my real life.

Seven days a week, four weeks a month, gone, like that; now it's May, and the glorious New York springtime I feared was never going to arrive is here at last. And I'm here too, at least for the time being. After London fashion week, where I managed to successfully navigate the catwalk without stumbling, I was back in New York for a couple of days, then back to Europe: Stockholm, where I shot a cover for *Elle*. From there, it was off to Istanbul, where I shot my first big ad job, for Gillette. A great gig, even if the ads are only going to run in the European editions of most magazines. From there, it was back to New York for one night, then to Punta Cana, in the Dominican Republic, where I shot a fashion story for *Self*. All told, I've had the lease on my apartment for almost three months now; I think I've actually slept there about eleven nights.

That's not to say I haven't been in New York more than ten or eleven nights—it's just that whenever possible, I crash at Jim's apartment. I've come to think of Irin's and my place as home, but I've probably spent more hours of my life at Jim's palatial duplex, on the Upper West Side, in this crazy fancy old building called the Beresford. After all the insane twists and turns mine has taken, I suppose I should be used to the fact that life is not much more than a random series of endless surprises. Still, I can't believe that my search for an apartment ended up leading me to the first serious relationship of my life. My life as Mac, that is. But that's precisely what's happened, and that's why we're here tonight, at Freeman's, a restaurant on the Lower East Side that's as popular as it is hard to find. It's our two-month anniversary.

I know two months isn't all that impressive, but Jim will take any excuse to throw a party. For our one-month anniversary, he took me an hour upstate, to the old Rockefeller farm outside of Tarrytown. There's a restaurant there now, and we spent hours lingering over the ten-course tasting menu. Thanks to

Dr. Gindi, I could actually eat about three-fifths of it. On Valentine's Day, Jim took me to dinner at Jean-Georges and then surprised me with ballroom dancing at the Rainbow Room, sixty-five stories above the city, which was like something out of a movie from the '50s. He's big on special occasions, and even bigger on giving presents: a white ceramic Chanel watch for our first month anniversary, a Bottega Veneta hobo for Valentine's Day, engraved sterling luggage tags from Asprey for no reason at all. Part of me isn't looking forward to later tonight, because I don't want to see what extravagant thing Jim's bought me now. I'm not in it for the fancy dinners and endless presents, as I've told him hundreds of times, but my protests only seem to lead to more gifts.

"This place is amazing!" Theo leans in and squeezes my hand.

Theo has a tendency to exaggerate, but I've got to agree: this place is amazing. The room is dark, lit only by flickering candles, and filled with the din of silverware clinking on plates and other diners whispering over dinner. I'm at the head of the long, rough-hewn wood-plank table, which is scattered with china and mismatched silverware, tumblers of ice water and goblets of wine, and tiny arrangements of magenta baby roses. Theo's to my left, Jim is to my right, and I can see all the way down the long table, and make eye contact with all fourteen of the friends who are here to celebrate with us: Irin, who was supposed to be only a roommate but who's become something of a buddy; Jim's sister Rebecca and her husband Averell; Ed Conley, a painter whose work Jim collects, and his boyfriends (yes, he has two) Diego and Mohammed; Stellene Graham, the actress, who's been a neighbor and friend of Jim's for years, and her husband Allen; Angelique Soro, the model I first met on that *W* shoot in San Francisco (she's alone—we're friendly but I still can't verify the lesbian rumors); Anthony Widmark, the state senator who ran an unsuccessful campaign for mayor last year, and his girlfriend Lakshmi; Alistair Burne-Jones and Rachel Smythe, the actors and real life young husband and wife who starred in a Chekhov play that Jim produced, and they have since become good friends.

"I think it's time we had a toast!" Stellene has such a commanding presence, she barely has to raise her voice and everyone at the table—everyone in the whole restaurant, even the servers—stops what they're doing and pays attention. I guess there is a reason she's got those two Oscars at home. "I don't mean to make a big production or anything." She pauses, taking her time to smile at everyone around the table. "I only wanted to say that I've known Jim a long time now. A long time. And I honestly think I've never seen him happier. I think we have Mac to thank for that."

There's the clatter of polite applause, and Ed puts two fingers into his mouth and whistles, the noise shrill and loud, startling everyone in the restaurant.

I lean to my right and whisper in Jim's ear. "This is too much." It must be the thousandth time I've said exactly that sentence to him in the two months since we met.

"I don't know when you'll learn." Jim squeezes my hand and slides a small, wrapped present across the table in my direction. "There's no such thing as too much."

Huge platters heaped with food keep making their way past me, literally under my nose, as Theo passes it to Jim, or Jim back across the table to his brother-in-law Averell. A few months ago, this would have been a very devious kind of torture. I would have eyed the platter of tenderly falling off the bone ribs, the basket of cornbread, glistening with its honeyed glaze, the massive bowl of mashed potatoes, sprinkled with grass green chives, and sipped my iced water and tried not to cry. Those days are behind me. So far, I've eaten a salad with an entire lemon squeezed over it, some delicious carpaccio, a tartare, and even a couple of spoonfuls of those mashed potatoes. I've taken to carrying snacks everywhere I go—plastic baggies of cashews and almonds, mostly in case I can't find anything raw on the menu—but I don't even feel any particular desire to break into those right now. I can sit back and enjoy the spectacle, focus my attention on trying to hold four different conversations at once.

"Mac, did you love Montreal? It's amazing, right?" asks Lakshmi.

"Mac," says Ed. "I'd love to have you sit for me sometime. You look incredible on film, but I'd like to see you in oil!"

"Mac, you've got such an expressive face. I think you should think about doing some stage work!" says Alistair.

"Mac, I think we have a friend in common. Shelly Pine! The photographer. She's amazing, isn't she?" says Allen.

The waitress deposits a dish of strawberries, raspberries, and plump, ebony blackberries on the table in front of me.

"I took the liberty of ordering you dessert." Jim strokes my hand, squeezing it gently.

"You're so thoughtful!" I know we're here celebrating how long this has been going on, but it still feels new to me. I still get a little flutter when I look at him, his perfectly trimmed silver hair, his beautifully tailored jackets, and think *He's mine.* Jim's basically most women's fantasy guy come to life.

He's handsome in a relaxed, classic way, with the kind of face you usually only see on older men in TV commercials—he's had years to grow into his looks, so he wears his own handsomeness comfortably. Of course, part of what makes his good looks stand out even more is the way he dresses; you can always tell that whatever he's wearing—nubby cardigans and wooly blazers in the cold weather, light as air cashmere v-necks and spotless, perfectly pressed button-down shirts the rest of the time—is expensive, but it's never trendy. He's absolutely polite and charming to everyone he meets, but if you study him closely you realize that he's got a way of talking to everyone like they're an employee. I guess that's what happens when you're rich from the time you're born, and you spend your days surrounded by people who actually do work for you.

Yes, he's nice to look at and incredibly generous—I've already slipped on the antique Indian necklace Jim purchased for me at auction at Philips & De Pury, from the estate of the heiress Doris Duke—but it's our time together that I love the most. Jim can discuss almost anything, and is always eager to hear what I've seen and learned on the road. In fact, when I am away I find myself thinking *I can't wait to tell Jim* about everything: people, restaurants, hotels, exotic places. In all the months I've been doing this, living this life, I think Jim is the first person who's truly bothered to get to know me, who at all understands me.

I pop one of the powdery blueberries into my mouth. It's delicious. "Thanks for that," I tell Jim. "And for this." I finger the dazzling stones hanging from my neck. They're so heavy— I can only imagine what he paid for this little bauble.

"You can thank me later." He winks. Sure, he's a little bit older, but when you come right down to it, Jim's as horny as any of the boys I knew in high school.

"Later, later," I say. "When we're alone. I'm on hostess duty right now."

"Mac!" calls Angelique. "What was the name of that restaurant, the one in San Francisco where that Vera made such a scene? I was just telling Anthony about it . . ."

"Mac? Tell me, what kind of a celebration do you think my brother will come up with for your three-month anniversary?" asks Rebecca.

"Mac! You must tell . . . did you do something new to your skin?" Mohammed gestures to his cheeks.

Under the cover of the table, Jim reaches past the short hem of my Tory Burch dress to stroke my bare thigh. "Is that a promise?"

My breath catches in my throat as his fingers trace a delicate pattern on the inside of my thigh. "It's a promise." I tell him, then get down to the business of hashing out my skincare regimen with Mohammed.

There's a lot to love about Jim's place. There's the stainless steel fridge in the kitchen, which his private chef Marcella keeps stocked with all kinds of treats I can eat, too, like unpasteurized cheese from Whole Foods and platters of prewashed and already bite-size veggies straight from the farmer's market. There's the whirlpool tub in the master bath, which faces the leaded glass windows that open onto a stunning, unobstructed view of Central Park. There's his bed, which is custom-made and bigger than my entire bedroom, and stuffed with horsehair, which sounds gross but is incredibly comfortable. But my very favorite thing about Jim's apartment has to be the terrace.

We're pretty high up—the twenty-second floor—so even though the night seemed still when we were at street level, there's quite a breeze. The mild spring air is a relief, a novelty after the long winter, and I know it's a temporary break until the summer heat descends. I might be shivering, but I don't mind; it's just a relief not to be shivering from hunger.

"You're cold." Jim drapes his soft linen blazer over my shoulders. "That better?"

"Mmmmm." It is a little better. "It's incredible out tonight, huh? I guess it's always incredible out here." I lean forward, my elbows on the wide railing, and gaze out into the New York night.

"You pay for the view." Jim sets his glass on the railing and drapes an arm around my waist, pulling me closer to him. "Did you have a good time tonight?"

"I did." We lingered for hours over dessert and coffee and more wine and cocktails, gossiping and giggling. It was precisely the sort of night I always envisioned having back when I was still living at home: a magical evening out in New York City, at a hip restaurant, surrounded by interesting people, talking and laughing, telling fascinating stories about traveling the world, acting in movies, collecting art, or anything. "I still think it's a little silly to celebrate a two-month anniversary, but I love being able to hang out like that, relax. Love your sister, and her husband. And Stellene, of course. And it's always nice to hear Ed's stories, or talk to

Alistair and Rachel." I used to date Patrick Carroll. Dinner with indie movie superstars is all in a day's work.

"They're good kids." Jim looks out onto the night thoughtfully, his expression so serious. "I do hate to share you, though."

I laugh. "Lighten up, Jimmy." I like to call him that—it's so incongruous it's funny. "This celebration was your idea, let me remind you."

"I did it for you!" Jim drains his drink, and flings the melting ice into a nearby planter. "You're always talking about how lonely you get on the road. I know you love having a bunch of people gathered around a table in some restaurant . . ."

"I do. You do too, though . . . In fact, they were your friends first." I pull away, looking at him seriously.

"Hey, hey. I'm not complaining. It's just that . . . I hate to share you with everyone. With anyone. You're always away. It's so hard to get any time together. "

"That's my life, Jim. Anyway, forget it. I'm right here." I turn and lean back against the railing—high up, but safely so, since the railing is wide, and Jim's got a tight grip on me. "And I'm all yours."

"So I see." Jim pulls me closer, kisses me gently but firmly on the mouth.

For a second it's like the wind is knocked out of me, like I've slipped and fallen, from his grasp, from the terrace, and I'm hurtling through the air. Then I open my eyes and I'm right where I was, in Jim's arms, in the middle of the dark New York night. "Happy anniversary, by the way." His whisper smells of whiskey, his neck of his spicy cologne; the aroma is intoxicating, and I bury my face in his broad chest and inhale deeply.

"Happy anniversary, Mac Croft." Jim takes my chin in his hand, bringing my mouth back up to his.

I kiss him back for a moment, and then we settle into one of those moments of silence you can only share with certain people. I rest my head against his chest, and the thrum of his heartbeat drowns out the sound of the breeze.

"Great night. Perfect night."

Jim wraps his arms around me, shielding me from the wind. "Very good night," I agree.

Jim drops kisses up my neck, nuzzles into my hair, and nibbles at my earlobe. "I wouldn't want to be anywhere else," he whispers, his hot breath tickling the inside of my ear. I wouldn't have thought my stomach and my ear were connected, but they must be, since the sensation of Jim's breath makes my stomach lurch and drop almost like I'm on a roller coaster. Without thinking, I sort of mumble and moan at once.

"What's that?" Jim asks, his breath like fire against my skin.

"I didn't, um, say anything." I'm flustered and fumbling and starting to feel drunk or something.

"Tell the truth," he teases, his tongue darting out of his mouth, tasting and teasing. Again, I moan and groan despite myself. Jim's quiet, but I can almost hear him thinking. "Are you happy?" he asks at last.

Before I can even think, the words tumble from my lips. "I am." The words just fly out of my mouth. I think about it for a moment. Am I happy? I'm standing in the New York night, in the arms of a rich and powerful man who dotes on me, who wants to throw a party just to celebrate the fact that we've known each other for eight weeks. I'd be a fool not to be happy, right? I'm living every woman's dream.

"I am," I say again. "I am happy."

Sixteen

The little red numbers tick up and up. We're not moving, but the seconds pass by, and with them, the number rises ever higher, in increments of twenty cents. It sounds like nothing, but in a little more than a minute, I've spent one dollar, and it's gotten me nowhere: the cab's still sitting here at the corner of Seventh Avenue and Thirty-seventh Street, a bus blocking the view out of my window, the honking horns of the impatient drivers trapped behind us making it damn near impossible to check my voicemail. I can't quite make out whatever it is Sloane's trying to tell me in her message. I jab at the button, ending the call, toss the phone into my bag, and turn my attention back to the meter. I'm working enough to justify the occasional cab, but this is exactly why I don't like them. It takes forever to get anywhere in traffic, and I'm convinced that the driver is going to cheat me if I don't watch the numbers carefully.

I lean toward the bulletproof plastic partition. "Maybe you want to take the highway instead?"

He glares at me in the rearview mirror and I lean back into the cheap vinyl seat. I'd roll down the window to get some air, but all I'll get is a lungful of exhaust. I suppose I should try to relax and enjoy the downtime while I have it.

I've been in New York the past few days, but working every one of them. I did a studio shoot with Walter Blackburn on Monday, a photographer I've heard of but never worked with before: we shot jewelry, necklaces and bracelets piled on my wrists and around my neck, clusters of rings on my fingers, huge chandelier earrings dangling from my ears. Yesterday and today I've been on a two-part shoot with *Vogue Nippon*. The entire crew (the photographer and his assistant, the hairstylist and makeup artist, the stylist and her two assistants, the editors) was in from Tokyo, so even though I've been in New York, shooting in a massive loft location tucked away on the outskirts of the garment district, I feel like I've been out of the country.

I tap my fingers impatiently on the seat beside me, ago-nizing over why Sloane called. Was it about Cover Girl? Does Renee want to see me? Is there a last-minute meeting that I am supposed to be at *right now*? It's been a couple of weeks now and I'm still dwelling on the fact that I fucked up: I never should have turned my phone off, that one winter afternoon in Pastis that now seems like years ago. That was the one and only day that the Cover Girl execs wanted to see me—and I'm in agony wondering if I'll get a second chance. I don't know if they've cast someone else (in my nightmares, that's exactly what's happened, and Vera or Jade or sometimes even Francesca is the new Cover Girl) or if they've decided that I'm not worth the trouble but every time Sloane calls or texts I assume it's going to be because Cover Girl wants me to drop by. So far it hasn't happened.

I can't help myself. "You're sure you don't want to take the highway?"

The second I say this, the bus moves magically out of the way, freeing up the avenue, and traffic streams downtown as quickly as it ever does in this town. The driver shoots me a triumphant glance.

"You see, miss? Now we go."

"Yes," I agree. "Now we go."

At this point, pushing through these swinging glass doors and into the lobby feels like coming home. It's all so familiar: the quiet clatter of phones ringing in offices all the way down the hallway, the frowns and sighs of the other girls waiting to see their bookers, the nervous patter of the would-be next big things, waiting with their mothers or best friends to see if they've got what it takes to be a model, and of course, above all that, Sloane, brassily answering the phone (*"Delicious, hold please."*) or barking orders (*"Down the hall! Francesca is waiting!"*).

"Mac Croft, ladies and gentlemen." Sloane barely looks up as I breeze in—she's nodding and typing quickly, clearly listening to someone chattering on her Bluetooth headset, but still she announces my arrival to the gawky girl and her beaming mom who are sitting on the waiting room couch. The mom smiles at me happily, but her daughter (bangs in her eyes, cheap jeans trying too hard to look high-end, elbows and bones jutting out awkwardly) looks miserable, poor thing.

"Great, thanks. I'll check in with you later. Mmm-hmmm." Sloane whips off her headset and drops it on the desk. "I need to talk to you."

"Me?" I can't tell from the urgency in her voice if this is good or bad. I'm either about to be canned or I'm on the verge of something major.

"I'm going on a break," Sloane declares loudly to no one in particular. I've never seen her do this before. Sloane does a lot, but she's always seemed to me like she's already on a break. She scoops a sheaf of papers up into her arms then stands, grabs me by the hand, and leads me down the hall, pulling me into an empty office. Slone tosses the armful of papers onto the unused desk dramatically, then whirls around and slides the opaque glass door behind us. It closes with a bang.

"What's going on?" I've never seen Sloane like this before. "Oh, I got you some more of those gourmet peanut butter cups you liked. From that place near my house . . ."

"Never mind that!" Sloane rifles through the papers scattered on the desk.

What is wrong? "Is this about Cover Girl?"

Sloane whirls around. "Can you please forget about Cover Girl for five minutes? They'll call again. I promise. Screw them. This is much more important." She rifles through the papers, grabs a piece torn from the newspaper and thrusts it at me accusingly.

"What's this?" I take the tattered page from her.

"Just read." Sloane crosses her arms sternly across her chest. "On second thought, I will take that chocolate . . ."

"It's in my bag." I tug the bag off my shoulder and drop it on a chair, then lean on the empty desk and start to read.

Model Mistress?

What's billionaire businessman Jim Segal's latest hobby? Word is spreading through the Segal Group that the CEO Segal (who started his real estate empire when he inherited Dad's millions on his twenty-first birthday) is up to his plucked eyebrows in some financial impropriety involving two models and a corner apartment at one of his company's signature ventures, the Clift, a luxury co-op building in Chelsea. A company insider told Page Six, *"There's definitely something shady happening. Records indicate we've given a professional courtesy rate to a handful of tenants in our projects, and we reserve that right only for members of the Segal family, in accordance with city rent laws and restrictions. This doesn't pass the smell test—it makes me wonder how these so-called models are earning their discount." Segal, who's been romantically linked to the actress* Celia Ash *in the past, was seen by spies at downtown fixture Freeman's last night, accompanied by one of the models in question, identified as* Mac Croft, *this spring's* Sports Illustrated *swimsuit issue cover girl.* Page Six *wasn't able to identify the second model, or obtain any Segal Group internal documents relating to the so-called "grandfather" regulations loophole. A spokeswoman for the Segal Group declined to comment.*

Sloane's unearthed the candy, and is chewing on it content-edly, watching me as I finish reading, then crumple the paper into a little ball.

I feel sick to my stomach. "Wow." I can't think of what else to say.

"Are you OK, Mac?" Sloane leans in, concern etched across her gorgeous, pale face.

"That article makes me sound like I'm some kind of . . ."

"Whore, I know." Sloane licks the chocolate smudges from the tips of her fingers. "Those fuckers. You should sue, I swear to God . . ."

"My parents." I cringe, imagining Dad. He always scours the papers and magazines for any mention of my name. Whenever my picture runs anywhere, he clips it out and pastes it into a big scrapbook. Sometimes he can't even tell if the model is me—there are clippings from a shoot Debbie Alexander did for *Seventeen* in that scrapbook; I don't have the heart to point out to Dad that it's not me.

"I left you a message," Sloane says. "I was worried you might have heard this on set . . ."

"Everyone on set today was Japanese," I tell her. "I haven't talked to anyone else. Damn!"

"Don't worry." Sloane smiles at me warmly. "It'll blow over."

"You don't think it's true, do you?" I don't know why I'm asking Sloane, but it's like the rug's been pulled out from under me. I'm not Jim's plaything. Am I? "I thought you were calling about Cover Girl." I sound pathetic, I know, but at the moment, that's how I feel. "Sloane, what is this garbage?"

"That garbage is all over the Internet right now." She unwraps another peanut butter cup. "You should eat one of these. They're ridiculous."

I shake my head. I've lost my appetite. "You don't think . . . Francesca? Renee? Paul? Oh God, please tell me Paul hasn't read this. He's running an agency, not a whorehouse."

"Page Six is the first thing everyone reads in the morning," Sloane tells me. "But don't worry. Paul loves when his girls are in the paper. It's good for buzz. And everyone here knows you. We know you're not some kind of . . ."

"Skank? Slut? Girl for hire? Shit, Sloane." Then it dawns on me—what if my clients read this? The last thing Cover Girl is going to want is a tramp as a spokesmodel.

Sloane leans on the desk beside me, drapes an arm around

my shoulders and gives me a reassuring squeeze. "Easy. There. I've seen this happen a million times."

"What do you mean?" I feel like I'm on the verge of tears.

Sloane sighs dramatically. "I've told you about my sister, right? Well, back in the day, at the height of her fame, you wouldn't believe the garbage the tabloids wrote about her. Utter horseshit, pardon my French. My sister—sweetest girl in the world. Truly. The nicest. But these reporters, they have a knack for twisting up words and facts. They love to tear you down. If you're prettier or richer or more successful or more talented—wham! That's when it happens."

"What did she do about it? How did she . . ."

"Survive?" Sloane laughs, and launched into an eerily spot-on Katharine Hepburn: "It's when they *stop* talking about you that you have to worry."

I know she's trying to help, but this isn't making me feel much better.

"Let me tell you a story." Sloane stands and starts pacing. "God I swear I could eat a thousand of those peanut butter cups. Anyway. Susie. My sister. This was like . . . ten years ago? I think. Anyway, she's on a shoot, she's doing her thing, you know, publicity. I think it was for the cover of her second record. You know—*Call Waiting*? So, she's on a shoot, and they're about to go out on tour, all the major US cities, so naturally, she's worried about her health. Her voice is her life, you know?"

I nod, to show I'm listening, but I can't stop myself from picturing Paul Anders, shaking his head, disappointed to learn that his up-and-comer is a cheap floozy.

"So, she's on this shoot, the makeup artist is doing his thing, and he starts to cough. Just cough. And Susie thinks—hey, this guy might be sick, maybe I should stay away? She asks is he's feeling OK, tells him he's looking a little rough, says maybe they should get someone else out there, right? Susie, you don't know her, but she and I . . . our parents raised us right. She's *worried* about the guy. Yes, she doesn't want to get a sore throat right before heading out on tour, and who can blame her, but she tells him maybe he should knock off, get some tea, take some herbs, and get this, she tells him she'll make sure he gets paid. Says she knows, it's a pain in the ass, you lug all your makeup and catch a cab and the whole thing, and she knows that when you're working for yourself you can't just call in sick. So she wants to call her record company, make sure they'll pay the guy even though he can't work, and that they'll call his agency and get them to send another makeup person, too, because obviously she's still got to get her makeup done and take a picture, you follow me?"

I think so. I nod again.

"So what do you think is in the paper the very next day? Susie Q is a homophobe. Susie Q hates people with AIDS, kicks an HIV-positive crewmember off of her set. I mean, can you imagine? She was worried about the guy. She thought he had a cold. Sure, she didn't want to catch it herself, but she was worried. My sister. My sister gave a fortune to AIDS research, a fortune. She was a Top Forty singer in the late eighties—all of her fans were gay guys, for Christ's sake!"

Sloane sits, her eyes glowing with fury at the memory of the incident. She's always over the top, Sloane, always funny and warm and a little silly, but I've never seen her like this before. She seems agitated, distressed.

"I'm sorry that happened," I say at last. "That's horrible."

She chokes back the tears. "I'm sorry. Look at me. I'm trying to tell you a story, make you feel better, and *I'm* getting all worked up."

"Are you . . ."

Sloane holds a hand up, silencing me. "I'm fine. My point is, they'll try to break you down, Mac. You can't let them get away with it."

She stares at me.

"Promise me you won't," she adds.

"I won't." I feel unexpectedly better. Fired up. Tough. Bring them on, I think.

"You go home," Sloane says. She stands and hugs me tight. "Go out this evening, hold your head high."

Hold my head high. I nod. That's just what I need to do.

The traffic is only worse now that it's later, but I need to clear my head anyway, so I decide to walk. I'm deep in thought, mulling over everything, and instead of west and downtown to my place, my subconscious directs me to walk east and uptown, toward the Park Avenue headquarters of the Segal Group.

I'm just pushing through the main lobby's revolving doors when I get a message from Theo: *Drink tonight? Abbot's?* I'm not much of a drinker, but at this moment that's exactly what I want. Theo must have seen Page Six. I text him back (*Yes!!!*) and check in with the security desk. It's funny having to check in and get a sticker with Jim's last name on it just to drop by his office. But that's how things are done at the Segal Group.

Jim's office is on the very top of the world: the thirty-eighth floor. It's a corner office, of course, with crazy views downtown and toward the East River. I've been there before, but still, it's the kind of place that actually takes your breath away—which is the whole point. Your adversaries can hardly negotiate fairly with you when they're in such daunting surroundings.

"Isn't this a surprise!" Jim drops his tiny sterling silver pen and stands as I enter the room. "You should have called!"

"Sorry." The office is so big I swear it takes a minute for me to walk from the door to his desk. I kiss him, quickly. I'm annoyed. I know it's not Jim's fault, but that article spoiled something for me.

"Uh-oh." Jim guides me by the shoulders, motions for me to sit in one of the low-slung leather chairs facing his desk. "Something's wrong." He clears a spot, and sits right on top of his desk, facing me. "Talk to me."

"Yeah, something's wrong. Did you see the *Post*?" I should have brought it with me. It's just a crumpled ball in the trash can of some unused office at Delicious now.

Jim laughs. "Is that what this is? Oh, Mac."

I'm pondering the ruin of my career, the loss of my reputation, and he's laughing? "What, *Oh, Mac*? I'm pissed."

"You're overreacting." Jim stands and walks around to his side of the desk, then slumps back in his Aeron chair. "You want something? Some tea? Anything?"

I shake my head. "I don't want anything but an explanation."

"An explanation? Let's see." Jim leans back and studies the ceiling for a minute. "There could be several. Number one. Some editor at the *Post* is mad at me because my new development blocks the view from his apartment. Number two. The so-called unnamed source at the Segal Group is some disgruntled wannabe trapped in a cubicle on the seventh floor. He or she recognized you, strolling around this office like you own the place, put two and two together, and called the press. Number three. The asshole who lives downstairs from you doesn't like it when you wear heels in the house, so he concocted this crap story about you being my mistress. Which, by the way, is especially hilarious since I'm not married. Number four. Your friend Irin called the paper because she wants a little attention. I'm not saying that happened, I'm just pointing out that it's possible." Jim stops, smiles at me. "Shall I go on?"

"Look, it's easy for you to be flip about this. You're the rich, powerful one. They made me sound like . . . some kind of whore. What if my parents see that?"

"Mac, come on. You're making too big a thing of this. You're a celebrity. You've got to expect that people are going to say things. And not always nice things. You know that's how the world works . . . And obviously, nothing in this item is true."

I'm a celebrity? This is news to me. I'm just . . . me. "But this is so unfair. And sexist. And . . . I'm sorry, it's just plain fucked up."

"How do you think I feel? Like an old man who can only buy companionship. It's bullshit, and I know that. You can't let it get to you at this stage of the game, Mac, because I guarantee you it'll only get worse. As long as you want a career as a model, as long as you're on the covers of magazines and running around New York City hotspots with actors and artists you've got to expect people are going to talk." Jim folds his hands on his desk and smiles, patiently.

I sigh. "OK, you win. I can't fight the press . . ."

"Not fight." Jim shakes his head. "Ignore. Ignore. Who cares? Let it go. Look. I've got some news that's going to cheer you up, I promise."

"I could certainly use some," I tell him.

"How about . . ." He smiles. "I have two tickets to the Costume Institute Gala. Next Monday."

I'm not sure what to say. A costume party? Dressing up like Wonder Woman doesn't sound like that much fun to me. "Oh, a costume party? But it's nowhere near Halloween . . ."

Jim laughs. "No, Mac. The Costume Institute. At the Met? The Metropolitan Museum of Art. It's a party—no, it's the party of the year. Or so I'm told. Anyway, it's some big fancy thing. They have it right in the museum. Dinner, and even dancing at the Temple of Dendur. Have you been there?"

I haven't been there, but I have seen it. I was shooting in Central Park, last summer, behind the Met, and the temple is in this huge glass room at the back of the museum building. "That sounds like it could be fun . . . but I don't have to wear a costume, right?"

Jim chuckles. "No, no, nothing like that. I was playing tennis this morning and I ran into Anna, and she heard that you and I are seeing each other, and she asked about you, and said we had to come . . ."

"Anna?"

"Anna Wintour. From *Vogue*. She chairs the party, you know. It's her thing. I figured it could be good for you to go, mingle with some fashion folks . . ."

"Wait a minute." Anna Wintour is the editor of American *Vogue*, one of the most powerful women in the fashion business and she wants me to come to her party? "You ran into Anna Wintour?"

Jim nods, like it's the most natural thing in the world to make small talk with Anna Wintour. "Sure. I saw her this morning. We play tennis together sometimes. Damn if that woman doesn't have the most incredible backhand . . ."

"And she asked you to bring me to this party? How does she even know we're going out? How does she even know who I am?" I can't get my head around the mental image of Anna Wintour on the tennis court, never mind the idea of her asking for me by name.

"Let's see . . ." Jim stands and walks to the window. "How does the most powerful woman in New York publishing know who you are? And how did she figure out that you and I are . . . involved?" Jim pauses. "Maybe she read it in Page Six, like the rest of the uncivilized world. Silver lining, Mac."

He's got a point. "OK, you win. I need to toughen up. Wait—when did you say this party is?"

"It's next Monday," he explains. "Week from yesterday."

"Shit! What . . . I mean, I need to get a dress. I mean, like, a dress. The big guns. I'm guessing that H&M isn't going to cut it. What am I going to do?"

"Come on, Mac Croft. You're not thinking. When you're in a jam, what do you do? You go to an expert."

"So . . . you're saying, I need to go to Anna?" I stand, and join him at the window. The view truly is astonishing.

"You could go that route." Jim nods. "Or you could go to your best friend Theo. The stylist."

Right. Obviously. "That's why you're the billionaire tycoon and I'm just a model." I squeeze him from behind. "You're a genius. I'm supposed to meet Theo for a drink later. He's going to love this."

"Oh." Jim sort of turns away, facing out at the river view. "I sort of thought. Well."

Now it's my turn to console him. "What's wrong?"

"I sort of thought we might have dinner. Or celebrate or something."

Dinner. Damn. "Oh. Well. We can . . . I just told Theo that I'd meet him for a drink."

"Well, if you'd rather see Theo than me. I've had a long day and you're in New York, I was excited to spend some time with you . . ."

I gesture to him to calm down. "OK, well. I guess I can postpone Theo? Though I feel bad canceling on him and then asking him to help me get a dress for this event."

"Come on . . . Let's get out of here. Go do something fun. We can take the copter to dinner in the Hamptons? Wherever you want. Whatever you want to do." He looks at me, almost pleading.

"Sure, sure." I nod. "Let's do that. We'll do something special. I'll meet up with Theo . . . later." I hate to cancel on him like this, but the look on Jim's face . . . well, it's clear what he wants me to do, and he did just get us tickets to this party. I hope this doesn't become a habit. . . .

"Atta girl." Jim smiles happily. "That's my girl."

Seventeen

At this point, we've dined together in Mexico City, sat beside one another on a much-delayed flight from London to New York, and, of course, he's seen me naked more times than Jim, so I don't think it's unreasonable to expect Zvi Zee to remember who I am. But apparently that's asking too much of the sensitive Israeli artiste, because when I get to the studio he looks at me blankly, not a trace of recognition on his face. For all he knows, I'm there to deliver the doughnuts.

"Hi Zvi!" I do my best to start the day on a positive note. Not easy because I'm irritated; I'm coming from Jim's, and when I woke up I realized I had nothing proper to wear, so I've got on the dirty jeans and dingy sweater I had on yesterday.

Zvi gawks at me like he can't believe I know his name, then wanders away, chattering into his always-present headset. Zvi Zee is one of the more hands-off stylists I've worked with. Everyone—the photographers, the models, the makeup artists—has their own working style, and Zvi's is to treat his assistants like they're marionettes, playing the role of master puppeteer, pulling the strings while his underlings tackle the heavy lifting.

I've been on shoots with stylists and top magazine editors who happily sit cross-legged on the floor, pinning up a dress. I once worked with an important fashion editor who wasn't afraid to slip his feet into a pair of Louboutins and show me how it's done. It's a good thing Zvi has Theo, a perfectionist who'll only hang ten items per rack, keeping the pieces six inches apart, who refuses to put shoes on the floor for fear of scuffing them, who lays out every piece of jewelry organized by type and then by color. Zvi's so hands-off that it sometimes seems like Theo's in charge, so I head right back to see him.

Theo's wearing a gray linen blazer with navy grosgrain piping and a big crest on the breast pocket, a pale blue gingham shirt, a hot pink tie, khaki shorts, gray and yellow striped socks, and brown leather horse-bit loafers.

"Mademoiselle!" Theo's cradling a dangerous-looking pink silk stiletto in his arms. "Let's get to work!"

"You look amazing, as usual." I bend down and drop a kiss on Theo's soft, stubbly cheek. "I'm so glad to see you."

"Is that so?" Theo puts the shoe delicately onto the table and studies me, head cocked. "If you wanted to see me, you had your chance last night, Miss Croft . . ."

"I'm sorry, I'm sorry!" I pull off my sunglasses and give Theo my most pathetic look. "I am. I mean it. Jim was . . ."

"Bros before hos, Mac Croft. That's all I'm saying . . ."

"Don't be like that!" It stings, though, because he's not wrong. I feel lame for having bailed on him. It's not like me—but in this one case I really felt like I had no choice.

"Make it up to me?" He smiles devilishly.

"Gosh, I almost can." I've got news that Theo's going to love. "You might want to sit down."

"You're getting married. You're pregnant. Oh my gosh, always a bridesmaid, never a bride. That's me. Show me the ring!" Theo hops up and down like a kid who has to pee.

"Settle down, sonny. It's nothing like that . . ."

"Yoo-hoo! Mac?" It's Brianne, a makeup artist I recognize. She's about four feet tall, and has a thick French/African accent. She's not exactly the kind of lady you forget. "I'm ready whenever you are."

"Sorry! I'm coming." I turn to Theo. "Walk with me." When the makeup artist beckons, I listen. I've worked with girls who treat the makeup artists like the help, and I think that's a huge mistake. You're trusting these people with your *face*. I think it's best to be as accommodating as possible.

"This better be worth it," he says. "I've got to organize the rings . . ."

"It's worth it." We stroll to the table where Brianne is set up, bottles and brushes all laid out like a surgeon's tools. I settle into the chair. "OK. Both of you. Guess where I'm going next Tuesday?"

"Where's that?" Brianne sweeps the hair out of my face, then starts dabbing at my skin with a toner-soaked cotton ball.

"Did you say Tuesday?" Theo clambers into the tall chair beside me. I've got my eyes closed but I can almost see the delirious expression on his face. "Tell me you didn't say Tuesday."

"What's Tuesday? What am I missing?" Brianne sponges foundation across my forehead. "I feel so out of it."

"What's Tuesday? Tuesday is only the *most* important night in the social calendar. It's the Costume Institute gala. Tell me you're going." Theo claps his hands.

I nod my head slowly, like a queen. "I'm going."

"Mmmm." Brianne's face is mere inches from mine, and she's studying her handiwork carefully. Being this close to the makeup artist used to unnerve me—I mean, you're close enough to kiss, or at least get a whiff of that morning's breakfast. "Oh, right, that party. I'm actually booked to do Posh Spice's makeup that night. Isn't that hilarious?"

"If by hilarious you mean amazing, then yes, it is." Theo sniffs, almost offended. "I've got to go deal with the shoes, ladies. Tell me Mac. You're going to the gala. This is a Jim Segal thing, isn't it? It has to be."

"It's a Jim Segal thing," I tell him. "I don't even know what this party is all about." A Jim Segal thing. I feel proud saying his name like this. Jim Segal. The Jim Segal. *My* Jim Segal.

"Mac, honestly. Do you know how lucky you are? It's going to be the most incredible . . . I'm so jealous it's not even . . . gosh."

"Don't be jealous." Brianne mimes at me to open my mouth, so I do, which makes it much harder to talk, of course. "*I eed ore el.*"

"My help?" Theo furrows his brow. "Why should I help the girl who ditched me for some dude?"

"Tsk-tsk." Brianne scolds. "Bros before hos, Mac."

"He's not a ho." I can't help but smile at hearing Jim described that way. "He's, um, my boyfriend. Anyway, I need your help, Theo, getting dressed."

"Oh heaven knows you do, Mac Croft." Theo hops down from the chair. "I've got to go deal or Mr. Zvi Zee is not going to be happy. But let's talk. You can't show up at the Costume Institute in jeans and a tee. Which is about as *haute* as your *couture* ever gets."

"Shut up!" I give him a little kick.

Theo scurries away. "Save it for after hours, please!"

Brianne laughs. "OK, Mac," she says. "Eyes closed. And tell me all about this um, 'boyfriend' of yours."

"Good! Mac! Good! Mac!" Audrey Jones is a screamer. She must have been a cheerleader in high school. She's a tiny lady, even smaller than Theo, something I didn't think was humanly possible, but her voice more than fills the cavernous studio, and when she barks—for a different lens, for a light reading, for an adjustment on the strobe—her assistant Kevin snaps into action like a man who fears for his life.

I smile. I turn. I preen, and pout, look pretty, and do the same vanishing act I always do when I'm in front of the camera. It's not about the photographer, it's not about the clothes, it's about that moment, those few seconds when the camera opens and reaches out and grabs me. Snap.

Thank goodness it's not about the clothes; we're shooting a fashion story for *Numero*, and of all the getups I've worn, today's are the most ridiculous. Jumpsuits. Still, I grin and bear it. I might tease a little, but I'm careful not to outright insult the clothes on any shoot. You never know who is friendly with what designer. It's entirely possible that Audrey wears jumpsuits every day. Better to keep quiet than get a bad reputation.

"I think we're done here." Audrey hands the camera to Kevin and pulls out her cell phone. "Nice job," she adds, before strolling away. What is it with people and their phones? Who is everyone talking to?

I slip the Sergio Rossi patent wedges off, and immediately the blood starts flowing again. Theo hurries to my side and takes the shoes from me as carefully as if they were his newborn sons.

"You were kidding before right?" Theo whispers. "You're not . . ."

Zvi studies us intently from the sidelines. The way he unfolds his long legs and stands, slowly, reminds me of an insect. He lopes toward me deliberately, like he's moving in for the kill. Then he stops, studies me carefully.

"Theo!" he barks, even though Theo is standing right there.

"Yes, Zvi?" Theo's voice is, as usual, all sweetness and light.

"This look." Zvi frowns, glaring at me like I'm wearing something from my local Wal-Mart. "It is not working."

"Yes, Zvi," Theo nods obediently. "This is the Comme des Garcons, the one you wanted . . ."

"No, no, no, no, no, no no." Zvi frowns. "No, no, no, no. I think, no."

"What's wrong?" Theo doesn't seem fazed by Zvi's disapproval—he's used to this.

"Theo, I feel so disappointed." Zvi shakes his head slowly.

"Next shot," says Theo, changing the subject. "The Sonia Rykiel."

Zvi holds up a finger, pointing to the ceiling. "I think," he says softly, "the shoes . . . the Prada."

"You're the boss," Theo mumbles.

Zvi turns and skulks back to his seat, so I guess we're dismissed.

"Let's go." Theo leads me off the set, his hand on the small of my back.

We disappear behind the racks and I carefully tug at the

zipper. I'm extra cautious with the clothes when I shoot with him; Theo takes fashion seriously.

"Mac . . ." Theo takes my wrist, starts removing the watch. "I think you've got a message." He nods at the accessories table, where my phone's blinking light is reflecting off the stacks of silver cuffs. He places the watch delicately in a velvet-lined case and hands me my phone. "It's probably Jim. Maybe you should ditch the shoot and go meet him . . ."

"Shhh." I stroke Theo's thick, curly locks. "I told you I'm sorry."

I skim through my messages as Theo tidies the already tidy dressing area. Then I freeze. There it is, the message I've been waiting for. From Renee: *Mitch Godfrey. CGirl. 5:30. 1400 Bway, 22 Fl.*

I feel like shouting, but my words come out steadily. "Theo. Cover Girl. I'm seeing them today."

"Shut the front door!" Theo is too gentlemanly to swear. "Mac! That's amazing."

"I know." It is amazing. "Five forty-five. You don't think we'll go late, do you?"

"With Audrey Jones?" Theo chuckles. "Not a chance. Miss Jones's nanny goes off the clock at 5:30 sharp. I've never known her to go even a minute past five. It's your lucky day."

We're way downtown, though. It'll take me a while to get up to the Cover Girl offices, even if we do wrap by five. "Shoot." I pick one of the watches up off the table and check the time. "I've got a commute though. You think I'll make it, right?"

With the plastic hanger in his hand Theo gestures at the rumpled pile of clothes on the floor. My clothes. "I think you'll be unfashionably on time," he says.

Shit. "My clothes. Damnit! Of all the nights to crash at Jim's . . ." I'm irritated by the inconvenience, but it was worth it. We didn't get much sleep last night, but I'm not complaining.

"That wouldn't have happened if you hadn't cancelled on me . . ."

The tears are welling up in my eyes. I've been waiting for this opportunity for weeks now. I can't go into this meeting in dirty jeans and a ratty sweater. It'll totally throw me off my game.

"OK, never mind that," Theo says. He drapes his arm around my waist. "Don't worry."

"I can just borrow some stuff from the racks, right?" I look down at my long purple canvas jumpsuit.

"Don't be ridiculous," Theo snaps. "You can't show up wearing *a jumpsuit*. You look like a gas station attendant."

"But what . . ."

"Give me your keys." Theo sighs dramatically. "When we break for lunch, I'll go to your place, pick out an outfit, and I'll be back before you're on to the next shot."

"I don't know what to say." I hug Theo tightly. "You are the best."

"I kind of am," he agrees. "Now, undress."

We're just finishing up lunch—pizza and Caesar salad for the crew, carrot sticks, a smoothie, and unsalted almonds for me—when Theo returns, my knight in shining armor, my knight in shorts and a blazer, garment bag flung jauntily over his shoulder.

"I should go." I stand and smile at Audrey, who's been regaling me with stories of her kids Violet and Rocky all through lunch, even showing me snapshots and home movies stored on her cellphone. "Get ready for the next look."

"Go, hon!" Audrey barks in that same, chipper cheerleader voice.

I hurry to the backstage dressing area.

"Was that OK?"

Theo whirls around, shaking the ice in his Starbucks cup. "I'm a stylist," he says coolly. "Emergencies are my thing. But Mac Croft, gosh, you could use a radical wardrobe makeover."

"What do you mean?" I unzip the garment bag. A silky purple dress I don't recognize pops out. "What's this?"

"That," Theo says, gently pushing me aside and removing the dresses from the bag, "is vintage Balmain, courtesy of Irin Churpacovich. Now there's a girl with a fabulous wardrobe. Her closet was exactly like Decades. That store on Melrose—do you know it?"

I'm no good at fashion speak. "Do you think it's OK if I borrow this stuff from Irin?" We've become pals, but with the exception of milk and toilet paper, we don't share anything.

Theo sniffs. "She's in Beijing with Patrick Demarchelier for the next four days. I'm sure she won't mind. Just don't spill coffee on it."

I'm not as sure as Theo is. Once on a job one of the girls I was working with helped herself to my belt and my sunglasses. Some girls are so used to just helping themselves to whatever is on the racks that they turn into kleptomaniacs. "I don't know, Theo." The dress is incredible, but it's more suitable for dinner with Jim than a meeting with a bunch of suits. "It's gorgeous, but I worry that it's too . . ."

Theo sighs. "I'm your best friend, so I knew you were going to say that. So, take a look at this." He pulls out a plain black dress. The neckline is a little daring, but the hemline is longer, and the sleeves are three-quarter length, and there's something very simple but confident about it. "It's Alaïa, and I like-a." Theo smiles happily.

I take the hanger from him, holding the dress up against my body and studying the effect in the mirror. I'm a little bustier than Irin, but I think that might work to my advantage in this dress. "I love it, Theo. You're a genius. You missed lunch because of me. You truly are my best friend."

"How about we start acting like it, then?" Theo gives me a pointed look.

"I get it. I'm sorry about last night. I mean it."

"All is forgiven, Mac Croft. Now put that dress down."

"Why? Did I get something on it?" I hang the dress on the rack.

"No," Theo says. "You're supposed to be wearing that Junya Watanabe jumpsuit, and you're supposed to be on set right now."

Theo wasn't kidding. Audrey hands the camera to Kevin, shouts out "That's a wrap!" swoops in and kisses me on the cheek, and is basically out the door at 4:55. I make a run for it, kicking off my Marc Jacobs spectator pumps, tugging at the zipper on this Maria Cornejo jumpsuit.

"Fifty minutes, fifty minutes." There's no time to be precious, so I toss the shoes onto the floor, tug the dozens of bangles off my wrist and drop them onto the table with a clatter.

"Let me." Theo intervenes, pulling the front zipper all the way down. I step out of the ridiculous garment and it falls to the floor, and Theo actually kicks it away. I pull the Alaïa dress over my head, and as I smooth out the front, Theo buttons up the back. "The fit is spot on." He gives me a little push. "Now get out there and see Brianne. You're supposed to be a fresh-faced gal next door cover girl with a capital C, and you've got about four pounds of gunk on your face."

Shit. A horrible realization dawns on me. "Theo . . ."

"Shoes, right?" Theo picks up a stunning, strappy black Louboutin sandal and dangles it mid-air, like he's hypnotizing me. "I'm taping the bottoms of these right now. Scuff them, and you're a dead woman."

I kiss him on the top of his head. "I would be lost without you."

I'm dangerously out of breath, my lungs aching like I've just run a marathon. I was out of the studio by 5:15, which must be some kind of world record, and on the subway seven minutes later. After much deliberation and consultation with Theo, Kevin the assistant, and Brianne, I opted for the train rather than taking my chances in the rush hour traffic. I can't decide what's more infuriating: sitting in the backseat of a taxi, listening to the honking horns, watching the fare climb higher by the minute, watching the lights change from green to yellow to red and back again without the car moving, or maneuvering between the disgruntled commuters on the train, searching in vain for a seat, gripping the disgustingly greasy pole, and wondering why the train has slowed to a crawl or stopped altogether in the middle of some dark tunnel. On the street, at least you can see what the holdup is; underground, in the dark, you're in a void. I spent seventeen minutes on the 1 train, tapping my foot impatiently as the train jerked and lurched its way toward Times Square.

Now at least I can see where I am. The problem is that I can't see where I'm *supposed* to be. I check my phone again. *1400 Bway.* I see 1440, and I just crossed the street for the fourth time and confirmed that the building on the corner is 1390. So where the hell is 1400? I don't even need to check my watch to know that I'm supposed to be at Cover Girl in two minutes. I dial the Delicious offices.

It only rings once. "Delicious . . ."

Oh thank God. "Sloane, it's Mac . . ."

"Hold please!" The line clicks.

Silence.

Fuck. I don't have time to wait. I end the call. I'm about to flag down a policeman, enlist random passerby in my quest when I spot it: halfway down the block a glass awning juts out into the street, with the big steel numbers I've been looking for. I dash toward it, the sweat dripping down my back, running down my forehead and into my eyes.

I fan myself with my hands, and try to catch my breath.

"I'm sorry." The receptionist stares up at me blankly. "You're here to see Mr. Mitchell?"

I can't believe this. "No." I'm trying to sound as nice as possible. "I'm here to see Mitchell Godfrey. Mr. *Godfrey.*" I check my Blackberry to confirm. "Executive vice president of marketing, North American division?"

"Oh, you said Mr. Mitchell!" The receptionist chuckles. "And I thought that was funny, because I've been working here three months now, and I don't think I've heard of a Mr. Mitchell in all that time! I thought I was going crazy . . ."

My smile is beginning to crack. It's 5:57. I'm twelve minutes late. "Can you tell me where his office is?"

He whistles, then starts tapping very slowly on his computer keyboard. "I think I'm going to have to get his assistant to come down and escort you up," he says. "Her name is Joelle. She's so nice."

"Oh, do you have to? I'm running late, you see, for a pretty big meeting with Mr. Godfrey . . ."

"A big meeting? Gee, you're not supposed to be in the presentation with the national sales force, are you? Are you a model?"

"Yes!" I feel like I'm negotiating with a particularly stupid child. "I'm a model. A very, very late model. Can you point me in the right direction?"

"You should have said something!" He smiles happily and points to his right. "It's down that hall, very last door on the left. You can't miss it."

I don't even bother with a thank you. I blotted most of the sweat off of my forehead on my way up in the elevator—where I also took the opportunity to change into my fancy shoes—and I don't want to get all doused again, so I walk slowly but deliberately down the long hallway, my steps silenced by the indoor carpeting, the gaffer tape Theo applied so lovingly to the red leather soles of these Louboutins sticking to the ground slightly. I wish I could take a quick look in the mirror before this meeting, but there's no sign of one. I'm at the last door on the left. I knock twice, then push the door open.

I step inside, and ten heads swivel in my direction in perfect unison. Great. Renee said this meeting was with Mitch Godfrey; she neglected to mention that nine of his closest friends would be joining us.

"Mac Croft?"

"I'm so sorry I'm late."

A man I assume is Mitch Godfrey waves me into the room. "Come in, come in. We saved you a seat." He nods toward the empty seat at the very head of the table.

I make my way toward the table, trying to move gracefully, breezily. I pull the chair out and settle in, daintily, I hope.

"I'm Mitch," he says. "And let's go around quickly, shall we?" He's a classic dorky business-guy type, with gold-framed eyeglasses, a blue shirt, and paisley tie. "This is Pamela Rifkin, our director of strategic partnerships; that's Angie Chang, our design director; there's Stuart Cole, the creative director for covergirl.com; this is Susannah Davis, our vice president for market research; Kara Stockton and Cindy Laski from our development and new products division; Jason Schorr, our executive vice president; Helen Conley Cox, our vice president of brand management; David Davis-Ellis, our chief creative director; and you know me already, so let's get this underway since we're a little behind schedule . . ."

"I'm so sorry, again, everyone." I summon up my warmest smile, turning my head slowly so that everyone at the table gets a look. I wish we were wearing nametags.

"No problem, dear," coos a woman in a Chanel suit. She's got the biggest diamond ring I've ever seen. I think she's Helen something or other, but I can't be sure. "We were going over your book . . ."

"Today is all about us getting acquainted." It's one of the

few men in the room, but the only one I can identify for sure is Mitch. I smile at him. "We're always looking for a woman with that certain something special, you know? Of course, you probably already know all about Cover Girl, but if you have any questions, you should feel free to ask."

Everyone is looking at me expectantly. My portfolio is lying on the conference table, and the strikingly beautiful Asian woman—was that Cindy? Angie?—is paging through it slowly. "You were the *SI* cover girl, right Mac? How was that?"

I clear my throat. "It was wonderful." That's so lame. Shit. "It was . . . a wonderful experience, first of all. We shot in Costa Rica, and I don't think I've ever been anywhere so beautiful. The crew was wonderful, and I'm very proud of those pictures. And naturally, it's been a wonderful launching point for me. That's wonderful exposure you know." Why am I saying *wonderful* so many times? I sound like a moron.

"Exposure is putting it mildly." This is Chanel Suit. She rolls her eyes, very subtly, smiling all the while. "It's quite a bare look, wouldn't you say?"

"Helen has some concerns about image. You understand, of course. The phrase Cover Girl—it's come to mean something. Our clients expect a great deal from our Cover Girls." This is Pamela or Cindy or someone. She seems nice enough. I'll take whatever friends I can get at this point.

"Sure. I'm sure you don't like your girls un-covered!" I laugh. The joke falls lamely onto the floor though. So much for trying to break the tension.

"I think what Kara is trying to say . . ." says another one of the men.

"Is that Alaïa?" interrupts Chanel Suit. Oh right, her name is Helen.

"It is, Helen," I say, graciously.

"I thought so!" she leans back in her chair, triumphant. "It's last season. I thought I recognized it. I had the same dress last year. Isn't that funny."

Oh. Ouch. I can tell from her tone of voice that wearing last season is an unforgivable sin.

"Sorry, David, please go on." Helen gives a little wave in his direction. I can't tell who the boss is, but clearly there are some complicated power dynamics in the room.

"I was saying," says David, "that I think what Kara was saying is that we have expectations. We know what makes a girl a Cover Girl. And the process of finding another Cover Girl is always the same, and always complicated. It's not about being the right size, or the right color."

"Right!" Mitch chimes in. "Cover Girl is every girl. What we need from you is . . ."

"Girl next door!" One of the other women who hasn't spoken yet slaps the table excitedly.

"I love these pictures," says the woman with my portfolio. "But I'm not sure I see it here. Do you . . . disagree?" She gives me a challenging look, but I'm not going to back down that easily.

"Well, you understand that the person in those pictures isn't me. It's . . . well, my job is to be whoever my client needs me to be." I lean forward, elbows on the table, staring down the girl with my portfolio.

"We worry, we do." Chanel Suit Helen shakes her head slowly. I'm starting to hate her. "The things you hear, the things you read in the papers. We expect the world of our girls . . ."

The things you read in the papers? I can feel my cheeks

turning red. Miss Chanel Suit has a very clever way of insulting the hell out of someone with a smile on her face all the while.

The Asian woman slams the portfolio shut and pushes it toward the middle of the conference table. "Helen, I thought we already discussed . . ."

Helen shrugs her shoulders theatrically. "I don't mean to insinuate . . ."

"Ladies, please." David clears his throat, silencing everyone. "Let's stay focused on the issue. Mac, we're so glad you were able to come in today."

"I am too." I shrug my shoulders to signal it's no big deal, smile plastered on my face all the while. "I'm so glad we were able to coordinate our schedules."

"How do you feel about going blond?" This is Kara or Cindy or someone, I truly have no idea.

"Can't get too attached to your hair in this business!" I laugh.

"I think the prototypical all-American girl next door is a natural blonde, frankly." Chanel Suit folds her arms across her chest and beams triumphantly.

I tuck my plain, brown, un-all-American hair back behind my ears. I'm about thirty seconds away from saying something I know I'll come to regret. Thankfully, Mitch steps in.

"I think we're set, for now, Mac. I do. I'm sorry you had to come all this way for a few minutes of face time."

"Don't apologize, please. It's my pleasure. Seeing someone in person can be so much more enlightening than the portfolio." I push my chair back and stand.

"Thanks again, Mac," Jim says.

There are a bunch of *thank yous* and *goodbyes*, and I sort of nod and bow, telling myself as I walk out of the room to keep smiling, and stand tall. They're all judging me. After all, that's the reason I'm here.

The hallway is quiet and empty, which is a relief. I've been in there for less than twenty minutes, but I'm winded. I've been on a lot of go-sees, but that was by far the most intense meeting of my career. And despite the rude comments, I want this, badly, more than I've ever wanted anything.

But first things first. I need to take these shoes off and unwind. I pick up my phone and call the only person in the world I feel like talking to right now.

For a quiet, neighborhood joint, Abbot's is packed. It is a Friday evening, though. I squeeze past in the front door, getting a friendly nod from Shannon, the buxom brunette hostess who by now recognizes me as a regular—or at least, the friend of a regular. The crowd by the bar is three people deep, but it's easy to spot Theo, perched on a stool at one of the tall tables against the wall. He waves excitedly and I maneuver between a well-dressed blond girl still wearing her office ensembles and a scruffy jeans and tee guy who's flirting up a storm.

"Crowded!" I hop up onto the soft leather stool. "Friday night, huh?"

"Time to celebrate!" Theo signals to the waiter. "What's your pleasure?"

I shake my head—another lesson from Dr. Gindi. "I'll stick to cranberry juice."

Theo frowns. "Come on. Let loose!"

The waiter, a tall, dancer type with plucked eyebrows and a deep, flawless tan leans in to the two of us intimately. "What can I get you?" His voice is gravelly and sexy.

"A cranberry juice for me, please."

Theo sighs. "I'll have another Grey Goose and soda." He winks at the waiter, who nods and wades back into the crowd.

"I'll have a sip of yours, I promise," I tell Theo.

"Don't do me any favors." Theo finishes the last of his first cocktail. "I thought you might want to celebrate!"

"Celebrate, not so much. Unwind, definitely." I can hear my phone vibrating inside my bag but I'm in no mood to deal with it. I know it's going to be Francesca, wondering how the big meeting went, or Jim, wondering if we're meeting up tonight, or Mitch from Cover Girl calling to tell me to thanks but no thanks, Cover Girl isn't in the habit of hiring brunettes who prostitute themselves to rich bachelors.

"You look incredible." Theo swirls the ice in his glass. "Alaïa. I'm brilliant."

I look down at the dress. "You don't think it's tacky to wear last season's Alaïa?"

He cocks an eyebrow. "What do you mean?"

"I mean Helen What's-Her-Face, some bigwig at Cover Girl, gave me grief for it. *I had the same dress! Last year!* Bitch."

Theo puts his glass down and stares at me in disbelief. "She didn't."

The waiter returns, our drinks in hand. "Can I get you anything else?"

I shake my head, and he winks before heading back to the bar.

"I can think of a few things he could get me!" Theo rolls his eyes dramatically. I think he's drunk. I wonder how many of those vodkas he put away before I got here. "Anyway. She said that? Gosh. Last year's Alaïa. Those are fighting words . . ."

"I think I blew it, Theo." The tears I've been holding back all the way over here are starting to well up.

"Don't be ridiculous!" Theo strokes my hand gently. "You're overreacting. Come on. You're amazing. I'm sure they loved you. You're the talk of the town, Mac Croft."

"Yeah, the town slut is more like it."

Theo giggles. "You're still worried about the *Post*? It's forgotten. There are much more pressing things in the gossip rags today. No offense or anything, but dish about Jim Segal isn't exactly juicy. The people care more about Madonna."

I dab at the corner of my eye with the cocktail napkin. "She made me feel like . . ." I can't find the right word.

Theo shrugs. "Forget it. I'm not kidding." He pushes his drink towards me. "Take a sip, get a buzz going. Call your boyfriend, make him take you to the most expensive restaurant in the city. Ask him to buy you something covered with diamonds. Go dancing all night long."

"My boyfriend." I know Theo's right—if there's one thing I can count on in the world, it's that Jim would do all those things. I could call Jim right now and ask him to take me shopping, out to dinner, out dancing, and he'd be here in twenty minutes, ready to go. I know I should want that—but I don't. Terrific as Jim is, I need some time and the chance to get some perspective on things. I'd rather hang out here all night with Theo. "Let's forget about him tonight."

"So it's the two of us tonight?" Theo clinks his glass against mine. "Cheers, girl. I'm down."

I reach for Theo's glass, take a small sip of the potent cocktail. "I'm hungry. What do you say we get a table?"

"Ten steps ahead of you, kiddo. My name's on the list. I was hoping you'd consent to dine with me after blowing me off last night . . ."

"OK, OK! Guilty as charged. Can we please . . ."

Theo winks. "Forgiven, forgiven. I'm only teasing. You know I kid."

"Let's forget about work, and boyfriends, and Cover Girl, and fashion, and all that stuff for one night, what do you say?"

"I'm down." Theo frowns into his drink. "I think I need a trial separation from Zvi Zee. We can discuss later. Oh! Before I forget, I wanted to give you something."

"A pick-me-up? You're too kind."

Theo shoves an envelope across the table. "Long story, I got these hockey tickets. You know me—sports? Not so much. Maybe if it were soccer. At least they wear those little shorts. But hockey? Anyway, I thought you might want them."

"Thanks Theo!" I take the envelope from him. I think Francesca's husband is into sports. Maybe I should use this opportunity to schmooze her a bit.

"I'm glad someone will get some use out of them." Theo polishes off the rest of his drink. "Yum."

Our dark, handsome waiter emerges from the crowd once again. "You guys? Your table's ready, if you are."

"Let's go!" I hop down from my perch, more than ready to put the day behind me.

Eighteen

"You're awfully quiet tonight." Jim reaches for my hand, grips it in his.

"I'm a little tired, that's all." I turn away, looking out of the window at the dark night, but I can still see him, reflected in the glass, dapper in his tuxedo. The Town Car inches forward, then stops again.

"Lot of traffic," Jim observes. "Must be the damn red carpet slowing things up."

"Must be."

He tries again. "You look incredible, you do, have I told you that already?"

"You have." I turn and look at him. "Not that I don't mind hearing it again. Theo did a good job." I don't know how he pulled it off with less than a week's notice, but somehow Theo charmed the right people and managed to get me this stunning, black Zac Posen halter gown. There's incredible beading all over the thing, and it hangs so sexily off of me, I can't help but feel like a movie star on my way to a premiere. I'm actually excited about emerging from the backseat and facing the photographers on the red carpet. But I am feeling a little bit off, since it's only been a couple of hours since Jim and I had our first real fight.

"You're never around when I need you," Jim had barked.

"You don't understand my life," I told him.

"How can you be this selfish?" he demanded.

It's always the same with fights—who can remember how it started? All I know is that if it hadn't been for our tickets to this party, and the fact that being late is not an option, lest you anger the all-powerful hostess, we'd still be in Jim's apartment, yelling at one another while the maid and the chef pretended nothing was happening. I pull my cropped sable coat closer. It's another gift from Jim, another present for no particular reason. His generosity when it comes to gifts is impossible to deny, but he doesn't seem to get that the thing I want most from him is a little understanding.

"At last." Jim squeezes my hand tighter. "Are you ready to make your entrance?"

I smile. The last thing in the world I feel like doing, but at this point, I'm an expert at smiling when I don't mean it.

For the first time, I understand the phrase "sensory overload."

There's an honest-to-God red carpet, and there are dozens, possibly hundreds of photographers penned up behind the ropes, jostling one another in a way that's downright frightening.

I reach behind me, taking Jim's hand in mine, and push forward, determined as a quarterback. "I think we can get through this way." I've got to shout to make myself heard over the din of honking horns and screaming photographers.

Jim grins happily, but I can't make out what he's saying. I'm trying to keep my ladylike composure, but that's hard when you're screaming "Huh?" at the top of your lungs.

"Miss Croft?" A persistent finger taps me repeatedly on my bare shoulder.

I whirl around, and am confronted by a smiling, freckle-faced girl whose headset doesn't exactly complement her formal gown.

"Sorry! I'm Jennah? From *Vogue*?"

I tug at Jim's arm, trying to pull him closer. I figure this girl is checking our tickets, and those are in Jim's pocket.

"Sorry," I tell her. "He's got the tickets."

The girl smiles. "No, Miss Croft. Not your tickets. I'm Jennah, from *Vogue* PR? I just wanted to let you know you can walk that way, with your escort of course. Straight down the carpet, please. It'll take you right to the main entrance."

"You want me to . . ."

"She wants you to walk the red carpet, gorgeous," Jim interjects, his hands on my waist, pulling me close to his body.

"That's right!" Jennah from *Vogue* nods chirpily, like a cheerleader during a routine. She glances at her clipboard. "Just follow me. I'll escort you down the carpet."

I look left, and then right, the explosions of flashes blinding me temporarily. I've seen this done. TV, in movies, but I'm not sure what to do. Do I just . . . walk? I guess so. Jennah is off, cradling her clipboard like it was a clutch, and I figure I should follow in her footsteps.

Jim squeezes me again, then takes my arm in his. "Let's go, doll." We begin ascending the steps, my heart pounding in my chest noisily, my shivers of giddy excitement running up and down my spine like electric current.

The photographers are calling out a chorus of names so famous they seem almost unremarkable: "Mary-Kate! Ashley!" "Tom! Gisele!" "Nicole! Keith!" "Beyonce!" When I hear my own name, my first instinct is to spin around in search of a familiar face. Who's calling me? Jim laughs, places his hand gently on my bare back, and with his other hand points to the scrum of photographers. "Mac! Over here honey!" I smile, and wave, and slip the sable jacket from my shoulders and hand it to Jim, turning to show off my dress. Some of the celebrities are a little uneasy on the red carpet—they're at their best up on the big screen. But I just found my element.

Jim and I glide up the carpet, nodding hello at the other guests, even the ones we don't know, or know only because, well, everyone knows them: David Bowie and Iman, the King and Queen of Jordan, a certain United States senator from New York and her husband, the former president. We follow the flow of traffic into the museum, checking in at the front desk, where security is as tight as you'd expect it to be at a party where the guest list includes royalty. We march through a couple of metal detectors, joking about how it's like being at the fanciest airport in the world. At the bar, I stand in line between Katie Couric and Venus Williams. It's that kind of party.

The exhibition we're here celebrating tonight is *Joie de Vivre: French Fashion from 1940 to the Present*, so many of my fellow guests are wearing French designs: Dior, Saint Laurent, Balmain, Leger. I want to see the show, but there's so much to distract us we haven't even made it all the way into the main hall where the dinner will be served. For starters, there's the people watching: celebrities wearing show-stopping gowns, beautiful people whose faces I can't quite place impeccably turned out, eccentrics wearing saris, or huge feathered headdresses, or ermine capes. Then there's the fact that you can't go more than ten feet without being offered a glass of champagne or some new tempting tray of canapés. Finally, of course, there's the fact that we're in a museum. Not any old museum, either—the Met, which is absolutely massive, big enough to hold an actual Egyptian temple, and the interiors of old churches and historic buildings, and has a collection that includes pretty much everything, and we have the run of it, just a few hundred party goers, able to stroll around, sip a kir royale, and study a Degas pastel in peace. I know I was skeptical about this whole event, and I know it's only been hours since our fight, but I'm starting to relax. I'm sipping champagne and making small talk with the mayor and his girlfriend. What's not to love?

Eventually the mayor continues on his way, working the room, and Jim and I are lingering in the corner, taking in the scene, when a stranger's hand squeezing my shoulder startles me so much I almost spill my champagne.

"Don't be scared, doll." It's Frank Lindo. I haven't seen him since last summer, or talked to him since I called him this winter out of desperation, but he's exactly as I remember him, except for the fact that he's wearing a tux.

"Frank!" I'm excited to see a familiar face here. We kiss our hellos.

"Mac Croft." Frank squeezes Jim's hand heartily. "You should be more careful about the company you keep."

"Easy, there," says Jim.

"So the rumors are true." Frank grabs a flute of champagne off the tray of a passing server. "I guess a toast is in order."

"Can't believe everything you read, Frank." I touch my glass to his. "Cheers."

He chuckles. "I've been around the block a few times, Mac." Frank drains his glass in one sip. "I know how to parse the gossip columns." He turns to Jim. "Who the fuck did you piss off, anyway, buddy?"

Jim gestures around the room. "Let's forget that. This is a party."

"Oh hell," Frank mutters into his glass. "Don't look now."

When someone tells you not to look, your first instinct is to look, of course. "What's wrong?" There's so much to look at in this museum, so much to see, but even so, the one thing that stands out is the figure of Caroline Gregory, floating toward us, swathed in a stunning asymmetrical purple gown that cascades off her body and to the floor, the massive diamond necklace around her throat catching the light beautifully. Oh right. For me, this moment is a fan sighting; for Frank, it's a run-in with the ex.

"Hello, Frank." Caroline's smile is even more startling in person than it in pictures. She's taller, too, more commanding—more like a statue than a human being. There's barely a trace of age on her face, though at this point she must be nearing forty, not old by any means, but it's been years since the most famous photographs of her were first published. "Fancy meeting you here."

"That's quite a dress, Caroline. Did I pay for that?" Frank signals to a passing waiter. "Let's get you some champagne, shall we?"

"No matter how drunk you get me, it's not going to happen." Caroline's smile is somehow icy and warm at the same time. "Hi, Jim." She kisses Jim on the cheek. "Still running with the wrong crowd, I see."

"Caroline." Jim smiles. "This is Mac Croft, a special friend of mine. Have you met?"

"So nice to meet you!" I can't stop myself from sounding like a fan.

"A pleasure, Mac." Caroline nods regally. "Lovely dress."

"Thanks!" Caroline Gregory just complimented me. Sometimes I can't believe this is my life. "Yours is . . ."

Caroline turns away, gesturing into the crowd like she's hailing a cab. "Over here! Helen!" She turns back to us. "Sorry. Just lost my friend . . ."

The friend in question waves back, then totters over unsteadily on some near-lethal looking heels, and as she gets closer, I recognize her pinched, post-facelift face. She's in a too-short, too-ruffled dress with a trim little bolero jacket, but to me, she's still Chanel Suit: Helen, my old pal from Cover Girl.

"Jim Segal, Mac Croft, this is Helen Conley Cox. Helen, you already know this gentleman." Caroline gestures toward her ex-husband dismissively.

"Frank!" Helen kisses him excitedly. "It's been ages. You're looking well." She turns to Jim, shakes his hand warmly. "Jim, so good to meet you at long last. And of course, I know Mac." She smiles at me limply.

Right. Helen Conley Cox. Of Cover Girl. With Caroline Gregory, former Cover Girl. It's all starting to make sense now.

"Hi Helen." I offer her my hand, force the warmest smile I can muster.

"Lovely to see you again." Helen grips me by the very tips of my fingers, like she can't bear to touch me.

"This is some party . . ." Jim starts to say, but he's interrupted by the sounds of a small, uniformed brass ensemble playing the Marseillaise.

"I think that's our cue." Frank drapes one arm around my waist and the other around Jim's shoulders. "Time for dinner. Saved by the bell, huh folks?"

I couldn't have said it better myself.

Theo outfitted me from head to toe tonight, and he did it beautifully, but my only complaint is the bag. My crocodile Erickson Beamon clutch is absolutely gorgeous, but it's so small there's almost no room for my keys and money, so snacks were out of the question. And I'm starving, surrounded by food (crusty bread smeared with pate, escargots swimming in pools of butter) that I can't eat.

The seated dinner is in a football field-sized interior courtyard in the museum. Etruscan vases and fragments of classical friezes are on display all around the room's perimeter, and at the center is a cluster of huge, round tables draped in red, white, and blue bunting and covered with lush floral arrangements and elegant place settings. It's breathtakingly beautiful—with all the French flourishes, I feel like Marie Antoinette.

But even the queen needs a minute to herself every now and then. It turns out that Frank is at our table, and the boy talk is getting a little boring anyway, so I slip away, hiking up my long dress, making my way carefully because the floor is slick and I don't completely trust these Stuart Weitzman stilettos. The dining room is already abuzz with the news that a certain model turned actress slipped and fell on the marble steps into the dining room. That's all I need—another public embarrassment that's perfect for the *Post*.

Even the bathroom is beautiful, with dripping candelabras and lush, fragrant arrangements of purple flowers, the flicker of the candles reflected in the gilt-framed mirrors. It's the kind of light that flatters anyone, but it's not the most practical for checking your hair and makeup. I lean closer to the mirror and turn my head slightly to the left to make sure my hair's not coming undone. I'm used to having my hair done for me now; my hands are out of practice.

"I think you're coming undone there." Caroline Gregory emerges from the shadows. She gently tucks the loose strands back into my chignon. "There. All better."

"Thanks." I smile gratefully. "I'm getting spoiled—used to having hair and makeup done for me!"

"Tell me about it." Caroline studies her face in the mirror. I can't help but study it too; it's actually flawless. Her eyes are electric blue, her skin naturally glowing. Her thick brown hair is down, hanging in gentle waves to her shoulders. Even her minor imperfections—the faint wrinkles at the edge of her eyes, the slightly askew front tooth—make her seem more beautiful. More human.

I'm staring, but I don't even think Caroline notices. We're models, so we both know what it's like to be studied, scrutinized, watched, appreciated. It's unnerving but eventually you get used to it. Then she catches my eye, in the mirror's reflection. I can feel myself blushing. I feel silly, like I'm watching a big sister, like I'm a freshman and she's the cool senior I am dying to be friends with. I'm glad the room is so dark, and glad too that we're alone.

"So." Caroline's studying me now, seriously, intently, like I'm one of the paintings just outside. "You and Jim, huh?"

"We're . . . close." That seems like a diplomatic answer. For all I know there might be a reporter inside one of those stalls, perched on the toilet, legs tucked up beneath her, scribbling eagerly on her notepad. Considering the crowd here tonight, there's going to be some pretty incredible gossip flying around this ladies' room.

"You're gorgeous, you know." It's not exactly a compliment. It's more like an observation. Caroline's not a jealous girl-friend; she's not an appreciative client. She's not hitting on me, and she's not screwing with me, either. This is just a comment, from one pro to another, and for that reason, it actually means something.

"Thanks." I want to tell her that she's gorgeous. I want to tell her that I'm a fan, that what little I did know of fashion magazines and models when I was a little girl was her. But she doesn't need to hear that from me. "I appreciate it."

"I've got a little advice for you, if you don't mind listening to an old woman." Caroline turns back to the mirror and dabs at her lips with a tissue.

"I'd love to . . ."

"Toughen up." She grins. "Fuck 'em. The papers, the trash talk. They're always going to talk, and you're always going to have to ignore them. You just be sure to have the last laugh, OK?"

I can't believe this: not only is Caroline Gregory talking to me, she's trying to tell me something meaningful, trying to pass along this pearl of wisdom. "Did someone say some-thing, Caroline? I appreciate your advice, and you're right, but am I . . ."

There's a mischievous twinkle in her beautiful blue eyes. "I can read the papers, Mac. I can put two and two together." She glances over her shoulder, then, satisfied we're alone, she continues. "Plus, I've worked with Helen Conley Cox. I know she's a bitch. A powerful bitch, though, so try to win her over."

I try to play innocent. "Helen?"

"She's been there since the days when I was a Cover Girl." Caroline winks at me. "Don't fall for her crap. She pretends to be all anti-brunette. It's an act." Caroline twirls a lock of her own chestnut-colored hair around her finger, playfully.

"I'm not used to being in the papers. I'm not used to the negative . . ."

Caroline holds up a hand, stopping me mid-sentence. "I had some good times with Frank, I did, and I've known Jim for years, and he's a wonderful guy. But if I could go back in time, get some face time with some mentor model, here's what I wish she'd tell me: work hard, forget about the men, don't listen to the naysayers. Keep your head down, and keep going." She tosses her lipstick-stained tissue into the bin. "You're going to be a star, Mac Croft. I can tell just by looking at you. It's as plain as the nose on your face. The only one who doesn't seem to know it is you."

She's gone before I even begin formulating my clever response.

Maneuvering through the crowd in the dining room is a bit like making my way through an obstacle course. Here's Calvin Klein, leaning in over a crowded table, telling a story to Oscar and Annette de la Renta. There's one of the New York Yankees, even more handsome in his tux than in his regular old uniform, winking at me as I squeeze past Henry Kissinger and Liza Minnelli, deep in conversation. I'm turning the corner, heading back toward our table when someone calls my name.

"Mac!" It's Shelly Pine, the photographer, waving at me eagerly like we're old friends.

I make my way to her table. "Hi Shelly." I kiss her on the cheek.

"You look incredible." Shelly bites into a cornichon, and munches happily. "Truly. You look terrific. Beautiful as usual, but so . . . healthy. Like you just got back from the spa. Have you been working or did you give up the rat race?"

God bless Dr. Gindi, wherever he is. "It's been a good spring," I tell her. "But why haven't we worked together lately?"

"I know!" Shelly squeezes my hand. "Everyone at *W* loved that film, you know? You've got it, girl. We should try to get together. In fact, I should introduce you to my friend Nikos. He's the creative director of L'Oreal. I think you could be . . ."

"Where have you been?" Jim's arm snakes around my waist. "I'm afraid you're going to miss the soup course."

Damn. She was on the verge of saying something good. "Jim, this is Shelly Pine. We worked together in San Francisco . . . gosh, when was that exactly?"

"Seems like ages," Shelly says. "So nice to meet you."

"A pleasure." Jim smiles warmly. "We'll let you get back to your dinner."

"Oh, it's no problem . . ."

Jim starts to pull me away. "Yes, you eat, Shelly." I wink. "The food looks outrageous."

"Totally," Shelly agrees. "OK, well, we'll catch up later?"

"A pleasure, truly." Jim guides me away from Shelly and back toward our table.

Now I'm irritated. "Jim. We were in the middle of . . ."

"Your soup, Mac. Come on. I paid a hundred grand for this table. We might as well get some use out of it."

I stop, stand my ground. "Jim, she was going to introduce me to . . . someone. I don't know who. But that's major. She's a big deal. I thought you wanted me to come tonight to network?" I feel a little silly having a mini-tantrum like this.

"Networking is all well and good, Mac." Jim frowns, looking like a sulking little boy. "But I kind of hoped we'd spend five minutes together."

I can't believe what I'm hearing. "Jim? I don't understand. This is important. This is my career we're talking about."

Jim scoffs. "It's *always* your career we're talking about. I'm getting tired of it, to tell you the truth."

Yeah, I noticed. "Well, by all means, don't hold back."

"Mac. Don't do this here, please," Jim mutters through a forced smile. "This is not the place."

Right place or not, I've got to speak my mind. "I don't know what to say, Jim. It's like you're jealous of my career!"

"Some relationships have the other man. We have Mac's career. Come on. It's a party." Jim winks.

His cheerful tone isn't going to dissuade me. I'm pissed. "This is no joke, Jim. Don't wink." I cross my arms across my chest. I'm suddenly very cold. "I don't like this side of you." Yes, Jim Segal has the ability to make me weak in the knees. Yes, I could spot him in this sea of men in tuxedos, feel that little twist in my stomach, that little catch in my throat that I think must mean love. But the people you love are also the ones who can annoy you like no one else.

"This side?" Jim looks like he has no idea what I'm talking about.

"This possessive side. You bring me here, telling me it'll be good for my career, then you interrupt me when I'm catching up with someone who is in a position to help my career? So I can come sit by your side while you eat soup? A soup, let me point out, that I can't eat? Come on, Jim."

"I don't care for this particular conversation, Mac. I don't think it's wrong for me to expect you to be by my side."

OK. Calm down. "Sure, by your side," I agree. "In bad times. Or when we're just having fun. But not every minute of my life."

"Mac." Jim smiles, pained. "I truly do not feel like having this conversation right here, right now, with all these people within earshot."

"Neither do I, Jim." I pause. "You know what? I've lost my appetite. And somehow I'm just not in the mood for dancing. Maybe we should pick this up later?"

"What are you talking about?"

"I think you know." I squeeze past him, and stroll out of the crowded hall, the sound of my heels clicking on the marble floor almost like applause.

"OMG. You look incredible!" Shannon steps out from behind the podium where she keeps the reservations book, grips me by the shoulders, and looks me up and down. "You seriously look like a princess. And this fur . . . is it real?"

"Thanks." I can feel my carefully pinned-up hair starting to fall, and even though I've had a ten-minute cab ride to calm myself down, I'm still angry, my heart pounding so noisily I think everyone must be able to hear it. "It's a fake." I stroke the jacket. It *is* pretty incredible. "Don't throw paint on me, OK?"

Shannon laughs. "Theo's in the back. Last booth. He's going to feel very underdressed when he sees you."

"Please." I wink. "Who do you think dressed me up like this?" I make my way through the restaurant. The back booth is at once the most private and most public table in the house. It's tucked away by the door to the back garden, so it's almost impossible for any of your fellow diners to overhear your conversation, but it's also raised up a half step, so it's a little like being on stage. It's also the best table for people watching, and Theo is watching me, intently, as I weave among the crowd and make my way to him.

"I should have put on my tux." Theo stands and kisses me hello. "Sit. I'm getting you a drink, and you're drinking it." He signals to the waiter, pointing at his own glass and holding up two fingers. "You look amazing, PS."

"PS nothing," I tell him. "This look is a Theo original. I owe you."

"OK. Go. Tell me. What the hell happened?" Theo props his elbows on the table and cradles his chin in his hands, staring at me like a little kid. "This was supposed to be total fantasy night."

"I don't know."

Shannon appears with two flutes of champagne. "On the house." She slides the glasses toward us, then winks and skips away.

"She is the best." I take a grateful sip.

"Cheers." Theo toasts me. "And cheer up."

"I'm so mad." I didn't know this happened in real life—I literally have a bad taste in my mouth. "Jim got so . . . weird. I was in the middle of a conversation with Shelly Pine and he freaked. It was bizarre."

"So that's that? You walked out? You walked out of the Costume Institute Gala because your boyfriend was feeling possessive?" Theo sips his champagne. "It would take a lot more than a jealous boyfriend to get me to bail on that party."

"No it wouldn't," I tell him. "What's the point in being at a party if you can't talk to anyone? And especially at a party like that. I mean, this woman from Cover Girl, the one who was so bitchy to me in that meeting? She was there and I didn't even get a chance to schmooze her a little. What a wasted opportunity."

"Gosh, Mac. Slow down." Theo pats my hand. "Pardon my saying so, but I mean . . . there's a time to work and there's a time to relax. Devil's advocate: Maybe Jim's feeling a little neglected for a reason."

I am not expecting this reaction. "Do you think so? I wasn't . . . I was just making conversation. Jim works the room all the time. All the time. He's always working on the next deal."

"Yeah, but that's lame," Theo points out. "All work, no play, etcetera. Especially with this Cover Girl stuff. You've got blinders on when it comes to Cover Girl. You want it so bad it's like . . . scary."

"Shut up! You think so?" I consider this for a second. "I don't know. It seems like a double standard to me. If Jim was closing a deal, he'd spend fourteen hours a day on it, talk about it nonstop. You know he would."

"So you think he wants you as arm candy, and nothing more?"

"No. That's not it. That's not fair. Jim's a good man. I worry that he wants me to settle down and be his sidekick, though.

And I don't think I can do it." I drain my glass, my head suddenly swimming from the champagne.

"You don't *think*?" asks Theo. "Or you don't *know*?"

"All I know at this moment," I say, "is that this stupid bag is so small I could barely fit an emergency snack inside. So I'm starving."

Theo smiles happily. "It's like you're reading my mind, Mac Croft."

It takes forty-five minutes, two orders of tuna tartare, and one more round of champagne (this one with a plump little raspberry at the bottom of the glass) for me to start feeling slightly better. I don't need to talk; I need to gossip, so we spend most of our time covering the many celebrity sightings I've had this evening.

"Was she a little thing?" Theo asks, referring to a certain chipper, blond romantic comedy mainstay. "I bet she's crazy short."

"She is kind of short!" I'm howling with laughter, and I can feel the eyes of other diners on us, but I ignore them. "How did you guess? You know who else is short? Like, pre-puberty short? That guy . . . what's his name. From the Yankees?"

Theo rolls his eyes. "Goodness gracious, Mac. I think you'd know me well enough not to ask me about an athlete. What the heck do I know about *sports*?"

"Come on! He's famous. You know. He's got kind of a . . . I don't know. A square head? He went out with that actress. You know who I'm talking about!"

Theo dabs at his lips daintily with his napkin. "No ma'am, I don't. But speaking of sports. You remember those tickets I gave you? Those hockey tickets?"

I nod. "I do. You made me a hero with my agent. Who knew? She's been texting me about it all week. I owe you one."

Theo shakes his head. "Nope. You owe him one." Theo points toward the bar. "That guy. Shaggy brown hair? Brown blazer?"

"What do you mean?" I turn a little, trying to spot the guy Theo's pointing to.

"He's a hockey player. Please don't ask me what team, or what position he plays, or anything. Because I guarantee you I have no idea. But he lives in the neighborhood. He's a regular here. Anyway, he knows Nate, the bartender. And Nate and I . . . also know each other . . ."

"Wait. You and Nate?" I turn all the way around and get a good look at Nate. His pale skin is dusted with freckles, and I don't know how he can see out of his huge blue eyes with all those eyelashes. "You never told me."

"It's still . . . new." Theo grins naughtily. "Anyway, Erik, that's his name, he's the hockey guy. Erik Baer. He plays for the Rangers. Erik and Nate are great pals, because Erik always stops in for a drink after a game. And I guess they got to talking, and Erik had these tickets, and he gave 'em to Nate, and Nate gave 'em to me, and I gave 'em to you and, well, that's that."

When he's been drinking a little, Theo's Southern accent comes out in full force. "Gosh, that's nice of him. I should thank him."

"Send him a drink," Theo suggests. "His drink is a whiskey and soda. Only thing he ever orders."

I flag down Shannon, who hurries over and starts clearing the plates—which we've completely picked clean. "Do you want another round?"

"Not for me," I tell her. "Maybe some green tea?"

"I'll have just a drop of whiskey," Theo adds.

"Just a drop. Right." Shannon's smoky, throaty laugh cheers me even further. "Anything else?"

"Yes, actually. Tell Erik that Mac wants to buy him a drink."

"Shh!" I playfully kick Theo under the table. "Don't tell him that."

"Ouch!" Theo cries. "Those Weitzmans are like weapons."

"Kids, don't fight," Shannon scolds. "So, you're buying this guy a drink, yes or no, what's happening?"

"Yes," Theo says. "You are. And tell Nate I said hello, too."

She sighs. "It's like a soap opera in this place. I'll be back with your tea."

I fold my arms across my chest and give Theo a disapproving frown.

"What?" he asks innocently.

"What nothing is what." I frown.

"That doesn't even make any sense." Theo crosses his arms like mine, mockingly. "Anyway, lighten up!"

That's easy for him to say. "I have a boyfriend, lest you forget."

"Please." Theo scoffs. "Number one: you're having a fight with him right now, which means that technically he doesn't exist. Number two: I don't know who you're trying to convince exactly. Number three: you're buying a semi-stranger a drink to say thank you for a courtesy he showed you. It's hardly a big deal."

"I don't know if Jim Segal would agree." I reach into my bag and find my phone. Despite my pledge to never do so again, I turn the phone off, ignoring the blinking light that means I have a message. I deserve a couple of hours to myself.

* * *

When Shannon comes back around to ask if I want my third refill, I shake my head, hand over the top of my mug. "I think I'm set, actually. Maybe we should get the check?"

"No!" Theo interjects. "What happened to Erik?"

Shannon shrugs. "Don't shoot the messenger, man. I told him a beautiful woman wanted to buy him a drink." She glances over her shoulder at the bar. "Looks like he's a bit preoccupied."

Sure enough, he's seated comfortably between a blonde and a redhead, turning his head back and forth between the two like he's taking in a tennis match.

I'm yawning. I'm beat. "Forget it," I tell them.

Theo leans out of the booth and cranes his neck to survey the scene. "He's talking to Nate. Not that I blame him. He's an entertaining fellow, that Nate. But you told him a gorgeous, stunning lady wanted to buy him a drink, yes?"

"Those were my exact words." Shannon rolls her eyes. "But what do I know? I'm a hostess, not a pimp."

"Never mind, Shannon." I slide out of the banquette. "I'm running to the bathroom anyway. Then let's go. I'm not going to wait around all night. I was only trying to do the polite thing."

I've had three cups of tea, so I hurry through the crowd quickly. But on my way back, I'm in no particular rush . . . and I do have to walk right past the bar.

"Excuse me." I don't know what comes over me, but I actually tap this man, this *stranger* on the shoulder three times. Tap. Tap. Tap. Just so there's no confusion about who I'm talking to.

He spins around on his stool and comes face to face with me. Up close, he's big, a lot bigger than he seemed from across the crowded restaurant. His thick hair is all mussed, almost like a little boy's after a heavy nap, and it has a strangely endearing effect. He smiles, but I'm determined not to be charmed. "Well, hello." He's got the faintest trace of an accent that I can't quite identify. "Can I help you with something?"

"As a matter of fact, you can." I smile back. "I was just wondering . . . did you get my message? I was going to offer to buy you a drink."

"That was you?" He looks amused. "I did get your message."

"And did you think about maybe . . . I don't know. Responding?"

He grins. "I just figured, I mean . . . why trade two for one, you know?"

"Let me save you the bother then. Just consider the offer retracted."

"Retracted?"

"Retracted. I don't know how you explain your appalling lack of manners. I'm sure girls just fall all over themselves, sending you drinks in bars. But I was simply trying to do the gracious thing and say thank you for the hockey tickets you so kindly gave to our mutual friend Theo." I glance to my right and I can make out Theo and Shannon, watching me, giggling to themselves.

"You're Theo's friend. Oh, wow. He said you were pretty. Will you join me for a drink?" The blonde and the redhead stare at me icily.

Is this guy an idiot? I'm mad. Mad at Jim for fighting with me before the party. Mad at Jim for freaking out at the party. Mad at myself for not kissing Helen Conley Cox's ass when I had the chance. Mad at Theo for convincing me to drink three glasses of champagne. Mad at this cocky jackass for . . . whatever. "Look, friend of Theo. I don't think you understand. If you didn't want to come over for a drink, that's fine. It's a free country. I was only trying to do the polite thing. You could have at least . . ."

"Hey!" He holds up both his hands like I'm robbing him. "I'm sorry. Sheesh. You must really want this drink."

"Actually, I think I'll take off. Thank you very much for the hockey tickets. That's all I wanted to say." As I turn to march away, I stumble a little on these ridiculous heels. I curse—and think I overhear a none-too-discreet laugh behind me.

"What was that all about?" Theo's grinning as I storm back, tossing my clutch angrily onto the table. "Hey! That's a loaner! I hope you didn't scuff it."

Accessories are the furthest thing from my mind right now. "It's fine. Crocodiles are tough—so is their skin. Did you get the check?"

Theo strokes the bag like it's a wounded puppy. "Hey, what's the hurry? I saw you talking to Erik. He's nice, right?"

Nice? "Wrong. He's an arrogant jerk. I mean, who does he think he is?"

"Relax, Mac. Sit down. You're getting all flustered about nothing. Or about . . ."

"Don't even say it, Theo." I shoot him a look that says I mean business. "It's not funny."

"I'm just saying." Theo shrugs, all innocent. "You're awfully worked up . . ."

"I can't tolerate rudeness." I reach down and grab my little fur wrap. "It's a personal peeve of mine. Did you pay or didn't you? Do I owe you cash?"

Theo's still got my purse, but he's not looking at me—he's looking past me.

"Hello again." Guess who? He's followed me back up to our table, which must not have been easy, because he's got a crutch tucked under his left arm.

"Erik." Theo smiles. "Good to see you."

Erik nods his hello. "Theo. How you doing tonight?"

"Can't complain." Theo puts my purse down onto the table.

Erik gives us both a sheepish look. "I think your friend might have a complaint. Do you mind if I sit?"

Well, he is injured. I step to one side and he eases himself down onto the banquette where I was sitting.

"That's better." He sighs. "You're not leaving, are you? We haven't even been properly introduced!"

"Gosh, where are my manners?" Theo clucks his tongue disapprovingly. "Mac Croft, Erik Baer."

"Hi, hi." I keep my arms folded across my chest. "You know, I think I'm going to take off."

"Please don't do that." Erik smiles up at me. "I'm sorry I didn't come over sooner. You should tell Theo's boyfriend not to be quite so charming. I totally lost track of time."

"Speaking of time." I glance at my wrist but I'm not wearing my watch. The watch I'm usually wearing. The watch Jim gave me. "It's late. It's a school night."

"You going to turn into a pumpkin, Cinderella?" Erik winks at me. "I'm ready for that drink now and you're running out the door."

This guy has some damn nerve. "No, I've got to go. Thanks again for the tickets. I'll try to think of some way to repay you, I'm sure."

"Promises, promises, right Theo?" Erik laughs—and his laugh is as loud as his voice. It's annoying. "Can I get that in writing?"

I am not amused. "Theo, we're working together Thursday, right?"

"Don't go like that, Cinderella." Erik clasps his hands together, begging. "I can see I'm not going to get my drink tonight, but don't hate me."

"I don't hate you. I don't even *know* you."

Erik pats the seat beside him. "Stay, Cinderella. Get to know me. Buy me that drink you owe me."

"Mac, come on." Theo looks at me, pleading.

I have the weirdest flash of a memory—my two big brothers, picking on me. I am standing my ground. "Can't do it, boys."

"All right, then." Erik frowns. "You're a tough negotiator. I'll drive you home."

"Drive me . . . I didn't ask . . ." I shake my head. "I think I'll grab a cab. Thanks, though."

"Why wait for a cab? I'm right here, madam, ready to take you wherever your heart desires."

"Sorry." I shrug. "Mom and Dad always warned me about taking rides from strangers."

"Ouch." Erik presses his hand up to his heart. "I'm no stranger. We're all friends here." Then, in a more serious tone of voice, "Listen, seriously—why wait for a cab? Let me drive you home. My car's right outside."

"Haven't you been . . ." I point to our own empty glasses on the table. "Celebrating?"

He points at his leg. "Injured, remember?" He grins. "Diet Coke, all night long."

"How is the leg?" Theo asks.

"I'm supposed to keep my spirits up. That's what the doc recommends. So let me see you home. Your company will be good for my mood." Erik pats at his jacket pocket, then digs out his keys.

"I don't know." Across the table, Theo is mouthing something at me dramatically. It is late. And I am tired. Suddenly, I feel ridiculous. I'm standing here, the two of them are looking at me, waiting for me to say something. "Fine." I sigh. "Take me home. Please."

"Uh, Mac . . ." Theo slides the check toward me. "Dinner."

"One last favor?" I pick up my clutch. "Pick up the check?"

"Twenty-fourth, right?" Erik accelerates slightly and we glide through a yellow light. "Whew. Made it."

"Yes, Twenty-fourth." I've told him four times already.

"Nice neighborhood." Erik whistles tunelessly. The radio's playing, but it's turned down so low it's impossible to understand the chatter of the voices on the all-news station.

I nod. "It's nice," I agree.

"I don't live far, myself. Little further downtown. West Village. Love it. Been there for years."

I nod. "That's nice."

Erik drums on the steering wheel absentmindedly. "So, that Theo is a funny guy, right?"

"That he is."

"You know Nate? His boyfriend?"

I shake my head.

"He's a good guy. Maybe they're not boyfriends yet. Maybe I shouldn't jinx it, right?"

"I guess not."

"Yeah." Erik pauses. "Yeah. Well."

I squeeze my hard little clutch like it's a doll. We speed through another intersection, and another. "That's it, on the left-hand side." I point out my building. "Just over there."

"Yeah. Twenty-fourth. Like you said." Erik slows the car, pulls up right in front of the building. I can see the night door-man, Eli, dozing at the front desk. Dad would not be pleased. "So. Here we are."

"Home sweet home." I pause. Under normal circumstances, I can strike up a conversation with almost anyone, but for some reason I cannot think of anything to say to this guy. I feel strange being here with him. I feel nervous. I feel guilty, and I'm not entirely certain why.

"So, this is it, then." Erik grins at me.

"This is it," I agree. I want to get out of that car, run inside, and go upstairs and collapse into bed. So why am I still sitting here, in a stranger's car, with a stranger, making mindless small talk?

"I'd get your door for you," Erik says, "but my leg. You know."

"Oh, no, I know. Please. I'm not some kind of princess." I pause. "OK, well, thanks for the ride." I step out of the car, slamming the door behind me more noisily than I mean to. I sort of shrug sheepishly and cross in front of the car, waving to Erik and I step up onto the sidewalk. I can feel his eyes on my back as I stroll toward to the door, and though I'm trying to ignore them I can't. I turn around.

The driver's side window slowly lowers and Erik leans out of the car toward me. "So, listen, Mac Croft, friend of Theo, hockey fan," Erik says, suddenly, and very quickly, his words all running together. "Would you like to go to lunch tomorrow?"

"Actually, I gave those tickets to Francesca. My booker. Her husband . . . he likes sports or something. I don't follow hockey." I pause. "And as for lunch, I don't think I can . . . Isn't tomorrow a weekday?"

"So what?" Erik shakes his head. "Say you'll have a meal with me. Skip work. You still owe me, let me remind you. I never did get my drink."

"I'm not sure you understand. I'm not exactly . . . available."

Erik is quiet for a minute, a minute that seems to go on forever. I don't know why I don't say thanks and goodnight, go upstairs, and forget all about today.

"I'm not sure I understand." Erik repeats. "Actually, I do understand. I understand that I'm going to go home, and I'm not going to be able to sleep at all tonight because I'm going to be thinking about you, and kicking myself for not asking you out. Which is why I'm asking you out now. But now you're saying no. Though, I have to tell you I don't think I can take no for an answer."

I laugh. "You're going to have to, my friend. I am . . . involved. I am not available. I am indisposed, or whatever they say."

"Say yes, Mac. Come on. Yes. One meal. It's no big deal."

"One meal. Any meal."

Erik nods enthusiastically.

"Dinner." I say it before I realize what I'm saying. I think it before I know what I'm thinking.

"Dinner." Erik smiles, happily. "Even better. Tomorrow."

"I don't know what I'm saying," I tell him. "But yes, dinner tomorrow. I can have dinner with you tomorrow." I don't know how I'm going to keep this promise. But somehow, on some level, I know that I have to. I say my goodbye, and it comes out sounding more breathless, throatier, than I want it. As I turn to walk away, I have the strangest feeling, a feeling I can't quite describe, a feeling I can't explain, a feeling that's both totally alien and strangely familiar. Maybe I just need to get some sleep.

Nineteen

It's not a wakeup call. That horrible noise I hear can't be a wakeup call, because I'm not in a hotel. For once, I'm in my own bed. It's not as comfortable as Jim's custom horsehair bed, and the sheets aren't ironed to perfection the way they are at the Four Seasons, but it's my bed, and waking up in your own bed is a pleasure I for one will not take for granted. Unless you're being awakened by a horrible piercing screech. What the hell is that?

I push aside the thin cotton blanket and stand up, a little wobbly. Is it Irin's alarm? She once accidentally left it on while she was in Panama and I was in London, and the neighbors wrote us an angry note. I stumble out into the hallway. Oh, right. It's not an alarm; it's the buzzer. I hurry down the hall-way and pick up the telephone.

"Yes?" My early morning voice comes out in a croak.

"Miss Mac, a delivery for you." It's Harry, my favorite doorman.

"Can you bring it up, please? Thanks!" I hang up and yawn. It seems odd that Harry would call up so early—but then, what do I know? This has been my home for months now and this is the first time I've ever had the doorman call up.

I pad into the kitchen, where the oven helpfully informs me that it's eight o'clock, a lot later than I thought. In high school, on Saturdays (when I didn't have an early shift at the Porter House), I'd stay in bed until ten—now that seems sinfully late. I'm scooping the coffee into the basket when there's a knock at the door. "Coming!" I call. I hurry over, unlocking the door and pulling it open.

"Morning, Mac!" When Harry smiles, his entire face disappears into wrinkles, which makes him look more like a cartoon than a person. He's wearing his uniform—blue pants, white shirt—and holding a gigantic arrangement of yellow and brown orchids, the glass vase wrapped in cellophane. "I didn't think you were here! You're never here."

"I'm not usually." I smile.

He hands me the huge arrangement. "Well, I hope I didn't wake you. They just arrived and I didn't want them to die . . ."

"It's no problem, Harry. Thanks for bringing them up. Have a good one."

The vase is heavier than it looks, but I manage to maneuver it over to the marble-topped kitchen island. The cellophane crinkles loudly as I tear it off, digging through the transparent layers for the card, my name written tidily on the envelope. It strikes me that these flowers could be from one of two people. I find this thought unnerving.

Mac—I was / am / have been a fool. Forgive me, if you can. Jim

Before I can think this through I am going to need some coffee.

I've always been able to get some good, serious thinking done in the shower—maybe the act of massaging shampoo into my hair stimulates the brain? Sure, the shower here might have a tangle of Irin's hair clogging the drain, and it's nowhere near as luxurious as Jim's glass-enclosed steam shower (with heated floors and a little cedar bench right in there with you, in case you need to sit while you exfoliate the soles of your feet) but like the bed, it's my own. Be it ever so humble, as the saying goes.

How many showers have I taken here in my own apartment? How much time have I actually spent in this place? Being here alone feels great: walking down *my* hallway, drinking *my* coffee out of *my* mug, putting *my* flowers on the center of *my* mantel, showering with my bathroom door wide open, because I can. I'm mad at myself for not taking advantage of this when I can, for not relishing every second I'm on my own, not only in this apartment but also in the city. This is the grown-up, big independent girl life I wanted so badly, and I'm spending every second of my adulthood either working or being a dutiful girlfriend.

But I can't think about this now. I've got work. Conveniently, that means I can't think about Erik either.

"Hi, Sloane." I love caller ID.

"Mac. Back on the hometown turf. Glad I caught you. I'm transferring Francesca, OK?"

"Definitely . . ." I start to say, but before I can finish, Francesca is on the line.

"How'd it go at DVF this morning?" she barks.

"Hey Francesca. It was cool," I tell her. "What exactly were they casting? I'm still not sure I understand."

"Something Diane does with American Express or something? I can't remember. I think it's TV. What's that? What? Oh. Renee says that would be good for you."

"Renee's there?" The walk sign just started flashing, so I dash into the intersection, trying to get across Fourteenth Street before the light changes. "What's she saying?"

"She's gone now, Mac. Let's stay focused, OK?"

"I'm focused." I make it back onto the sidewalk in time to avoid being flattened by a cab rounding the corner. "Watch it, asshole!" I scream after him.

Francesca laughs. "That's my girl. A New Yorker now, huh? Anyway, I am calling for a *reason*. And you're going to love it. Are you ready?"

I check my watch for the millionth time, and think of Jim again, for the millionth time. The only communication I've had with him was a text message, to say thanks for the flowers. I can't bring myself to call him. I'm not ready, and I've got a lot on my plate already today. "I'm ready. I've got forty minutes before I'm supposed to see J. Crew."

"Can you get up to Cover Girl again this afternoon?"

Can I? "I can. Of course I can. I can't believe they want to see me again!" My heart starts pounding faster, and I'd swear louder. Nothing is going to stop me.

"Can the modesty, Mac. They love you. Everyone loves you. You are, as Renee might say, *chaud*." Francesca giggles. "Which reminds me. I'm mad at you."

"Mad? You're kidding, right?"

"Well, you're too busy now to come in and see your favorite member of the Delicious team. I get it. You're in demand, and that's a good thing. But today of all days? The day after the Costume Institute Gala? Please . . . I've looked at every single picture on style.com four times already. I need some dispatches from the front lines."

I sigh. "I'll give you the full rundown next time I see you. A sneak preview: guess who I stood in line behind at the bar?"

It's Francesca's turn to sigh. "I don't know if I can wait . . . anyway. I need a clue."

"Broadcasting pioneer. And tennis superstar."

"Dan Rather? And Martina Navratilova?"

I start laughing. "You work on that. I'll fill you in later, I promise." There's no point telling Francesca the disappointing truth about my big night out. I'd rather think about the people watching.

"I am holding you to that. I gotta go. I'll text you when I confirm a time with Cover Girl, OK? Be good, and check in after J. Crew."

Francesca hangs up, and I tuck my phone into my pocket. I can't quite believe it. I'm seeing Cover Girl today. Style.com and all the gossip sites and the papers are full of pictures of everyone from last night, including myself and Jim. This seems like too much for one person to think about.

Even the elevator at Bergdorf Goodman is fancy. I've never had occasion to come in here before—I usually only handle Balenciaga bags and Philip Treacy hats on set. The mirrored glass doors open silently onto a surprisingly dark hallway, and there, as promised, is the restaurant. I never knew there was a restaurant tucked up here, out of the way like this, but apparently this is where Mitchell Godfrey prefers to do his early-evening business. I'd have met him at the McDonald's in Penn Station if he asked.

"I have a reservation . . ." I start to tell the host, but then I spot Mitchell, at a big comfortable table by the window. With

Helen Conley Cox. I'm not thrilled to see her again, but it is kind of a relief; it means Mitch isn't just going to try to seduce me. Unless he and Helen get into the kinky stuff. "I see him, actually, thanks."

"Mac!" Mitch is in casual mode, his tie loosened, his sleeves rolled up to the elbow, his jacket hanging on the back of his seat. He shakes my hand vigorously. "So glad that you could make it. You remember Helen."

Helen nods at me regally, her blond and silver mane flawlessly hair-sprayed into place. "Mac, so nice to see you again. We missed you last night."

"Oh?" Mitch sits, gestures to me to do the same. "What was last night?"

"Mitch, come on now. The Costume Institute?" Helen picks up the unwieldy martini glass and takes a sip. "Mac was there. And then . . . she wasn't!"

I settle into the comfortable, velvet-lined chair. From my spot, I can see past Helen and through the window, out to the beautiful spring evening. I've had a great day, I remind myself: a fine meeting at DVF, an excellent meeting at J. Crew. The weather is great, I feel rested and ready for whatever happens. I'm even having a good hair day. "Helen, good to see you again. Sorry I had to run off last night."

"Nothing bad, I hope?" Mitch flags down a waiter. "What can we get you, Mac? I'm afraid Helen and I have a head start on you."

"Just a green tea, please," I tell the waiter.

"You're sure?" Jim toys with his glass, the ice tinkling musically. "It's almost six, you know."

"Tea's great. That'll do me. So."

"So." Mitch repeats. "Like I said, I'm glad you could make it today. Last minute and all."

"It's no problem. I'm in town for a couple of days, catching up on appointments. "

"Anything good?" Helen asks. She plucks a peanut from the dish of mixed nuts and pops it into her mouth. "Anything we should know about?"

Way back when, Francesca gave me some very sage advice—never speak badly about anyone in front of anyone else, and never tell anyone everything you're up to. To me, they're all clients; to one another, they're competition. "I always like getting out there, meeting people. It's one of my favorite things about this job."

"You've been working . . . almost two years now, right?" Mitch picks his Blackberry up off the table, glances at it, then puts it down.

"A year and a half. Quite a whirlwind. The time really flies, you know?"

"What do you like doing, Mac? You like the high fashion stuff? You do the runway? You prefer being in studio or out on location?"

Helen shakes her head like she's disappointed. "You're not tall enough for the runway, are you, Mac?"

"I've done a little runway." The waiter sets the steaming pot of tea in front of me. "I enjoy it. Generally, I think I'm just lucky to be able to do this for a living. It's a great job. It's hard work, but I wouldn't trade a minute of it for anything." I feel like a contestant in a beauty pageant. What's next—my vision for world peace?

"So, you like it all then?" Mitch chuckles.

"Sure, why not? I get to travel, I get to talk to interesting people. What's not to like?"

"I like your attitude, Mac. Count your blessings! That's the spirit. I bet your parents brought you up that way, didn't they?"

"Mitch, uh, did you hear back from Paul?" Helen checks her watch showily. "What about dinner tonight? Lever House?"

"Right, right. We'll get to that. Oh, actually, Mac, maybe you should join us for dinner?"

Paul . . . does she mean my Paul, Paul Anders, Paul the big boss? "Dinner? Oh, no, I couldn't."

"What do you mean, you couldn't? Come on. You models get to travel and see the world. Us suits get to have free dinners at fancy restaurants."

Helen isn't paying attention in the least. She's taken her Blackberry out, too, and is typing away on it with both hands. I don't know what to say. Clearly Mitch wants me to join him for dinner, and clearly I want to do whatever Mitch wants me to do, even if it does involve going to dinner with a woman who obviously hates my guts. As an added bonus, going to dinner with Mitch gives me an excuse to bail on dinner with Erik. I don't know what I was thinking, agreeing to that last night. Three glasses of champagne and I'll say anything. "You know, I am free tonight. Maybe we should get dinner."

Mitch claps his hands. "Terrific! You can entertain me with stories from the road. Like I said, us suits hardly ever get out of the building, you know."

"If you'll excuse me for one minute, Mitch, Helen." Even though I'm speaking directly to her, Helen doesn't even look up. Classy!

"Of course!" Mitch stands as I slip away from the table, and out into the hallway toward the ladies' room. I need a little privacy to make the two phone calls I've been putting off all day, even though I had plenty of time to make them. I need to call Erik to cancel dinner. And I need to call Jim and tell him . . . well, I don't know what I'm going to tell him, but I do know that I can't put this off any longer.

There's a huge, ornately framed mirror in the foyer of Jim's apartment, and I pause, examining my reflection for a second. The weirdest sense of déjà vu washes over me: a moment in some hotel I can't quite remember, in some city who knows where. I was only passing by, on my way out or on my way back, and in the unfamiliar place I at first mistook the mirror for a window, mistook my reflection for another girl. Who is that, I wondered, before the eerie realization: that girl, with the gaunt cheeks and sleepy eyes and pale skin was me. So much has changed since then. Changed for the better. I'm happier, I'm healthier, and even though every day is hard work, the days feel like a challenge, not a struggle. A challenge I've faced, a challenge I've risen to. Even tonight: I was on top of my game, chatting comfortably with Mitch, and even getting Helen to warm up to me. It's not phony, it's not slimy; it's work. Schmoozing is part of the job description. Ironically, this is lesson number one from the Jim Segal school of life.

"Mac? Is that you?" Jim hurries into the foyer, tipped off by the clatter of my set of his keys in the Hermes ashtray full of odds and ends he keeps on the console.

I won't be needing those keys again.

"It's me." I stand, arms folded across my chest and smile weakly at Jim. He looks worried. He looks . . . older. He's still his same, handsome self, dressed impeccably as ever in simple khakis, a blue button-down shirt with the sleeves rolled up over his arms, which are surprisingly tan considering it's barely summer. But even so, it's like he's aged five years in the twenty-four hours since I saw him last.

"Come in! Come here."

Jim takes me into his arms, and even though I know I should stand my ground, I kiss him. In that moment, his lips on my mine, his hands in my hair and on my back, at my waist and gripping my wrist, all is momentarily forgotten. I pull away. "Sorry I'm so late."

"I'm just so glad to see you, Mac." Jim takes me by the hand and leads me into the living room. The lights are turned low, and Mahler is playing on the stereo. Mahler—Jim's unwinding music. "Sit. Can I get you a drink?"

"I don't think so, thanks." I sink onto one of the two leather club chairs by the fireplace and watch Jim, busy at the bar.

"Did you close the deal tonight?" Jim drops a couple of ice cubes into a tumbler and pours something from the decanter into his glass.

"It was Cover Girl. Did I mention that?"

"You mentioned that," Jim says. "So, how did it go? You charmed them, didn't you?"

I laugh. "I learned from the master."

"Well, why are you sitting all the way over there?" Jim leans on the mantel, studying me thoughtfully. "This can't be good."

"Jim . . ."

"Wait." He sighs. "This is about last night. I was a jerk. I was . . . I don't know what I was. Something came over me. It's only because I like you, Mac, so much. I could . . . I mean, I want us to be together, truly together. No more of this one dinner here, sneaking away for lunch there. I'm ready for more."

"I know, Jim. I know you are. And you deserve it. You're the greatest. We have such a good time together. But I'm afraid that I can't give you what you want the most." There. Whew. I feel a hundred pounds lighter having said that. It's funny how these things work—sometimes you don't even realize that something is weighing you down until after it's not anymore.

"Don't do that." Jim shakes his head. "Don't say that. Come on, Mac. I think you owe me a little more than the classic Hollywood breakup scene."

"Ouch." I pull the Missoni throw off the back of the chair and wrap it around my shoulders. "No need to get ugly."

"I don't mean it like that. Sorry. I only meant . . . don't walk out on this, not now. We have so much fun together." Jim slumps into the chair next to me.

"We do." I nod. "We do have fun together. There's no denying it. I really enjoy spending time with you. The problem is that I don't have all that much time to spare. What I have, what I can give . . . it's not enough for you. Don't pretend it is, either, and don't pretend it could be, because we both know that isn't true."

"I can change, Mac. I can change. You'll see. I won't want as much. I won't ask you for so much . . ."

"That's the thing, Jim." I reach out and squeeze his knee. "You're a wonderful man. You shouldn't have to change. Not for me, not for anyone."

Jim swirls the ice in his drink. He takes a sip, leans back into his chair with a sigh. "So we're doing this, aren't we?" he asks after a minute.

* * *

The light's on. Did I leave the light on? Am I being robbed? I push my way into the apartment, drop my bag onto the floor. "Hello?"

"Mac! I'm home!"

I kick off my red Marc by Marc Jacobs patent flats (a present, from Theo, naturally) and shuffle into the kitchen, feeling utterly defeated, utterly exhausted, but weirdly pleased that Irin is home. The whole way here, in the taxi, I felt so alone; it's kind of nice to have some company.

"Howdy, stranger." Irin is sprawled on the living room floor, on her stomach, paging through a massive stack of fashion magazines, a glass of white wine on the weird, stained coffee table we salvaged from my folks' basement. "How was . . . China?"

"China, yes." Irin nods. "Was amazing. But so far, Mac! You don't know. Is late now, but my body is awake. I think I might come home and sleep, but then I feel awake."

"Nothing quite like jet lag." I sit on the floor, rest my elbows on the coffee table.

"Mac, the flowers? Where are they from? So beautiful."

The flowers. The arrangement Jim sent me this morning is on the mantel, where I left it, a beautiful and painful reminder that immediately brings the tears to my eyes. "That, Irin, is a long story."

Twenty

"Jim! Jim! Can I get a reading?"

My breath catches in my chest. What are the odds that the photo assistant on today's shoot would be named Jim? Why is it that the universe sometimes just screws with us?

"Sorry." This Jim is a scruffy kid with a faux-hawk and tattoos all over his neck, so the only thing he and my ex have in common is their first name. He hurries over to me, holds the light meter right under my chin, then calls out a stream of numbers. Even after all these shoots, and I still haven't learned all the technical things photographers do.

"Mac, right at me, please, look right at me." Alain Davis dresses like a skater boy, but scolds like a schoolteacher.

I'm in no position to insult the way he dresses though; I'm standing in Brooklyn Bridge Park, in the middle of a June afternoon, wearing woolly trousers, a black cashmere turtleneck, and to-the-elbow leather gloves with soft fur trim at the ends. That's the fashion game—you're always months ahead of reality. Thus, I'm dressed for a blizzard in the middle of a heatwave, and I've attracted quite a crowd of tourists, who have gathered to gawk at the spectacle of a fashion shoot right here in the most scenic park in Brooklyn.

"Good, Mac. That's it, Mac. So pretty, give me more, yes, that's it, all right!" Something about Alain's patter is vaguely pornographic. I glance at the watching crowd, hoping there are no kids around.

I feel like a moron, but sometimes that's part of the job description. Whether I'm sweating bullets in my woolen pants or swooning on set in a couture gown, my role is the same: to sell it. I hold my head up high, determined to do my best, even though I've sweat so much I'm starting to feel faint. It's a disturbing flashback to my pre–Dr. Gindi life.

"That's incredible, Mac. Incredible. I think we're good here."

Good, but not done; there are racks of fur stoles and sweaters, puffy vests and knit dresses waiting for me inside the motor home. There are so many looks on the schedule today that Danielle, the stylist, has brought along three assistants— poor Ricky is stuck inside, endlessly steaming, while Valerie and Katherine stay by my side constantly, keeping me lint and wrinkle free, and also hydrated, with ice cold bottles of water. Bless them.

"I think I've sweat off four pounds." I laugh. The three of us are slogging from the low, grassy hill where Alain is set up, which has a beautiful view of the harbor, to the motor home parked only a few yards away, but it's slow going.

"I feel like a lady-in-waiting." Valerie totters behind me, carrying the little wool capelet I discarded the second Alain gave me the all clear.

"I feel faint." I can't help laughing.

"Miss! Miss!" A woman about a dozen feet away is waving, flagging me down like I'm a taxi. She's jumping up and down enthusiastically like the crowds you see waiting outside the studio on the morning talk shows. I don't know why she doesn't just walk up to me; it's not like there are any barricades holding back the crowd. I wave back, smiling, even though I feel ridiculous.

"Can I take your picture?" The woman brandishes a digital camera. There's a guy standing next to her, he must be her husband, and he's turning bright red from embarrassment.

"Hang on a second, guys." She's still not coming any closer, maybe out of respect, so I walk toward the couple. They're definitely tourists—the fanny packs and bottled water are a dead giveaway. Clearly, they've heard that the views of lower Manhattan from this point in Brooklyn are spectacular, and I bet they've come in search of snapshots to impress all their friends back home in Illinois or Texas or wherever they're from. "Hi!" I shoot the two a winning smile.

"Oh my gosh, hi." The lady is smiling maniacally, her cheeks even redder from heat and nerves than mine. "I don't believe it. Hi!"

Sometimes crowds gather on location shoots like this. It bothers some of the other girls—once, I was shooting on the steps of the New York Public Library with this girl Imani and she shielded her face, waving away the onlookers like she was Princess Diana. But I don't mind. In fact, I kind of like the attention. The two of them both just sort of stand and gawk at me like I'm a painting in a museum. Up close, I see they're younger than I'd thought from her mom jeans and his receding hairline. In fact, I suspect they might be honeymooners.

I'm charmed by their big, warm smiles. There's something so sweet about the fact that they're this excited about seeing me at work.

"Are you . . . is this for a magazine or something?"

"It is," I tell her. "For *Glamour*."

"Oh my gosh, oh my gosh." The lady grabs her man's hand and squeezes it excitedly. "*Glamour*! I get that magazine! I can't believe this. Dave, honey, *Glamour*!"

Poor Dave nods. "Hi," he says to me, sheepishly.

"So, um." I better get this show on the road. "I've got to get changed in a second but did you want to take a picture?"

"I would love to!" She gets the camera into position and starts snapping eagerly, flash exploding—even though it's bright and sunny out. She'd make a terrific paparazzo.

"Oh . . ." I grin through the blinding light. "I thought maybe you wanted to take a picture . . . with me."

"Would you?" She grins at me excitedly.

I don't know why other models overreact about this kind of thing. Taking pictures is what we do for a living. One more picture is no big thing. "Of course!" I drape my arm around her shoulder and we mug for the camera. There's one flash, then another, then another.

"I think you've got it!" I laugh. "I have to get back to work. But have a great day!" I give them a wave and hurry toward the motor home, where Katherine is holding the door open for me. I climb the steps.

"There she is, the woman of the hour." Danielle is at the rack, examining our next look. "Are you holding up, hon? I know it's hot . . ."

"All in a day's work." I stand still as the assistants do their thing, unpinning and unbuttoning. I'm dying, but we're all working, we're all hot, and I'm just not a complainer.

"Mac!" Ricky waves to me from the back of the narrow motor home. "Your phone is ringing."

Ricky passes the phone to Danielle, who hands it to Katherine, who's kneeling at my feet unbuckling the ankle straps on my black Loeffler Randall booties. I can barely press the buttons on the phone because my arms are sheathed in these ridiculous gloves. I probably shouldn't take this call when I'm in the middle of getting undressed, but something clicks inside me. I've been on the road for a week, shooting a swim story in St. Maarten for *Self*, a fashion story in Miami for *In Style*, and the time away, the relative seclusion of anonymous hotel rooms and dinners with people I don't know all that well has been just what I needed. I feel like myself again, and I feel ready at last to take Erik Baer up on his offer of dinner. I only hope that's why he's calling now.

"Erik!" Even I'm surprised at how excited I sound.

"Hello, stranger." Even though we've only spoken once since I cancelled our dinner, while I was at the airport in Miami waiting for a flight, his voice sounds familiar. "You back in New York yet?"

"I am in New York," I tell him. "Brooklyn, to be exact." Valerie tugs at the fingertips of the glove on my left hand.

"Exotic. The model's life. I'm a little jealous."

"Where are you?" I ask him, switching hands so Valerie can get the other glove off.

"Just back from Toronto," he says. "Sitting on the sidelines, you know. Even if I don't take the ice, I've got to go support the team."

"Did you win?"

"They eked out a victory without me. Wouldn't even have been close if I'd been playing . . ."

"Modest. I like that."

"So, are you going to blow me off again? Let me remind you that about two weeks ago you told me, promised me, that you'd have dinner with me. I'm not letting you off the hook."

"Aren't you?" Valerie starts undoing the clamps that are all over the backs of my legs, pulling the trousers tight. As each one comes off, I can breathe that much more easily.

"I am not." Erik does sound determined. "I'm in New York, you're in New York, what about tonight?"

I'm genuinely conflicted. I am in New York, and I don't have any real plans—was hoping to catch up on my laundry, maybe see Theo later. I'm still raw from the whole Jim thing, and the reason I broke up with him was to devote my energy and attention to myself, right? Going out to dinner with Erik doesn't qualify as "me time." Then again, it can't hurt, can it? Maybe? "Tonight. Well, Erik, I have an early morning tomorrow." I'm shooting with Shelly Pine tomorrow, another story for *W.* I guess my networking efforts at the Costume Institute Gala weren't such a bust after all.

"You do turn into a pumpkin at midnight, don't you? I'm asking you to dinner, Mac Croft. I'm sure you're a charming conversationalist, but I bet we can wrap it up before eleven. What do you say?"

"I say fine," I tell him. "I say that sounds like a plan."

"This is my favorite restaurant." Erik smears butter across a piece of bread and bites into it happily. "Ask me why."

"Why?"

There's a twinkle in his eyes. "Couple of seasons ago? Broke both my clavicles. Like that." He snaps his fingers. "Couldn't lift my damn arms. And you know what? I sat right there at that bar, and the head waitress sat right next to me and fed me. Like a baby. Never complained, refused to take a bigger than normal tip."

"You're joking." I've never been to the Odeon before, but I've heard of it, of course—it's one of the most famous spots downtown, a big, noisy French bistro that's been a celebrity hangout since the eighties. It's a Wednesday night, but the place is packed, the high ceiling amplifying the sounds of conversation into a quiet, background roar that makes the cavernous space more intimate. We're surrounded by hundreds of other diners, but I feel like we're in a world all our own.

"Honest. This place is like a second home to me." Erik grins through his mouthful of bread.

"Your clavicle, your leg." I stab at the little mound of goat cheese, flaking it apart, playing with my food, despite everything my Dad ever taught me. "Hockey is dangerous."

"That it is." Erik sips his beer, his eyes boring right into mine. "Is something bothering you, Mac Croft?"

I put my fork down on my plate. I've barely eaten, and weirdly, don't have much of an appetite. "I should be honest with you, Erik."

"You should be," he agrees. "You should be honest with me. You should also run away with me." He winks.

"I'm being serious." I pause. "I'm still a little . . . I just ended a relationship. Not even two weeks ago. So, if I seem distracted, or you know. Defensive? That might be it."

Erik helps himself to a cherry tomato from my plate. "Let's take this one day at a time, what do you say?"

"What do you mean?" I'm starting to blush.

"I mean," Erik chuckles, "let's try to relax. Have a nice evening. We don't have to get married tomorrow. Can't two people have dinner?"

He's right, of course. Maybe I'm making too big a deal out of this—part of the problem with my last relationship was that we got too serious, too quickly. Who says I can't have a little fun? This realization is weirdly reassuring. I can feel my appetite starting to kick in. I've been putting off seeing Erik because I've been feeling so conflicted about Jim—but the reality is that the two don't have anything to do with each other. I can't treat Erik like he's Jim any more than I could treat Jim like he was Patrick. I don't even know this guy yet. Now I've got to figure out if I *want* to get to know him. "Yes," I agree. "Two people can have dinner."

Erik tears off another piece of bread. "So tell me about this shoot today."

"Not much to tell. You know how it goes."

"Tell me." Erik's smile is bright, unguarded. He's a big guy, with the physique of the professional athlete that he is, but when he smiles, he seems like a kid. "I want to hear all about it."

"Fine. Then you can tell me what's the story behind the bum leg."

His boyish smile dissolves. "It's a long story, Mac," he says simply.

"I'm in no rush," I say. I'm surprised how much I mean it, too.

"It's just up here," Erik says. Somehow he's managed to take my hand without my noticing—my hand in his, and it doesn't feel odd in the least. It feels . . . comfortable. Normal.

In the cab on our way here, Erik refused to tell me where we were going. The most he'd say was that he wanted to show me one of his favorite things about living in New York. And despite the fact that it's now past eleven, my self-imposed curfew for school nights, despite the fact that I've got a job tomorrow at nine, despite the fact that he'd assured me I'd be safe at home by now, I agreed to this errand. I want to see what it is that he loves best about New York. And, though I thought I would be, I'm not anxious to see our date end. I'm booked on a job in New Mexico next Monday, and the Rangers are heading into the finals; this might be our only chance to hang out together for a while. Not that I'm planning ahead or anything.

Erik had the taxi drop us on a quiet corner, on Fifty-eighth Street, a few blocks uptown from the United Nations. I haven't spent much time on the Upper East Side, but this particular stretch is all sidewalk and late night traffic. It's quiet out, and then it occurs to me—is this safe?

"Where are you taking me?" I try to sound amused, but I must sound nervous, because Erik starts laughing.

"It's safe, don't worry, Mac. Just come on up and take in this view." We're climbing some steps now, poor Erik hobbling without complaining on his crutch, and then we're on a wide, open plaza, tucked away up here right on the edge of Manhattan. It's dark so I can't quite make out the water, but I can see Queens, glimmering in the distance, across the East River, and the massive bridge high overhead.

"Wow." It's the only appropriate response. I had no idea there were secret little nooks like this in New York City. We're totally alone in this big, open space, the sounds of traffic from the bridge drifting down toward us. I let go of Erik's hand and walk toward the very edge, lean on the railing and look out into the night. "This is incredible."

Erik grins triumphantly. "I told you so."

I feel a little twinge of something—guilt, regret, I don't know what—thinking of Jim, washed over with the strong sensory memory of leaning on the railing of his balcony, taking in the view of Central Park, the wind in my face just like it is right now. I push the thought away. I don't want to think anymore; I don't want to be sad. I want to just be, enjoy this moment.

"What do you think?" Erik drapes his arm across my shoulders and pulls me closer. "It's amazing, right?"

"It's beautiful here. I had no idea."

"I'm just a guy from the middle of nowhere, Canada," Erik says. "I never saw anything like this. Hell, I never imagined anything like this. I never thought I'd think something like this, you know, the city, the lights, the bridge, I never though I'd think all this could be beautiful, but look at that. There's no arguing with this view."

He's so earnest, Erik; seeing the city through his eyes makes me love it even more. It's like I was always telling Jim—I don't need fancy watches and fur coats. The simplest things, a view, a moment, can be magical. Not that I'm dwelling on Jim or anything.

"You OK?" Erik sounds genuinely concerned. His sweetness, his attentiveness, somehow make me feel even worse.

"Fine, yeah. Thinking."

"You're a mysterious woman."

I'm surprised he doesn't press me, ask me what's on my mind, but glad he doesn't. I've only known this guy for a few hours, and here we are, standing together, comfortable in our silence like we've known each other for years.

"I've got to be up early," I say finally.

"No. No, don't say that."

"It's true." I walk away from the ledge and sit on a nearby bench. "I should be tired, too. I worked all day. But weirdly, I'm wide awake."

"Sometimes? When we're on the road?" Erik sits beside me. "I'll get back to the hotel. You know, exhausted, sore, totally beat. And then—I'm wired. I don't want to sleep. Sometimes I think it's because there's never any time, when you live on the road like this. Like I do, like you do. You're so used to not having any time to yourself that even when you're tired, beat, whatever, you stay awake, or I do, watching TV or talking on the phone or doing nothing. Just because I can."

"That sounds familiar." I nod. "I've definitely done that." Not five days ago, I was in St. Maarten, reading a two-day-old newspaper and watching some horrible movie on HBO at midnight, even though I should have been asleep. It's true, the feeling Erik is describing—I get possessive over my time. Even now; I should be home, getting into bed. Tomorrow belongs to *W* magazine, but tonight belongs to me.

"So, are we done here, then? Are we calling it a night?"

"No," I tell him. "No, we're not."

It was a little after midnight when we showed up Abbot's, and the post-post-dinner crowd had started to head home for the night. Now even the post-club-going crowd has come in, devoured their fries and desserts—the late night menu, I've discovered tonight, is a lot shorter than the regular dinner offerings—and headed out, and the only people left in the place, though it's still open for business, should anyone stumble in, are the staff, plus Theo, Erik, and I. It's almost four in the morning, and I'm doing a superb job of not thinking about the fact that I have to be at work in five hours.

"I don't know what I'm doing here." Theo sighs, plucks another fry from the plate, dips it halfheartedly into the little bowl of mayonnaise.

"You're visiting your boyfriend." It's late, I'm exhausted, and my faculties are all out of whack. I've gone this far—why not go further? I reach over and snag two fries for myself.

"True." Theo looks longingly in Nate's direction, but he's busy flipping the unoccupied bar stools up onto the bar so he can mop. "He works late, I work early. I'm never going to be able to make this relationship work."

"Try dating someone when you're on the road almost three weeks a month." I scoff. "It's a pain in the ass." Oops. I forgot, for the moment, that Erik is sitting right between us. I hope he doesn't take this the wrong way. I'm not talking about him, of course.

I'm not.

"I've got to get out of this line of work," Theo says glumly.

"Theo, you're the sharpest dressed man I know. Look at you." Erik shakes his head. "It would be a crime if you didn't work in fashion."

It's true—tonight Theo's wearing a crisp white button-down shirt, a yellow paisley ascot, slim khaki trousers, and velvet slippers emblazoned with his monogram.

"Zvi Zee is sucking all the pleasure out of it." Theo reaches for more fries. "Look at me—binge eating."

"I feel your pain, kiddo." I pat Theo's hand reassuringly. "He's not being dramatic, Erik. This Zvi guy . . . he's a weirdo."

"Theo, my friend." Erik sips his beer thoughtfully. "Sounds to me like it's time to go free agent. Get out on your own. You're probably much more valuable than you think."

"That's not a bad idea!" I slap the counter enthusiastically.

"Calm down over there!" Nate leans on the mop. "I don't want to have to ask you to leave."

"Mac, please." Erik drains his glass and sets it on his coaster. "You're embarrassing Theo and I. Try to control yourself."

"Shush," I tell him. "Theo, actually, that's not a bad idea. Why don't you just make the big break? Just quit? It's time to get out there on your own."

"That's easy for you to say, miss top model." Theo stands on his tiptoes, reaches over the bar and fills his own glass from the beer tap. "You're in demand. You're a star! I'm a nobody."

"You're the best, Theo. I know you could get work styling . . ."

"Yeah, for *Cat Fancy*, maybe. Nate! Can we get some more fries?"

Nate rests the mop handle against the bar and walks back behind the bar. He leans in across the countertop, whisking away the soiled, empty plate. "You all stop causing trouble!" He looks delicate, Nate, with his white-blond hair and his skinny arms, but he's got the firm, swaggering voice of a native New Yorker, loud enough to keep even the rowdiest bar flies under control. "Mac," he says, "can I get you something? Have you tried the brownie sundae? It's ridiculous."

"She can't eat that kind of stuff!" Theo interjects. "Bring her some fruit! Make her a fruit plate. Or a fruit and cheese plate."

"Shall I, Mac?" Nate cocks his eyebrow playfully.

"It's weird," I reply. "I am kind of hungry. But we just had dinner . . ."

"Actually, Mac," Erik points out. "That was about eight hours ago. So it's about time for another meal."

"Eight hours?" Fuck. I look at my watch. Fuck again. *The watch Jim gave me.* "Eight hours?"

"I'll get the fruit plate." Nate winks.

I might as well. At this point . . . "Actually, Nate. How about a bottle of champagne? For all four of us. On me."

"I'm done." Theo sets his glass down on the bar and yawns. "It is officially bedtime."

"Hate to break it to you," says Nate, nodding toward the window. "It's officially *breakfast* time."

Oh boy. He's right: outside the big plate glass window, I can see that the darkness of night is beginning to fade. I can even make out the sounds of birds singing. What was I thinking?

"I've got to go!" I stand, the legs of my stool scraping the tile floor noisily. The restaurant is spotless, now, and everyone else left long ago, but Nate and Theo and Erik and I have just been camped out, working our way through one bottle of champagne, then another, some more fries and my fruit plate. I reach for my phone to check the time, and the battery is almost dead. "Oh gosh." I'm starting to panic, my heart beating louder, and faster. I've got to get home. I've go to rest. I've got to shower, and wash my hair, and . . . what have I done?

"It's late." Erik stifles a yawn. "How about I walk you home?"

"Walk? Walk? Yes. Walk. That'll be faster than trying to get a cab, right?"

"OK, boys," Erik says, laughing. "I'm taking Mac home. You guys have a good evening. Or morning. Whatever it is."

Theo and Nate stand, too, and Theo rests his head on Nate's shoulder. "Bye Mac. Good luck tomorrow! Call me if you have any bright ideas about the future of my career."

We've been talking about his next step for the past thirty minutes or so, but at the moment the only thing on my mind is the future of my own career—which is far from assured if I blow this shoot tomorrow. Or four hours from now. Shit. I don't know what I was thinking.

"If you're coming, let's go." I undo the latch and push open the door, stepping out into the very early New York morning. It's funny—sometimes the city seems so overwhelming, so crowded, but right now it's empty, quiet, and the only sign of life is the singing of the birds. But I don't have time to stop and take it all in. I start almost jogging up the street.

"Hey, wait up . . ." Erik comes hobbling up along beside me. "I've got a disadvantage here."

"I'm sorry," I say. "But you don't understand. It's so late. I've got to get home, I've got to get ready, I've got to . . ."

"Easy, easy," Erik says. "Look, your place is about eight blocks away. We'll be there in ten minutes. Running there now is going to make things worse, not better. It's already late. Ten minutes is not going to make or break you."

He's right, though I'm still annoyed. I can't believe I would do something so irresponsible. What if I have dark circles under my eyes tomorrow morning? Or, in three hours, or whatever. "Fine. You're right." I slow down, and Erik falls in beside me, breathing heavily with the effort of pushing himself up on his crutches.

"You want my jacket? You're shivering."

It is cold, this early in the morning, and my flimsy Philip Lim minidress does leave me pretty exposed. "That would be great, actually."

Erik shrugs off his jacket and hands it to me. I pull it on.

"So, I kept you out a little later than I'd planned on tonight."

"You could say that." I know I'll probably laugh about this someday years from now, but at the moment I can't find any humor in this situation.

"I know you're mad, but I'm flattered. I seem to recall that you didn't even want to go to dinner. And now looks like you've spent almost the entire night with me." Erik grins, the little boy smile again.

"So you tricked me into staying out all night. You happy now?"

"You're trying to blame this on me? You're the one who ordered the second bottle of champagne. And dessert. And the one who made Theo tell us the saga of how he and Nate met."

"They're cute! Besides, I was . . . I don't know what I was doing. I don't know what I was thinking." I stuff my hands in the pockets of Erik's too-big jacket. We walk in silence for a couple of minutes, crossing the street against the light because there's so little traffic at this hour.

"That's not true," I say after a while. "I do know what I was doing."

"So do I," Erik says. "You were doing just what I was talking about before. You had tonight. You wanted it to yourself. No one understands that more than me."

"I'm tired of always being so responsible," I say. "I know I'll regret it when I show up for work but . . ."

"It's a drag," Erik agrees. "The late nights and early mornings. Hustling to make a plane, hustling because you're part of a team and everyone's counting on you. It's work, but it's not quite like a job, like a normal job. We don't get weekends off, we don't always get the holidays. So sometimes you've got to cut loose a little bit, be a little irresponsible."

"Something like that." It's true, what he's saying. I've done a damn good job of putting everything I have into my career. I deserve a couple of hours to myself. I'll find a way to get through tomorrow. Or today. Whichever.

"Well, I suppose this is it." Erik pauses.

I can't tell if we've made good time walking here or I'm just well and truly out of my mind. Either way. We're in front of my building. The sky is even lighter now, a rich blue that's streaked with purple and pink. I slip off Erik's jacket and hand it back to him—but I'm cold still, cross my arms and rub them for a bit of warmth. I need to get inside, I need to face this day, but I'm not quite ready. I've spent the past nine hours with Erik, and I'm not tired of his company. I could easily invite him in, drink coffee and talk to him until we both just fall asleep from exhaustion. But not tonight. Another night. When, I don't know. But there will be another night. I can feel it.

"I should run. Thanks for seeing me home."

"Thank you, for a lovely evening. You know, I'd love to do it again sometime. Sooner rather than later."

"Well . . ."

"I know. You're still a little raw from your last relationship. I get it." Erik leans in closer. "But I don't think you'd have stayed out all night long if you weren't just a little interested in seeing where things might go."

"You may be onto something." It's one of those moments, those pivotal moments that come along every so often in life— I've got to decide what to do, and I don't feel equipped to make this decision right now. "Let's do it again. Soon." That last word slips out, but it's the key. I'm not ready, I am ready. I don't even know anymore. But I can admit to myself what was evident even a couple of weeks ago, when this guy was nothing more than a stranger driving me home. There is something between us.

"Oh. Soon. Good. How about . . . what's tomorrow? Or today? Today's Thursday? How about Saturday?"

"Can't do it. I'm leaving for New Mexico on Saturday afternoon. I'm back . . . uh, Tuesday afternoon, though. I think. How about Tuesday?"

"Shoot. Can't. I'm leaving Tuesday for a week. Shit."

I can't help laughing. "So, I guess it's a good thing we had tonight. Looks like it's going to have to tide us over for a while."

"In that case, well." Erik leans closer, takes my chin in his big, calloused right hand, and pulls my face closer, right to his. He's smiling, that same naughty, boyish smile, and then my eyes are closed, and he's kissing me, his lips surprisingly soft on mine. Then he's got his arm around my waist, and has pulled me closer to him, and his other hand is on the back of my neck. His tongue is hot and thick, and somehow everywhere, in my mouth, on my neck, near my ear. It feels electric, almost dangerous, his stubbly chin grazing my skin, his calloused palms on my wrists.

We stop. I breathe in the crisp morning air. I look up at Erik, who's still holding me close to him, which can't be easy considering he's standing on crutches. "I ought to go," I tell him.

"I guess that kiss will have to last me for a while." Erik smiles. "But I'm a patient man, Mac Croft. I will be waiting."

"I'm glad to hear it." I hug him, quickly, resting my cheek against his shoulder for just a second. "I've got to go." I pull out of his embrace and dash away, pushing through the glass door of the lobby quickly, before he can call out to me to wait, because if he does, I know I will, and if I do . . . well, I don't know what will happen next. I jab at the elevator button, and the car is already there, so the doors open immediately. Before I step inside, I turn to my right, and Erik's still there, alone in the pale, very early morning light, watching me as I disappear back into my real life.

Twenty-one

I feel slightly more human after a shower. At least, I feel more human while I'm in the shower, warm, alive, clean. But now, tiptoeing around the apartment and trying my best not to disturb Irin, I am starting to feel sleepy. I brew some coffee, wincing while the machine does its work. I never realized before that our coffee maker is kind of noisy.

I can't stop yawning, deep yawns that make my whole body shake. But I can't give in. It's too late now, or too early now; if I try to take a nap, I don't know if I'll wake up, and I can't risk anything going wrong today. I just need to keep myself busy for a little while. Then it'll be time to get dressed and go to work. I need to talk to someone. That will wake me up. And I only know two people who will possibly be awake this early, so I dial the number.

"Hello?"

I can picture Mom, still in her nightgown, her robe knotted loosely around her waist, her hair pulled back in a no-nonsense ponytail, making her own pot of coffee in the kitchen I know so well I could navigate it with my eyes closed. "Hi, Mom."

"What's wrong?" Suddenly, her voice is clear, alert.

"Mom." I laugh. "Nothing's wrong. I'm calling to say hi."

"Oh thank God." I can hear her blowing across the top of her coffee. "Melody. What's going on? Where are you?"

"Home, right now. I've got a job in a little while, here in the city, but I'm up early." A little white lie won't hurt. I don't feel like trying to explain that I'm up late, not early.

"Up early. Just like your mother. Your dad's in the shower. I'll put him on when he's out."

"Leave him be," I tell her. "There's no big news to report or anything. I just wanted to check in."

"There's certainly nothing to report here. Oh, wait! Yes there is. Your brother Teddy? He's bringing a friend to dinner on Saturday. A friend! A girl. I put two and two together—a girlfriend."

"A girlfriend? Teddy's bringing a girl . . . home? Wow. That's huge!" Teddy's the family ladies' man, but he's never been serious enough about any of his many loves to bother bringing them over to meet our folks. Until now. This must mean something.

"Your father's thrilled. He's pretending to be cool about it, but you know your dad. Nothing would make him happier than you kids getting married, settling down."

"I could have gotten married yesterday," I say. "I was dressed for it. The ugliest wedding dress you've ever seen, Mom, seriously."

"My little girl's gone high fashion, I see. I suppose once you've walked the runway, a normal wedding dress seems a little boring."

I tuck the phone between my shoulder and my ear, and fill my own coffee cup. "Hardly. If you could see this dress, you wouldn't be defending it. I looked like a cross between a Barbie and a drag queen. Rhinestones everywhere."

"Now, Melody. Some girls like a little sparkle." She pauses. "What else is going on? How are things with you and Jim?"

Right. I haven't broken the news to Mom yet. "We're . . . well, actually, Mom, Jim and I aren't . . . we're not . . . together anymore."

"Oh no!" She sounds upset. "Melody, what happened?"

"It's a long story, Mom. It's nothing bad, it's just . . ." I wish I could sum it up easily. "I just don't think we were right for each other. Or. We're at different places in life. I've got my career . . ."

"Melody." I can practically hear Mom shaking her head over the phone. "Your career?"

"What? Did I say something wrong?" I'm trying to stir soymilk into my coffee as quietly as possible.

"I just want to be sure that you're not putting off too much for this career. Look how much you've missed."

"What do you mean?" I settle into the most comfortable part of our old, overstuffed couch, knees pulled up to my chin.

"There's college, for starters. And holidays, and special occasions, and just seeing your family on a regular basis. I like Jim, I do. I think maybe he's a bit old for you, but that's my opinion. I hate to hear you giving up on anything else for your career."

"It wasn't only my career, Mom." I don't think it was. It was part of it, but not the biggest part of it. Now that I've had a couple of days to think it over, it's become clear to me that Jim and I were never going to make it. I don't think we were doomed, necessarily. I think it's probably for the best, though, that I ended it. It would have happened anyway. "It was time. I probably need some time on my own."

"On your own?" Mom pauses. "If you think that's best."

"I do." It sounds reasonable enough right now. Me, on my own. Of course, that doesn't necessarily account for the fact that not two hours ago I was standing on the street, in the middle of the night, kissing a stranger. "I've got a lot going on at the moment, and a lot of plans, and . . . you know."

"What's going on, at the moment, then?" Mom wants to know.

"Well, don't get excited because nothing has actually happened, but I've had some meetings with the people at Cover Girl."

"Cover Girl? Melody, that's fantastic! Sam! Melody's on the phone. Oh, honey, your father is going to be so excited."

"Mom, I told you . . ." I hold my phone away from my ear for a second, checking the time. "Nothing is set in stone. All we've had is one meeting and one dinner. It could mean nothing."

"Sam!" Mom calls out, louder this time.

"Mom, please. Don't get Dad all worked up about nothing. Which is just what it could be. And don't put him on—I've got to run. Tell him I said hi, though?"

"Do you have to go? Already?" Mom sounds disappointed.

"I do, Mom. Shooting for *W* today. Uptown. It's this photographer Shelly, who I worked with in San Francisco."

"Melody, I can't keep track of all your comings and goings, you know that . . ."

"Well, I met her in San Francisco. She's a famous fashion

photographer. She's nice. But she might not be that nice if I'm late, so I ought to go get ready."

Mom sighs. "OK. You're in a rush. I do wish, though . . ."

"What's that Mom? Is something wrong?"

"No, nothing's wrong. But we miss you. We miss seeing you, having you around. You can't come to dinner on Saturday, can you? Because I know your brother would love it if you showed up. . . ."

"I can't do it, Mom. I'm leaving for New Mexico that afternoon."

The line is quiet for a minute—a long minute, and I almost think I've lost the connection. "No, you can't do it, can you?" Mom says at last.

"I'm sorry." I don't know what else to say.

"Don't be sorry, Melody. I can't help wishing things could be different. But they're good the way they are. Aren't they?"

Are they? Are things good? I never get to see my family. I just ended the most serious relationship I've had to date. I'm absolutely exhausted, dying to crawl into bed and sleep the day away. But she's right. Things are good. There's so much that's good—work, my friends, my life, my success. One late night, one missed family dinner. How can I choose?

"Yeah, Mom. Things are good. But I've got to go."

"OK, Melody. You go. I love you."

I'm in such a hurry, and half asleep too, that I hang up the phone before I can tell her that I love her too. But I know she already knows that.

It's too bad we're shooting inside today, because this is one of those too-beautiful-to-be-believed days: the purple sky of the

early morning has cooled to a rich, deep blue, utterly cloud-
less, and bright with sun. There's a gentle breeze whispering
through the branches of the trees, enough to cool you down
if the strong sun feels too warm. The air even smells clean,
tinged with a hint of flowers, and fresh laundry, though that's
because there's a Laundromat at the end of Shelly Pine's block.
I double-check the address in my phone once more—it's #112,
and I'm standing right in front of it. It's a massive mansion,
with a heavy iron gate painted a glossy black. The house has
big bay windows, and ivy climbing up its gorgeous façade.
How fitting—the quintessential summer day, spent inside the
quintessential New York townhouse.

I swing the heavy black gate open, and climb the steps to
the front door, careful not to spill my coffee. I am going to
need lots of caffeine to get through today without completely
losing my mind. Even the doorbell is grand: I can hear it echoing deep within the house seconds after I press the illuminated
button.

After a minute, the door flies open. The doorway is so tall
that Shelly—a tall woman, with a big halo of frizzy red hair—
seems small, like a little girl.

"Mac, Mac. So good to see you." Shelly kisses me on both
cheeks, pulls me into the house. "You didn't have any trouble
finding the place?"

"No, Shelly, it was fine. Gosh, your place is beautiful!"

It is. The parlor floor has a big, open foyer, with marble
floors, lots of pictures in gilded frames, and a glittering crystal chandelier overhead. A graceful staircase winds up into the
house, the stairs lined with elegant oil paintings of horses and
gray-haired men in old-fashioned clothes.

"Oh, thanks," Shelly says, scurrying into the drawing room.

"It was my mother-in-law's. It's a little fancy for my taste, but what can you do?"

I follow her into the room, which has low leather sofas and built-in bookcases crammed with books and tchotchkes.

"Come on back, Mac, come on." Shelly beckons to me with her finger like I'm a stubborn dog. "It's a big house for the two of us, but it's a nice place to shoot. Tons of light in the back."

Tons of light, and tons of space. This place is incredible—we cut through another room lined with books, then through a narrow hallway that runs past the kitchen, and then I see what she means by light. We're standing in an atrium, with double-height ceilings and a huge glass wall, the sunlight spilling in.

"It's chaos," Shelly says, loudly. "But that's par for the course, right Mac?"

Chaos, indeed: A couple of assistants are rigging up a background front of the room's exposed brick wall, Shelly is consulting with a woman I vaguely recognize, and two other assistants are organizing a messy corner that's clearly going to be the dressing room today, for me . . . and for the three male models who are lounging around on some folding chairs. Huh.

"Hi." I give the guys a friendly wave and set my coffee down on a table.

"How's it going." One of the guys nods in my direction. "I'm Evan."

"Hi. Mac."

"I'm Jake, and this is Christian." Even though they're not even all the same race, the three of them look eerily identical, in that way that so many male models do.

"Hi guys."

"They're doing makeup back there," Christian points toward the hall I just came through.

"Great." Then I get a closer look at the racks. Gowns. Long, elaborate gowns, some with feathers, some beaded. I start to piece it together: fancy gowns, male models. What a relief. I can picture how this story is going to work, and it's going to be an easy day; me, in my party best, swooning in the muscled arms of these three boys. There are certainly worse ways to spend a day. And I'm so tired, I'm seeing spots. Leaning on a bunch of hunky male models is about all I can handle right now. "I guess I'll go get into makeup, then."

I feel like a princess in some cartoon movie. I'm wearing a long, slinky Cavalli gown, scarlet red and covered in crystal beads, strolling through this beautiful, brightly lit space toward a trio of handsome tuxedo-clad suitors.

"Mac." Shelly studies me carefully. "That's good. You look good."

I was right—the lady who looked familiar did for a reason: It's Laurie, the same stylist I worked with last time I shot with Shelly. Oh, of course—she works for the magazine. She's as deadpan as I remember her (she referred to the dress I'm wearing right now as "an STD waiting to happen") but she's fun. Despite my almost blinding exhaustion, this whole job has been fun so far: the makeup artist was cracking me up, Laurie's hilarious too, I like working with Shelly, and I'm looking forward to working with the boys, even though I'm usually pretty skeptical about male models—they love to hog the mirror, and the camera, and are generally bigger divas than the girls.

"I can't take the credit." In these Prada heels, I'm towering over everyone, including Shelly. "It's all Laurie's doing."

"Please." Laurie puts her sunglasses over her eyes. "My styling. Your DNA."

"So, today." Shelly grabs my wrist and pulls me toward a folding ladder. "You're going to be here. And the boys are going to be here." She points. "Boys. I need the boys."

The other models hurry over. Laurie grabs them each by the shoulders, sizing them up carefully, plucking at an uneven pocket square, picking off barely visible specks of lint.

"Boys," continues Shelly. "Stand here. And here. And here. There. Good." She's got the boys where she wants them, stationed around the perimeter of the ladder. I don't think I like where this is going. "And Mac, you climb up there." She points to the top of the ladder.

Climb. In these shoes. "Up there?" I nod. "Got it."

"Give me some Polaroid." Shelly's warmed to me, but when she talks to anyone else, she barks. And people listen. One of her assistants dashes over, offering the camera like it's a sacrifice to a vengeful god.

"Shoes off, Mac." Laurie frowns, thoughtfully. "Hold them in your right hand, both in one hand."

That makes things a little easier. I slip off the shoes and hold them as instructed. One of the boys steadies me as I step on the first rung, and then the second. This isn't so bad.

"Higher please, Mac," says Shelly patiently.

"Keep going, girl," adds Laurie.

One more rung then. So, I'm not lounging on some chaise, surrounded by gorgeous men. It could be worse. At least the caffeine has kicked in and I'm thinking a little more clearly. I can do this. It's seven shots today. Not a short day, but not the longest of my life. I can do this. I have to do this. There's no choice.

"Good. That's good," says Shelly, her face hidden by her big camera.

"Boys, in more please." Laurie studies them dispassionately, gesturing with her hands. "Closer. Closer."

"That's it. Perfect," says Shelly. "Now jump."

What did she say?

"Jump, please." Shelly says it again, and this time it's unmistakable. "To the ground. Just right there."

Jump? Off of a ladder?

"But the shoes, hold onto them, steady," Laurie chimes in.

"Just jump, please." Shelly's voice leaves no room for argument.

All of a sudden, I don't feel asleep at all. I feel wide-awake, and panicked. This woman wants me to jump off of this ladder and to the ground, in a party dress, and she's acting like it's a perfectly reasonable request. Like there's absolutely nothing out of the ordinary. Jump. I'm all dressed up, now I have to jump. In a way, it's fitting. It's the story of my life.

I jump.

It's possible that my ankles are broken. Seriously. We've moved on from the ladder setup, and now I'm leaping into the air, the train of my ivory Dolce and Gabanna dress fluttering.

"Great. Wonderful." Shelly's pleased, but still all business. She's a lot more involved in this shoot than our last, maybe because we're on her home turf.

"We're ready for the next look when you are." Laurie's sitting on the ground like a kid, watching me. "Whenever."

"I think we're done here." Shelly hands the camera to one of her assistants. "Let's move on."

Wonderful. I can't imagine what torture lies ahead. "Sounds good." I don't bother putting on my Giuseppe Zanotti heels, just walk in bare feet back to the corner where Laurie's assistant Rachel is waiting.

"How you holding up?" Rachel looks concerned. She's possibly the only person on set today who's deduced that jumping from a ladder isn't the most comfortable thing in the world.

"I'm holding up." I turn and to let her unzip me. She does, and I step out of the dress and into a robe.

"Sit for a minute." Rachel pulls out a metal folding chair. "I'll check with Laurie about the next look."

I don't need her to tell me twice. I cinch the robe tight and collapse into the chair. I'm sort of hidden behind the rack, which suits me fine, since I'm so tired I need a minute to clear my head, focus my thoughts, otherwise I have no idea how I'll get through the two looks or three looks or however many looks we have left to do. But I can't resist the urge to multitask. My phone's in the pocket of my little cotton cardigan, which is lying on the floor in a heap. I dig it out and scroll through my text messages. I've got two from Theo, and one from Francesca. *Call ASAP.*

That's interesting. It's by far the most urgent-sounding message she's ever sent me, so I do as instructed and dial the main number at Delicious.

"Delicious Models."

"Sloane. Hey." I can barely get the words out—I am *tired*. "It's Mac."

"Damn, woman. You sound rough. Hold on. I'm transferring you to Paul."

"Wait, Paul? I'm calling for Francesca."

"No, you're not," Sloane says. "Trust me."

The line goes quiet before I can say anything else, then starts to ring again.

"Paul Anders' office."

"Hi, Stephanie." Out of nowhere, I remember Paul's assistant's name—thankfully. "It's Mac Croft."

"Oh, good. He's waiting for your call. One sec."

"Wait, Stephanie. What's this all about?"

"Just a sec." She puts me on hold.

"Mac Croft." Even over the phone, Paul's seductive—a born charmer.

"Hi Paul." My voice sounds shakier than I want it to be, a combination of exhaustion, too much caffeine, and confusion; I rarely talk to Paul, and have never been on the phone with him before.

"Mac, my girl. How's it going? What are you up to right now?"

"I'm shooting. With Shelly Pine."

"You in the city? You are, right?" Paul starts laughing. "You're at Shelly's house, aren't you?"

"I am!"

"Jesus. That place. Ask her about her mother-in-law," Paul adds in a tone of voice that makes it clear to me I most definitely should not. "Anyway. Hey, listen, I'm going to put you on speaker, OK?"

What can I possibly say? "OK."

There's a pause, then the crackle of static, so Paul sounds far away. "Mac, you there?"

"I'm here!" I tell him.

"Good. Renee's here. So is Francesca."

"Hi Mac," they both say, in unison.

"Hi, everyone . . ." I don't know what to say. Am I being fired? A midday conference call—it's unprecedented.

"Mac."

I can almost picture Paul, leaning back in his Aeron chair, feet kicked up onto his big, glass desk.

"Mac," he continues. "Don't worry. This is good news. As you know, we run a tight ship here. We've got tons of different girls, everyone's doing their own thing. I trust that to Renee and Francesca and the experts. And this was their idea. But you're working like crazy, you're all over the newsstand, we're only hearing good things. So effective immediately, we're moving you up to our next division."

Wow. I don't know how to respond. "That's great! Thank you so much . . ."

"Moch, you wouldn't believe the response to your ad. Gillette? In Europe?"

"Looks like you've convinced millions of European women to shave under their arms, Mac." Paul chuckles. "That's no small feat. Well done."

"Wow. This is so exciting. I'm so . . . Thank you, all of you. This is fantastic." I'm babbling, but I'm overwhelmed. This is the most tangible evidence yet that my hard work is, in fact, paying off.

"That's nothing," says Paul. "Renee and I just had lunch with Mitch and Helen, and we shook hands on it and everything. Congratulations."

I'm so tired I'm not entirely confident that I'm not hallucinating. "What?"

"You got it, Mac! Cover Girl!" Francesca claps her hands together happily.

"You're kidding."

"Now, Moch, this is going to change things a lot for you. This you won't notice, maybe, but we're raising your rates . . ."

" . . . and your schedule just got a lot crazier," adds Francesca. "I know you're leaving this weekend, but the Cover Girl people are going to want you almost immediately, not next week, but the following. I'm already putting out the word; you're only available for covers and features right now."

"And the covers, they'll all be Cover Girl makeup, from here on out," Renee points out. "You and Cover Girl—you're one now. You're a Cover Girl. So, you must be on covers." She laughs.

I'm swooning, or fainting, or something. This is all moving too quickly. "I don't understand. What? When did this . . ."

"There's nothing to understand," Paul says. "Celebrate. Go out to dinner. Have some fun. You're on your way. This is all great news."

"It is. It is." I'm nodding, clutching the phone in a death grip, and have totally tuned out everything that's happening around me. "This . . . I don't know what to say. Thanks so much for this, all of you." I'm starting to tear up, and I can't tell if it's my weakened state or genuine emotion. "This is incredible."

"I'm taking you off speaker." Suddenly, Paul's voice is loud and clear. "Mac, kid, we're all so proud. You've done good work for us, and you've earned this. And trust me. This is only the beginning. We'll talk to you later."

I stuff my phone back in the pocket of my sweater and sit, staring at the rack of clothes in front of me. What's just happened?

"Hey, Mac." Rachel has returned, clutching a diamond necklace and frowning. "I've got some bad news."

"Hm?"

"Gosh, are you OK? You look . . . do you need some coffee or something?"

"No, thanks." I shake my head. "I'm fine. What's the bad news?"

"Laurie wasn't crazy about that Carolina Herrera look. So she wants to add a shot. Which means you've got four more, not three. I'm sorry."

"Don't be sorry." I'm still dead tired, so exhausted I'm shaking. But something has changed. Actually, everything has changed. I feel invincible. "I can handle it."

"You're sure?" Rachel smiles down at me, genuinely concerned.

"Suddenly," I say, "I feel like I can handle just about anything."

"I can't believe you wanted to come back here!" Theo stirs his tea. He's swearing off booze tonight, or so he claims. "Honestly, we spend so much time here, maybe I should quit working for Zvi and get a job waiting tables?"

"I don't think it's a good idea for you and your boyfriend to work in the same place. It'll kill the romance, I guarantee it." I sip my own tea—herbal. The last thing I need right now is more caffeine. I'm on such a high, I can't stop jiggling my legs. I kept the big news to myself on set, but the second we wrapped, I called Mom and Dad. And Jim. I figured I owed him that at the very least; I don't think I could have gotten as far as I have without Jim in my corner. Things might be tricky between us at the moment—Jim was happy for me, but there was a twinge of sadness to his voice that he couldn't disguise—but I hope one day we'll be friends, real friends. I think it'll happen. These things take time. Mom was thrilled, of course. Not exactly jumping up and down screaming, but I know she's happy for me, even if she doesn't entirely understand what this means for me.

"I don't know what I'm going to do, I honestly don't." Theo frowns into his steaming cup.

"I have an idea." And I do. The Jim Segal school of business has taught me many things, and I've been turning this plan over in my head all afternoon. "I know of a job."

"For me?" Theo looks up excitedly. "You don't. Tell me!"

"What if you were able to work with a good friend, every day? Someone who knows and trusts you, someone you know and trust, and more importantly, someone you like? What if you got to travel, but didn't have to be on the road all the time, and weren't schlepping trunks of clothes for Zvi but just . . . coordinating things. Details, itineraries, schedules." My phone buzzes; it's a text message from Francesca. *Elle, Monday the 27th. Cover.* In my exhausted, delirious state, I can barely process any more information.

"That's the dream, Mac. To have a job I love, working with a normal human being. But how am I going to get this fantasy job?"

"Easy." I lean back into the banquette and smile right at him. "Come work with me."

Theo cocks his head sassily. "What are you going on about, Mac Croft? I'm cute as a button and all, but I'm hardly model material."

"You would make a terrific companion though. Assistant. Friend. Personal stylist. Emergency shopper. Confidante.

Things are about to change for me." I pause for effect—of all the people I know, no one will understand what this means more than Theo. "I'm the new Cover Girl."

The sound that comes out of Theo's mouth is unlike anything I've ever heard—so high-pitched I bet dogs all over the neighborhood are stopping in their tracks, looking around nervously. As it is, every head inside Abbot's swivels in unison, eighty pairs of eyes fixed right on the two of us. "Stop. Stop. You're kidding. That's all. You're kidding. You must be trying to hurt me. Mac, why would you toy with me like this? Oh, you're so bad."

"Honest," I tell him, pushing my cup aside and propping my elbows on the table. "Dead serious."

"OK, first of all? That's amazing. You're amazing, that's amazing. You deserve this, girl. I am so proud. Seriously." He starts laughing. "Gosh, I swear, you were so green when I first met you. And look at you now! You're literally America's next top model."

"Well, I don't know about that. But what do you say?"

Theo frowns. "Mac, I don't know. We're friends. It's like you were just saying two seconds ago about Nate. Are you sure we should work together? I mean, won't it be weird if I'm your assistant?"

I shake my head vigorously. "Don't think of yourself as my assistant. Not ever. This is so much more than that. Theo. You know what this business is like. For every Theo I meet, I run into a hundred . . . Zvis. Or worse. I need someone who I trust. Whom I like. This isn't being an assistant. It's being my always-on-call genius. You're the man I trust to find that dress that makes my tits look good, helps convince the suits at Cover Girl to hire me. Even if that dress is last season Alaïa. You know that text message I just got? I booked the cover of *Elle*. Things were already going fast—now they're moving at light speed. I can't even think straight."

"Holy heck, the cover of *Elle*? Oh my. Look at you go." Theo lowers his voice to a whisper, like it's a word so bad it can't be spoken aloud. "Aren't you worried, though? That we'll fight?"

"Nope. Not really. If you can work for Zvi, trust me, you can work for me."

Theo grins. "That would be an incredible campaign slogan." He drums on the table, mindlessly. "So, you're gonna pay me, and I'm gonna . . ."

"Let's talk about the details another time. My head's spinning, I'm freaking out, and I need to you to start immediately."

"What do you mean?"

"I mean, let's order dinner. I'm paying. We're celebrating." I turn and signal to Shannon for a menu.

"Oh! Mmmmm." Theo coos. "Mac Croft, I saw what you just did."

"What do you mean?" I whirl back around.

"Woman, please. Don't even try it." Theo winks at me. "He's not here, you know."

"I don't know what you're talking about." I can feel my ears turning purple.

"Please, Mac. If we're going to be working together, traveling together, there can't be any secrets. Besides. I know you too well."

"Seriously, I have no idea what you're talking about. Where are those menus . . ."

"Nice try, lady. Anyway, they've got a game tonight, and even though he's injured he has to be there. Something to do with team spirit. Not that I'd know anything about that, having never been on a team myself. He was telling me about it last night. Or this morning. I don't know which."

"I was looking for Shannon, for your information."

"He might come in after the game. He usually does. But then, he probably didn't get any sleep, so maybe not tonight."

"Theo, shut up. Please." I pluck a packet of artificial sweetener from its dish and toss it at him. "Besides. I just got out of a relationship."

Theo shrugs his shoulders. "So? That doesn't have anything to do with this. Mac, he walked you home last night. I'm no fool."

"Theo. I have not had one second to think about this. But it's too soon. Isn't it?"

"Mac, sometimes you don't get to choose. Sometimes we fall in love and it's not necessarily great for our schedule . . ."

"Wait. Who said anything about love?"

"Methinks the lady doth protest way too much." Theo grins. "Look, it's like being on the cover of *Elle*. Or being the next Cover Girl. You don't get to decide these things. They just sort of . . . happen."

Hm. I mull this over for a minute. "Theo. That is the stupidest analogy I've ever heard."

"Shut up!" Theo retaliates by tossing the sweetener packet back in my direction. "I'm tired, and that's your fault because you made me stay up all night. Which goes right back to my original point, which is that you would never stay out all night long with a gentleman who you didn't have some special feelings for . . ."

"I don't even know his last name."

"Does that matter?" Theo leans back, crosses his arms triumphantly.

I have nothing to say.

"I thought so."

At last, Shannon approaches; drops two leather bound menus onto the table. "I am so sorry. We're a little slammed tonight."

"No problem." I tell her.

"Do you need a minute? You must have the menu memorized by now—do you know what you want?"

"No, hon." Theo shakes his head sadly. "She doesn't know what she wants."

If I didn't love Theo, I'd be mad. As it is, I just start laughing. What else can I do? Maybe he's right.

Twenty-two

"Melody, this is so exciting. I can't believe it!" Mom reaches over and squeezes my hand.

"I'm glad, Mom. I'm so glad you guys were able to come along." It's a bright July morning, and the sun is streaming in through the little porthole window, so I reach past Mom and slide the shade down firmly.

"This is so nice of them." She whispers, like there's someone lurking around who might overhear, but it's just the two of, ensconced in the luxurious, leather-upholstered belly of the plane, the private plane, the Cover Girl executive plane.

This trip to LA is for business, of course, but taking the private jet, and bringing my parents along—that's strictly pleasure, a little signing bonus from my new best pal, Mitch Godfrey. Helen Conley Cox was in on the meeting when Mitch proposed it, and the look of disgust on her face was priceless. I'm glad she's not tagging along.

I can't help but laugh. It is nice of them, and it's pretty sweet having this big plane all to ourselves. "We're going to have the best time in California. Wait until you see the hotel, Mom. You're going to freak out."

Theo comes huffing up the steps and into the cabin, groaning, a bag in each hand. "She's right, Margaret. The Chateau Marmont is incredible."

"Mac!" Mom stands. "You're working Theo to death. Let me help you with those bags, hon."

"Please Mom." I roll my eyes. "Those are *his* carry-ons."

"I travel in style." Theo tosses the bags onto an empty seat. "So sue me."

Dad follows Theo into the plane, ducking his head a little. The plane doesn't seem quite as big when he's inside. "Now this . . . this I could get used to." Dad collapses into the seat across the aisle from me.

"Well, don't. I think this is a one-time deal. So enjoy it while it lasts."

"Seriously, Mac, I think you should try to get this into the contract. *Ms. Croft is to travel via Cover Girl private plane only.* That would be so awesome." Theo settles into one of the seats opposite, facing us. "Think about it."

"Way too late, my friend. The contracts are signed. The deal is done. This is a little bonus, but let's not forget, it's work. We're on . . ."

"You're on for tomorrow. You're shooting at Smashbox, call time is nine. Tomorrow evening there's the reception . . ." Theo digs out the travel wallet—my travel wallet—and flips through it until he finds my agenda. "The reception with the West Coast team from Cover Girl, at the Roosevelt Hotel. That's at eight. Then I made dinner reservations for you, me, and your parents at Craft, at ten. That's late, I know, but I figured with the time difference and everything our body clocks will be off anyway. Plus I double confirmed and there will be passed appetizers at the reception, so hopefully we won't be starving. Then Thursday, you've got early morning TV appearances scheduled, so we're starting at five, I know it's early, but we need the time, you know how the TV stuff works. Then after TV you're free for an hour or so before your lunch with the packaging people from Cover Girl. They need to do some consultations with you about . . ."

"Hang on, Theo. Sorry." My phone is ringing insistently. My stomach lurches when I see who's calling. "I'm going to take this outside. Is that OK?"

Theo laughs. "I don't think we'll leave without you."

I hurry down the aisle and out the door into the blinding late afternoon sun. I shield my eyes from the sun with one hand and answer the phone with the other. "Hello?"

"You." Erik laughs. "You are a hard woman to get on the phone."

I settle onto the top step of the gangplank. "I'm sorry. After New Mexico, I was in town, and you know, it was all about Cover Girl. Then you were in Canada, and then I was doing *Elle* in Kenya. My phone didn't work in Africa."

"Never mind all that. Where are you now? Because I'm heading to Abbot's for happy hour, and I could be persuaded to walk by your place and pick you up."

"I wish I could." I do. My heart's pounding, and I feel jittery and nervous. As excited as I am for this trip, I wish we could call it off, go to my favorite restaurant and talk. We haven't had the chance to, not since our first and only date, just trading text messages and voicemail. I'd love to tell Erik about everything, about signing this contract, about the way my life is going. "I'm at Teterboro. We're taking the company jet to LA."

"You're kidding. Well, you travel in style."

"No, not really. It's a little present from my pals at Cover Girl. My bosses, I should say. It's nice, though. I'm bringing my parents along. They're getting a kick out of it. I'm excited for them to see what it's like, you know, my life on the road?"

"That's great. Very cool. Your parents must be proud."

"They are, I think. No, I know. They are. I'm lucky to have them on my side. It makes all this so much easier."

"I'm sure it does." Erik's quiet for a second. "So, it's a funny thing, but I'm done for the season. Actually, I'm heading out to see my brother and his wife. I've got a little nephew, I never get out to see them during the season. And it happens that they live in Santa Monica."

"Oh. You're going to LA."

"Don't sound so excited."

I laugh. "No, I am. I mean, I'll be in LA, you'll be in LA. Maybe we can coordinate our schedules?"

"I was hoping you'd say that. I've been thinking about you almost nonstop for the past few weeks, Mac. I know you said you weren't ready, then, but it's been a while, and I was hoping . . ."

"You were hoping. I see. Well, I don't know Erik Baer. I don't know . . ."

"When will you know?"

"I don't know when I'll know." I'm laughing now, teasing him.

"I can wait," Erik says. "I'm a very patient man. But I don't know if I can stand you and me being in the same town and not sneaking away for dinner or something. I'm staying at the Chateau. Let's try and coordinate, OK?"

I'm laughing out loud now. "I think we can work something out. I'm staying at the Chateau too. I'm guessing you already knew that, though. I have a feeling a little birdie might have told you what I'm up to . . ."

Erik's quiet a second, but I can almost hear his smile. "I will see you tomorrow night then. Not taking no for an answer."

"I'm not giving no for an answer," I tell him. "I'll see you then."

I end the call, and just sit for a minute. The warm sun is beating down on me, and I should get inside before it takes its toll on my skin. It's ironic that a noisy airport seems peaceful to me, but not that surprising, I suppose, given what the past few weeks have been like. I watch a plane speed down the tarmac, tilt up and climb—like magic—into the air. It seems impossible, air travel. It seems miraculous. It's one of those things I take for granted, one of those things that are a central part of my everyday life. But that's the thing about life; when you can slow things down, stop and really look at it, it's pretty incredible. Maybe it's the sun, maybe it's simply exhaustion, but I'm feeling awfully philosophical. I better snap out of it. Mom, Dad, and Theo are going to wonder where I am—not to mention the flight crew. I need to get inside so we can get this show on the road . . . or in the air. After all, I have to work tomorrow.

A+

**AUTHOR
INSIGHTS,
EXTRAS, &
MORE...**

FROM

**CAROL
ALT**

AND

AVON A

Advice from Carol Alt

Every woman who decides to be a model should be aware that this is a business. Many girls first start out thinking that this will be one big party: great clothes, beautiful shoes, gorgeous makeup and hair, industry parties . . .

But in reality, unless you conduct yourself like a business-woman, even the most promising young model cannot make it to the top. You see, there are thousands of young women who want to become models. How do you distinguish yourself in the fray?

Here are ten ideas . . .

1. *Be on time for go-sees.* No client likes to wait for a girl they may or may not hire. Showing disrespect now can lead them to think you are unreliable.

2. *Be clean.* Remember you will share a studio space with other people. And the poor hairdresser has to touch your hair . . . if it is dirty or you smell (even too much perfume is offensive to many people), they can send you home.

3. *Be on time for the job if you are lucky enough to get it.* And remember it is LUCK! There could be hundreds of girls vying for each job. If you get it, it is PURE LUCK! So don't let all the attention go to your head.

4. *Don't let it go to your head!!* Modeling is a HEADY business. People will be telling you that you are beautiful as a way to get you to work harder or better or longer or to feel good so that their pictures of you are the best they can be. They will tell you anything to get what they need from you. Do not believe that you are any better or any different from the waitress at the corner diner—remember she came to town to model, too AND she may even have gotten a few jobs herself!

5. *Be respectful!* The client is your link to future rewards . . . they all talk and everyone in the industry knows one another. They talk about girls, business, the day's shoot—who is good, who is not, who is hot, and who never to work with!!

6. *Look at every job as a link to another job and every client as a repeat customer*—and remember, the customer is ALWAYS right . . . to a point!

7. *Protect yourself, for sure, but do it in a polite and kind way.* Remember no one protects you but you. Yet every client may be a repeat customer—this is a fine line to walk. Learn to finesse.

8. *Learn telephone etiquette.* This is a part of not only being respectful, but of earning respect. Silence your cellphone and don't look at it until you are alone. You need to be "present" in the studio and to give your focus to the client, your colleagues, and to your work. This shows you care! And when you are fighting for each and every job, people want to know you care.

9. *Do not take that which does not belong to you!* I have seen even big names take things . . . and MAYBE (and I do mean

maybe) they get away with it sometimes. But seriously, I have seen models put designers in desperate straits when they shoot-lift things. Most of the time, the designer has only ONE of a sample. And taking his one-off sample can set him back—it is a prototype. And believe me, he will know it was you who took it and he will complain if you are a thief. What goes around comes around.

10. *Bookkeeping is important—receipts, money in, and money out.* Keep track. Even if the media likes to tell you that models make a lot of money, our taxes are paid at the END OF THE YEAR. Our employer does not deduct taxes. So be careful what you spend because half of everything you get belongs to the government. And they WILL come looking for it. Even models get into debt from overspending.

Carol Alt

For more than two decades, **CAROL ALT** has been one of the world's most recognizable names and faces. In addition to being the first American to be the face of Lancôme and gracing the cover of more than seven hundred magazines, she has made calendars, posters, and exercise videos, all of which have sold millions of copies. An accomplished spokesperson and frequent guest on talk shows, she has acted on stage and television and in more than sixty-five movies.